SHADOWS AND WALLS

By

Meade Saeedi

ISBN 978-0-578-04013-4

Printed by Signature Book Printing,
www.sbpbooks.com

Also by Meade Saeedi

Balancing Act

To Denise,

With best wishes,

Maeve Binchy

ACKNOWLEDGMENTS

First and foremost, I thank my husband Saeed Leon Saeedi for insights into the Persian culture he has provided me over nearly forty years of marriage. With him I have visited Iran twice, including being in that country on September 11, 2001. The American public never saw the candlelight vigils held throughout Iran on behalf of the victims of that terrible day, nor did the American media show the moment of silence held in Tehran before the World Cup Soccer games a few days later.

I also thank my friends, Audrey Lynch and Joanna der Stepanian, both of whom thoughtfully reviewed this book and provided exquisitely wise guidance, and I thank my Germantown Writer's Group for re-reading this story so many, many times as I struggled to get it right.

To the Persian friends I have made over the years, many of your stories and anecdotes have found their way into this novel. This is a novel of hope, a tribute to the ability of humans to change behaviors that no longer work well for them. I have witnessed such change both in my personal life and in my life as a citizen of the world.

SHIRAZ

CHAPTER 1

Tahirih paused for a moment to collect her thoughts as well as some energy. Although pregnant for the fourth time in six years, she had been working ferociously all morning, cleaning the house, supervising arguments between the older children, and feeding and changing the eight month old twins. Soon her husband Ismail would be arriving for his noontime meal.

As always, she wanted his home to be warm and welcoming when he returned from the bazaar. Tahirih considered herself unimaginably fortunate to be married to a man who was almost always generous and thoughtful, even though he did hold some very firm ideas, some of which ran counter to her own thinking.

As she was working, she had been mulling over Ismail's response to her supplication that morning. Although nine out of ten of her fellow Persians were illiterate, Tahirih had long felt a burning desire to learn to read. In the society where she lived, however, reading was considered not only unnecessary, but even unseemly for the well-to-do, who could easily afford to hire a scribe for the occasional letter that might need to be written. If a man learned to read, it was only so he could immerse himself in the glory of the Koran. However, reading religious works was strictly forbidden to women. Tahirih understood that in the Persian society of the late nineteenth century, a woman had to have either her husband's or her father's permission to undertake such a radical proposition as acquiring literacy skills.

"Absolutely not," had been Ismail's unmitigated response. "I am dumbfounded that you would even consider voicing such a request," he had added, shaking his head in consternation. "Women's brains are not designed to comprehend the meaning of written words."

"But Ismail," Tahirih had countered gently, "if I learned to read, and possibly even to cipher, then I could guard your invoices so no one could ever cheat you again the way Ahmad did. You were so furious about that. My beloved husband, you work so hard every day, and since you do not wish to learn to read, perhaps I should. It distresses me when you are not happy."

"Tahirih," her husband had replied, obviously drawing on every ounce of his patience, "I appreciate your concern for my well being, but I happen to be one of the most successful businessmen in all of Shiraz. I achieved this prosperity before I married you, and I achieved it without your knowing how to read. Please constrain your enthusiasm to caring for the household and the children. I will always protect you. You know that. There is no need for you to be able to read. It is a woman's duty to obey her husband. Now please do so." Then he had lovingly patted her protruding belly and left to spend the morning at the bazaar.

Although disappointed, Tahirih had not been particularly surprised by this response, since she had often heard her husband express the opinion that lowly scribes in the bazaar could be paid a few cents to write a letter or read an invoice. She was also well aware that he shared the opinion of most Persians that only the male mind could ponder the magnificence of the writings of the Koran. Although he occasionally discussed the teachings of Islam with her, it was more in an instructive mode rather than to solicit her ideas. Somehow, though, Tahirih believed that she would be able to understand written language, and indeed even to think critically about what she read. Therefore, even though her husband had forbidden it, she knew that the desire to read was still in her heart.

This presented an impasse to the twenty-one year old woman. Although she certainly did not want to oppose her beloved husband, she did want to help him with duties he did not want to undertake himself, and those related largely to tasks involving literacy. She also believed there was a whole different world out there for someone who could read stories and learn about things beyond the small world where she existed. Forlornly, she turned to her household duties as she reflected on what led to her marriage.

Tahirih was the youngest daughter in a well-to-do landowning family of fourteen children. Her mother did not want to allow her to marry, choosing instead to retain the youngest daughter at home to care for her parents in their old age. Although her father disagreed with this decision, in order to maintain peace with his wife, he turned away many suitors for their lively, beautiful youngest daughter until finally his nephew Ismail had made an offer too good to refuse.

Ismail had been just short of thirty and well established as a tea merchant when he had approached his uncle for Tahirih, whom he had known since she was a toddler. Marrying a first cousin was typical in Persian society where families did not want to risk bringing an outsider into their lineage. Tahirih found herself betrothed when she was fourteen and married a few days following her fifteenth birthday.

Now she had shared nearly one third of her twenty-one years of life with this man. They lived in a splendid home in a prosperous neighborhood of Shiraz, where they were respected by everyone who was important. Tahirih understood that Ismail did not mean her any harm by refusing her request for learning to read. It was just what he thought best. Although she disagreed, she knew that she would, for the time being, abide by his decision, as was a wife's duty. To do otherwise would bring disgrace on herself and all her family. But still, she was sure that there were people somewhere who must believe as she did. Someday she would find them.

Her reverie was interrupted by a servant's mild but urgent voice. "Tahirih Khanem, I beg your pardon for disturbing you. Little Husayn has fallen from a chair in the kitchen, and he is calling for you."

Panicked, Tahirih rushed to the room where her five year old son was angrily yelling. "Husayn Jan, what happened?" she asked tenderly, running her hands over him quickly to assess the extent of his injuries, as a servant brought a cold compress which Tahirih lovingly applied to the bruised arm and ribs.

"I fell. It was the fault of the *jinn*. They pushed me."

The child, just past babyhood, sniffed as he sought comfort

from his mother, while at the same time trying to meet his father's standards of bravery, which included accepting pain without crying. Tahirih could see the bruises darkening, so she soothed the pain with loving words and a silly song to make the child smile. Little by little, she succeeded, until he finally agreed to take a nap, after which she promised that he could play with his favorite new toy.

After he was taken away, Tahirih sat on a divan and allowed her annoyance to take hold of her. She, too, had been brought up to be afraid of spirits who returned from the netherworld to play tricks on the living. But now, as a mother herself, she had come to believe that the *jinn* were just a tool that adults used to keep children meek and obedient. She no longer believed that *jinn* really existed, and she was sure there were better ways to control a child's behavior. Fear did not lead to anything positive, so far as she could see. But the servants, especially the elderly Parvin, frequently told the children stories about both good and bad spirits. Tahirih recalled one day overhearing Parvin relating a story about the *jinn*.

"Did you know, little Husayn," Parvin had said, "that the *jinn* are spirits of the dead. I remember one day I saw a man stealing from his neighbor, but suddenly a *jinn* caused him great pain and he cried out, and the neighbors caught him and beat him severely. The *jinn* have a very special obligation to remind us of Allah's love for us. Always remember, my precious little man, that Allah has a plan for each of us, and if we stray from that chosen path, the good *jinn* will bring us back even if they must terrify us to do so. But you must also remember that not all people who have died were good throughout their lives. There are also bad *jinn* and they must be avoided, especially at night when there is no moon."

Husayn had been so frightened of the unseeable spirits that he had refused to go outside for several weeks thereafter, so one night Tahirih decided to ask Ismail for his advice about teaching children about *jinn*.

"Ismail," she had said, "I don't think Husayn should be frightened into good behavior. Although telling him stories about the *jinn* might cause him to obey me, the obedience would come from fear but not respect. I would rather have him understand that what I tell him is for his own well being and that obedience is a way of protecting himself."

But Ismail had had a different opinion. "What is important, my wife," he admonished Tahirih, "is that a child learn to do as he is told. Whatever causes this to happen is good. I myself was raised to be afraid of the *jinn* and surely that helped me to become the honest and upright man that I am today. It is acceptable to introduce fear into a child's life, to assure that he is learning the right lessons."

Here again, Tahirih had not agreed with her husband's reasoning. What would happen, she wondered, when the child himself used the same methods to get what he wanted? Just the other day she heard Husayn frightening a neighbor's child with exhortations about the *jinn* just so that he could be first in line for something. Little Husayn was only a child, after all, but he could learn adult strategies. Tahirih wanted something better for her child than being able to win disagreements by bullying.

CHAPTER 2

Although Ismail seemed to assume that everything in the household spontaneously took care of itself, Tahirih understood first hand the complexities a woman faced each day so that her husband could come home to a comfortable abode in the evening.

That morning the butcher had sent very old lamb again, for the third time in two weeks. Ordinarily, servants took care of problems like that. This time, however, Tahirih had been too incensed to allow the matter to be handled by servants. She herself took the meat back this time, shaking it in the butcher's face.

"Sniff this meat," she commanded, thrusting the decaying flesh under the startled man's nose. "It smells worse than rotten eggs." She glared at him, then proceeded with her tirade. "Not once, not twice, but three times now you have delivered inedible food to me, expecting that I would just accept it. Well, I won't. My family will not be made sick because of your greed. Know this, mighty butcher. Hereafter I will not buy anything from you, not even a scrap for the chickens. Nor will my neighbors, when they hear."

This unexpected outburst brought the butcher to her door an hour later with a basket of fruit. "Oh wife of Ismail, please accept this small token of my respect for you and your family. I humbly beg your forgiveness for my son's ineptitude. He has been punished for his carelessness. Always hereafter I will attend to your needs myself when you come to my shop."

"Don't hide behind your son," Tahirih retorted sharply. "It has always been you who sold my servants the meat, never your son. You think you can just sell whatever garbage you want to get rid of and I will continue to buy from you because I don't know the difference. Well, you are wrong. Be gone."

The butcher, incensed at being spoken to in such a manner by a woman, had his own last words. "May Allah curse those who refuse to patronize poor hardworking people like me," he shouted. "I, too, have a family that must eat. May your home be struck by hailstones and may all your father's orchards dry up and become barren." He stomped off, furiously muttering imprecations against the wealthy.

Then there was the problem with the carpet. Earlier that week, Ismail had told Tahirih that he was expecting Mullah Mohsin to visit. In preparation, therefore, Tahirih hired a carpet beater to clean Ismail's favorite carpet, the one he proudly displayed in the large salon. The cleaning took place on the street in front of the house. That morning some children had been playing outside by kicking around a rock. One child kicked too hard and the rock slammed into a neighbor's flower pot, causing shards to fly out and cut the rug beater's arm. To Tahirih's horror, a few drops of blood splashed across a cream colored portion of the carpet, causing stains which could not be removed despite all the tricks she and the servants could muster.

Tahirih had been alarmed. Not only were the stains ugly to see, but bloodstains on a carpet were considered an omen of a future calamity. She fretted about what terrible thing might happen because she had given an order to clean a rug that was not really dirty. Maybe she tried to do things too well, she mused, and this was a message from Allah not to be so faultless. She thought carefully about her pride.

At noon, she heard her husband enter the front door and remove his shoes. She joyfully hurried through the house to welcome him home for his midday meal. "Good afternoon, my husband," she greeted warmly. "Do you prefer to eat immediately, or shall we first sit in the garden for a few moments?"

Ismail took a moment to survey his wife, who still had a good figure after three childbirths, including a pair of twins. Just now she was quite large, since she expected his fifth child in less than three months. Nonetheless, she was still attractive.

Although he occasionally favored other women with his presence for an evening, Tahirih remained the center of his life. He answered assertively. "I prefer to sit outside and enjoy the smell of the roses and singing of the birds. Tell Parvin to bring a tray of fruit and some tea. Actually, something happened this morning that I want to tell you about."

Ismail enjoyed telling his wife about his daily escapades, which puffed him up in her eyes, he was sure. They sat beneath the apricot tree and inhaled the fragrance of the blossoms while they sipped their tea. Ismail pointed out the beauty of the fish in the pond he had designed, then finally got around to telling his story.

"You know Ali, the fruit vendor?" he began. 'The one who knows how to run everyone else's business, but not his own? He claims to be such a good Muslim, but today he did something reprehensible, and then he had the audacity to brag about it." Ismail paused for effect before continuing. "Business was slow so he was walking around the bazaar -- actually he was strutting the way he likes to -- while two of his sons watched his shop. Well, this little kid who couldn't have been more than six years old tried to steal a fig. Instead of just shooing him away, which he could easily have done, Ali kicked the child. Up and down the whole avenue, everyone heard the bone in the boy's leg crack. Then when the child fell, Ali struck him several more times with a metal rod, yelling that this was Allah's punishment for someone who tried to steal." Ismail shook his head in dismay. "No one, absolutely no one, came to the defense of the little tyke. After a long time, the boy managed to drag himself back to the entrance of the bazaar where he collapsed beside a blind beggar who was probably his father. By the time I heard about it, they were gone or I would have given them some money. Now the poor kid won't ever be able to walk right, and he will be as much of a burden to his father as his father is to him."

Tahirih's heart ached for the child, but she knew that this was the way the destitute were treated, especially by wealthy men like Ali. Her heart burned at the injustice, and she was proud of her husband because he showed concern. Tahirih told him how proud she was to have a husband who cared about the misfortune of others, and Ismail took in the praise with practiced nonchalance.

After a few more moments of conversation, they returned to the house and sat down in the formal dining room. At Tahirih's direction, Cook had prepared several of Ismail's favorite dishes, including two kinds of rice, one with lima beans and the other with saffron decorating the top in beautiful yellow and orange swirls. There was also a savory stew of vegetables and lamb cooked together so that their flavors and aromas intermingled, and Tahirih had ordered a variety of fruit for dessert.

After the meal, Ismail took a short nap while his wife proceeded with cleaning up. Two hours later, Ismail returned to the bazaar for an afternoon of trading and gossiping, while Tahirih spent the rest of the day supervising the children's care and preparing the house for her husband's evening guests.

CHAPTER 3

Ismail gazed at the arched entrance to the bazaar that opened onto a cavernous maze of passages with neither signs nor numbers. The only reliable guide to navigating the labyrinth was experience, since signs would have been of no use to the illiterate populace. Each specialty -- jewelers, fabric sellers, leather designers, food merchants, carpet dealers and the myriad of other shopkeepers in this huge marketplace -- had its own section, with avenues twisting and turning in a design known only to the frequent patron.

Ismail strolled past several shops toward the center of the maze where his tea stall was located, stopping along the way to chat with some fellow bazaaris. To his distress, he learned that his friend Suleiman had been attacked by highway robbers while returning from an excursion to purchase supplies. Ismail made a mental note to visit Suleiman on his way home that afternoon, before continuing on through the winding passageways toward his own place of business.

"Good afternoon, Mahmoud," he called out to the merchant just across from him. "Did you leave your son at home for the afternoon?"

Mahmoud grinned. That morning his seven year old son had been with him, helping to set up the shop, preparing tea to serve to potential customers, and observing the techniques of salesmanship that would one day secure his own place in the bazaar.

"My wife does not think he is old enough to spend the whole day here yet. She thinks he should have time to play, so he will be with me only in the mornings for a while."

Ismail nodded his head in acceptance of a woman's belief that children were still children, but he himself believed that a male child needed to follow in his father's footsteps as soon as possible. He intended to start teaching Husayn the methods of a businessman in the near future, and he knew that he would need several more sons to enable him to meet his dreams of expanding his business far beyond the Shiraz bazaar.

As he sat awaiting afternoon business, he chatted with Mahmoud about the latest gossip that seeped through the bazaar like a mist.

"Have you heard about the Kurdish uprising out in the west? I hear that several people were killed."

"Those abominable Kurds are always looking for a fight," Mahmoud replied angrily. "They don't look like real Persians, and they do nothing but create trouble. I have relatives in Urmieh and I pray to gracious Allah that none of them were hurt."

Although Ismail agreed that the Kurds could be aggressive, he had a somewhat different attitude toward them because as a young man, he had traveled extensively throughout Persia. In the western mountains near the border with Turkey he had encountered several Kurdish families and over a period of time, he had had an opportunity to experience a culture very different from his own. From the Kurdish men, he heard horrific stories of how they had been driven from one place to another for centuries, never allowed to establish their own homeland anywhere. Ismail supposed that would be enough to cause anyone to become fierce and rebellious.

However, he kept these thoughts to himself, not wanting to dispute Mahmoud's point of view, which would have been rude. Fortunately the arrival of customers put an end to the discussion and they were both occupied with transactions for the rest of the afternoon.

Ismail loved bargaining, and considered himself successful when the price he got was at least two thirds of what he had originally asked. His was both a wholesale and retail business. As such, he not only sold small portions of tea to daily customers, but he was also the major source of tea for the Shah's palace. Although this was prestigious, it was not profitable. The royal family rarely paid bills, assuming that the honor of serving the court was sufficient recompense for a businessman. Accordingly, Ismail had to figure losses from that part of his business into the prices he charged other customers, but he did so sparingly and his business flourished.

At the end of the day he sent a messenger to tell Tahirih that he intended to visit his injured friend Suleiman, since he did not want her to worry when he did not come home at the usual time. At Suleiman's home, he was admitted by a servant and escorted to Suleiman's sleeping quarters, where the man lay in bed with an elevated leg and bandages covering nearly every inch of his body.

"Ah, my friend, you are looking well," Ismail greeted heartily, being obliged to follow Persian manners even though he knew perfectly well that Suleiman knew how awful he looked. "The color in your face is good and I am certain that you will soon be back at your stall in the bazaar."

"I fear not, my friend. Nonetheless, I thank you for coming to visit. I am sorry I cannot be a proper host, but that fool of a doctor absolutely forbids me to move. He says that my ribs will puncture my lungs if I breathe too heavily. But never mind that. First, tell me how your family is doing, then we will talk about what is happening at the bazaar."

They spoke briefly about Tahirih and the children, as was customary, and then Suleiman told of his own family. Only after that did Ismail broach a subject he had not yet discussed with anyone else.

"Suleiman Agha, you are a wise man and I have therefore come to you for guidance," he said deferentially. "This is my concern." Ismail took a deep breath, then pressed on. "Because my business is doing well, I know I can financially afford to support another wife and more children, along with servants to take care of them all. But I have heard that there are appalling problems with more than one woman in the house. You, however, have many wives and your home is always calm and peaceful. How do you do it?"

Suleiman chortled, which in turn caused him to grimace because of his tightly wrapped ribs. "Yes, Ismail, it can be done," he answered, "and indeed you are correct to have more than one wife. Because you have shown that you are prosperous in the bazaar, you must now demonstrate your affluence in other ways.

A man must have many children, especially sons. That is why I married four times. In total, all my wives together have given me nine sons, as well as many daughters. We men must do as Muhammad instructed us and take many wives so no woman will be left without a husband to watch after her.

"Now this is how you do it. Find a girl whose father has too many daughters, so she will be grateful to be taken as a second wife. Be sure, however, that you never slight Tahirih and remember that she was your first wife. Always treat her accordingly. Be kind and gentle with them both and give each her own area of the household to manage. It will work well, I assure you. Maybe in the future you will take even more."

Ismail thanked Suleiman profusely for the advice, then they began to talk about rumors floating through the bazaar. "Have you heard that the Shah's emissary Mojtabeh Amuzegar is visiting Shiraz? Officially, it is for a shopping trip to buy jewelry before returning to Russia as the Assistant to the Ambassador. But I have also heard that he is here to look into gossip being told about a heretical group called the Baha'is. Do you know anything about them?"

"Who did you say? Baha'is? No, I don't recall ever hearing about them. But if they are heretics, they must be wiped out immediately. The supremacy of Islam cannot be challenged." Suleiman was aghast that heresy was being spread in his beloved city, and he began to twist in his bed.

Ismail explained more about what he had heard. "The Baha'is claim that their prophet is the successor to Muhammad. But the Koran unequivocally states that Muhammad is the Seal of the

Prophets, so that is impossible. I suppose there will always be some fanatic trying to stir up trouble. It will all disappear soon, I am sure. In the meantime, however, I'm afraid that I might unwittingly associate with one of them, which would be disastrous for my business. The Shah confiscates the property of anyone affiliated with a Baha'i."

"Don't worry. It will come to nothing," Suleiman pronounced.

However, Ismail was disturbed that religious heretics might infiltrate the bazaar, which was not only where he made his living but also where he associated companionably with fellow merchants. To Ismail's way of thinking, Islam and the bazaar were one, just as Islam and all social interactions were one. Islam was the basis for everything a Persian man did, the guiding point for all decisions. Nothing could be allowed to disrupt that.

CHAPTER 4

The same afternoon, at Ismail's house, Tahirih called to the cook's teenaged daughter. "Zahreh, have the children been fed?"

"Yes, Mistress," the slow witted girl replied. "While you cut flowers. Maryam feed Husayn. Parvin feed Scheherazade. And babies eat right now."

Because Zahreh did not speak in the flowery manner exhibited by most Persians, Tahirih had at first thought the girl to be a bit impertinent. In time, however, she came to realize that the child simply lacked the capacity to produce elaborate speech. She also noticed that Zahreh had difficulty responding to very basic instructions. When told to fetch something, she would return with the wrong item, and had to be reminded over and over how to do even the simplest chore.

Zahreh's father, the cook for the household, became exasperated with his child and frequently beat her for being disobedient. Since his wife had died two years before during one of the many smallpox epidemics that crisscrossed Persia, he had been left to raise this youngest offspring by himself. Now he was stuck with her forever, since he was sure no one would ever agree to marry such a stupid person.

Tahirih, on the other hand, understood that Zahreh was not deliberately obstinate. The child simply could not understand what people expected of her, and her distress exacerbated her confusion when people showed impatience. As a result, Tahirih tried to be as kind as possible.

"All right. Go tell your father that Mullah Mohsin is coming to visit my husband tonight. We will need lots of fruits and sweets in the salon."

"Yes, Tahirih Khanem, I tell him."

Zahreh went outdoors and walked down the street, stopping to play with some neighbor's children, completely forgetting to give her father the message.

An hour or so later Tahirih left to visit her parents. They lived outside Shiraz on a large farm with vineyards, fruit tree orchards and enormous fields of wheat. Because her parents were planning an important party, she wanted to stop by to see what last minute help they might need. Remembering why her mother initially opposed her marriage, Tahirih made extra efforts to remain available to help her parents whenever she could.

When she arrived, Tahirih's mother was in the kitchen supervising the cooks. "Good morning, dearest Mother. How are preparations coming?" Tahirih smiled warmly as Manizheh Khanem walked out from the kitchen area.

Her mother rolled her eyes in pretended exasperation, and they both giggled. Tahirih's mother had confided that this event could be the means to launching a diplomatic career for Tahirih's father, and perhaps some of her brothers as well, which was exactly as her mother felt it should be.

"Tahirih," Manizheh said, "my servants work hard, and so do I. Your father has no idea how much effort is required to get ready for a party of this magnitude. We expect at least ninety guests. The food will be served on time, the house will be spectacularly decorated, everything will be clean and sparkling, and none of it will be noticed. But, of course, if all goes well, Mojtabeh might be persuaded to recommend your father for a position in the palace."

Tahirih knew that her mother's reasoning was that, thanks to the present Shah's grandfather who had reportedly sired at least two thousand offspring, most important Persian families were related in some fashion to the royal house. So, thanks to the former Shah's philandering ways, her father was just as closely related to the Shah as was his cousin who would be their prime guest at the upcoming party.

"Is Papa excited about moving to Tehran?" she asked, knowing full well that the intriguing was all on her mother's part. Her father was perfectly content to remain in Shiraz as a well respected landowner.

"I have been planting seeds in his head for a long time, and little by little they will grow. We shall see tonight if the tree begins to take shape."

Tahirih marveled at her mother's hopes. To be part of the palace, that would be beyond the wildest dreams of all but a few Persians. Over the years, however, Tahirih had seen the power of her mother's quiet influence. She would not be at all surprised if it worked out exactly as Manizheh contrived.

"Have you been able to talk Shahjari into coming?" she inquired. "He is so old. I am surprised that he still agrees to perform."

"He is very fond of your father. He will come and give his famous recitation of the <u>Shah Nameh</u>. Everyone loves to hear about the days of ancient Persia and no one can tell tales quite the way Shahjari can."

Indeed, even as an adult, Tahirih still enjoyed listening to the legends of the mighty Rustam, most powerful of all Persian warriors. Although she had heard these stories hundreds of times throughout her childhood, the legacy they imparted was so wonderful that she still thrilled to hear them repeated. Eighty year old Shahjari was the best of storytellers. When he recited poetry composed by the renowned Ferdowsi hundreds of years before, it seemed as if the listeners were right there at the scene of battle, watching the blows and hearing the cries of victory.

"What a wonderful treat for everyone, Mama. They will be spellbound. And what kind of music will there be?"

"Everything. Flutists and violinists and santoor players, some hand drummers and even cymbal players. Men love to show their agility, you know, waving their arms, snapping their fingers and swaying to the rhythm of the music. We women, of course, pretend not to watch, but you know we always do. Yes, indeed, there will be plenty of music."

Again, both women laughed in agreement, and began to talk about food preparation. For more than two weeks the household had been preparing for this feast. Garlic pickled twelve years before would be brought out as a special treat. Trays would be loaded with almond macaroons, rice cookies, and several versions of baklava. Sholezard, that wonderful pudding made from sugar, saffron, rose water, almonds and pulped rice, then sprinkled with cinnamon and pistachios, would decorate yet more platters. A variety of zoolbieh, some shaped in lacy designs and some formed like little tubes, would be deep fried and dipped in sugar water just hours in advance so they would be fresh and perfect.

All that, of course, was either appetizer or dessert. The main dishes would be yet more elaborate. Several kinds of rice would be served, some with dill and lima beans, others sweetened with sugared orange rind and raisins. If the rice had no added fruits or vegetables, it would be decorated with saffron, not only to enhance the taste, but also to provide a beautiful sight

Meat dishes would include *fesenjun*, which was chicken simmered in pomegranate juice and combined with finely chopped walnuts, as well as some beef dishes to which various vegetables had been added so all the flavors intermingled.

Festive looking salads made of watercress, scallions, radishes, feta cheese, black olives and parsley would be put out on all the tables. Mixed salads such as the local favorite, salad Shirazi, made of finely chopped tomatoes, onions, cucumbers and parsley then sprinkled with lemon juice, would complement the other offerings. Tahirih's absolute favorite salad was made from ground chicken breast, mashed potatoes, green peas, pickles, and onions, then coated with a mixture of eggs and oil and decorated with sliced green olives. Tahirih reminded her mother to be sure to have plenty of that, and Manizheh laughingly assured her daughter that there would be enough even for a greedy little girl like her.

Finally, of course, there would be the lamb dishes. Due to availability, Persians ate lamb more than any other meat. Chickens raised in Persia were usually scrawny and tough, and beef just did not have a good enough flavor. But lamb, ah, Persian lamb was the most succulent of meats. For this party there would be *ab goosht* prepared with lamb, potatoes, tomatoes, onions various kinds of beans, limes and turmeric. There would also be eggplant and tomatoes with lamb, okra with lamb, split peas with lamb, and string beans with lamb. Of course, there would also be *dolmeh*, which was spiced ground lamb and rice wrapped in grape or cabbage leaves. Finally in the center of the table would be the *koofteh*, an enormous ball of ground lamb, mashed split peas, onions, parsley, dill, mint, salt and a raw egg. Inside would be hidden surprises of walnuts, raisins, apricots or prunes.

Beside the tea, which Ismail would provide, other drinks would include *doogh,* made of yogurt, water and a pinch of salt served over ice with a sprig of mint, as well as a variety of fruit juices.

It was well understood, however, that there would be no alcohol. Tahirih's father, Haji Youssef, scrupulously observed Muslim injunctions against imbibing any type of alcohol. The title Haji told people that he had traveled to Mecca, and this particular Haji, unlike many of his fellow Muslims, unswervingly followed the teachings of his faith regarding the drinking of alcohol.

Finally, after one final survey of the preparations, the women had a chance to sit in the salon for a short while and just chat amiably. They discussed childrearing issues, and Tahirih begged her mother's pardon for not bringing the children with her that day, as she normally did. "Now that I am in my sixth month, I just cannot keep up with the four of them all the time. I am blessed with capable servants, and I trust them to keep my children safe for a couple of hours," she explained.

They then turned to local gossip for a few minutes, but eventually Tahirih made her apologies for not being more help to her mother and asked permission to return to her own home to prepare for company coming that evening.

By the time she walked in the door, it was late afternoon. Although she really wanted to lie down and rest for a few minutes, she knew she couldn't. After easing her mind about the well being of her children, she gave orders for dinner and checked on the readiness of the large salon. Just then the baby in her belly gave a sudden kick, and she grunted with the unexpected ferocity of the movement. An active baby, she thought. It must be a boy. Ismail would be happy.

CHAPTER 5

"I will be home sometime this evening, I don't know when. Have my supper waiting."

With that, Mullah Mohsin stomped out of his house and headed toward the home of Ismail Agha, his adopted benefactor, whether Ismail knew it or not. Mohsin always enjoyed visiting Ismail's home, where the atmosphere was inevitably peaceful and pleasant, so different from his own.

Earlier in the week Ismail had approached him and asked that he come to visit. Then began the game that was always played for the alleged purpose of showing courtesy. Ismail extended the invitation, Mohsin declined for fear of imposing, Ismail insisted, and after several more 'Please come -- No, I can't intrude on your time' exchanges, ultimately the invitation was accepted. This was called *taarof*, and Mohsin found it a bother and a waste of time, but it was ingrained into Persian behavior and had to be followed.

Mohsin was always delighted to be invited to Ismail's home for reasons other than just the atmosphere. The food was plentiful, the conversation enjoyable, and even more importantly, it was a perfect excuse to cause distress to his own wife.   Out of spite, Mohsin would deliberately not inform her that he had no intention of coming home for the evening meal, so she would prepare dinner, then wait for hours before eating a little bit herself and discarding the rest or giving it to the street urchins. He would then have an admirable excuse to berate her for wasting their limited income.

In Mohsin's opinion, his wife had become a liability. Many years before he had married above himself socially, thinking that through her family connections he could become an independent businessman. His loving new wife had convinced her well-to-do father to loan Mohsin enough money to start a jewelry business. Although Mohsin tried to emulate the other jewelry merchants in the bazaar, he could not select the proper inventory, nor could he deal satisfactorily with customers who were frequently unhappy with his sales.   He squandered his father-in-law's stake in less than a year, and no amount of pleading could secure him another loan.

Mohsin began to blame his wife for her father's attitude, and ultimately decided that being a mullah would be a better career choice for him anyway. After he decided that he no longer needed her father's money, he convinced himself that his wife was displaying an arrogant attitude toward him, and consequently spent as little time at home as possible. They never had children, which he blamed entirely on her. Yes, he was sure that she deserved not to be told that he would not be eating at home that evening.

Like most mullahs, and indeed most Persians of the late nineteenth century, Mohsin was poorly educated. He was gifted, however, with an excellent memory, and had the ability to recite lengthy portions of the Koran at the mosque. This facility led people to believe that he was divinely inspired. So far as he was concerned, it really did not matter whether the recitations were accurate or not. Because the people seeking his religious services could not read anyway, no one really knew what the Koran said, so a bit of invention here and there rarely caused him problems. Thus he became a purveyor of his own words, interspersed with a few well known quotations here and there. The more he could convince people that his interpretation of the Koran met their needs, the wealthier he became; and because he did not receive a regular income from the mosque, his day-to-day existence depended on how well he could reassure people that he was knowledgeable, sincere and capable of imparting good advice. He quickly learned that what was most needed to succeed as a mullah was a facile tongue, not a thorough knowledge of the faith he preached.

When he arrived at Ismail's home, he found a warm greeting and a comfortable room awaiting him. Ismail invited him to sit on the large pillows scattered on the floor of the largest salon in the house, the one reserved for important guests. There were platters of sweets and fruits on several small tables. Tea was immediately served by the good looking servant girl Mohsin had noticed several times before. He fantasized about catching her sometime when she was out shopping and enticing her to a location where he could take his pleasure and then send her away. However, because she was Ismail's servant, he knew that he had better not act on that fantasy.

Mohsin sated his appetite with desserts because he had not eaten a real dinner, and he deliberately led Ismail to believe that his wife did not bother to prepare food for him as a good wife should.

Meanwhile, Ismail had his own reasons for inviting the mullah to his home. They began by discussing crops, weather and travel conditions, all as a prelude to what Ismail really wanted to know, which was why the Shah's son, Prince Masoud, had recently been in Shiraz. The Prince had come unexpectedly, and that always foretold trouble. But that subject would be approached slowly. For the moment, the conversation had turned to water distribution problems, with Mohsin voicing what he pretended were his own opinions.

"The foreigners want to force us to build irrigation ditches and canals. They say we will be able to have better water supply for dry areas and fewer problems with disease. But I tell you, Ismail Agha, these ideas, coming from outside Persia, are erroneous and dangerous. They do not come from Muslim minds. They are not to be trusted. The foreigners want to control us and to take over our tobacco sales. Their true desire is to undermine the supremacy of Islam, to change Persia from a devoutly Muslim society to one where Allah is no longer worshipped and unquestioningly obeyed. We must resist foreign evil with all our strength."

Mohsin worked his mind into quite a frenzy as he heatedly repeated what he had heard other mullahs say. He rarely thought critically about what his ears heard, but merely mouthed it back because other mullahs, whose opinions he considered to be indisputably correct, had expressed such thoughts.

Ismail, although not better educated, did think more critically about how much of what he heard could be reconciled with and integrated into his own understanding of the world. Although he agreed that foreigners were an evil within Persian society, he did not automatically reject any ideas they might bring with them. Actually, the idea of irrigating arid areas made sense to him, as did the concept of conserving water for dry times. However, again in keeping with Persian courtesy, he did not overtly disagree with his guest. Instead, he turned the course of the conversation to his own purposes.

"Mullah Mohsin, have you heard that Prince Masoud was recently here in Shiraz?" he asked politely. "Do you have any idea why? Perhaps it was to evaluate the financial condition of this area so he could report to his father. Or was he here for other reasons?"

Through his networks in the mosque, Mohsin had heard a lot about this subject. He became even more incensed as he remembered being told that Prince Masoud, like the Assistant Ambassador, had been tracking down heretical Baha'is.

"Prince Masoud has nobly come to hold high the banner of Islam and do away with those who would question the eternal sovereignty of the Prophet Muhammad," Mohsin arrogantly asserted. "Indeed, the Prince located some families practicing this heresy and punished them severely. From the rich ones he confiscated all their property, and the poor ones had their homes burned down around them. Yes, the Prince is a true guardian of the Faith."

In reality, the Prince was well known for being more interested in causing misery and stirring up trouble than trying to eradicate heresy. But Mohsin, lacking the capacity to understand that the royal behavior was more for sport than religious fervor, saw only that the Prince was fighting for the cause of Islam.

As Ismail politely listened, he realized that he had secured the information he wanted. Expanding his business over the next few years was his major concern, so it was critical that he adopt all necessary precautions. Because he did not want to jeopardize his family's well being by offending either the palace or the clergy, he began to devise ways to ferret out possible heretics intruding into the bazaar. The most critical thing for him, he decided, was to avoid dealing with newcomers, since he was certain that the bazaaris with whom he had dealt for many years would not be heretics. Gradually, he would ask strategic questions of the new merchants, and judge their devotion to Allah according to their responses.

When he was comfortable in his mind that he knew what he was going to do, he gradually turned the conversation away from Baha'is and toward Muharram, the upcoming celebration to honor the prophet Muhammad's grandson Husayn, the most beloved of all martyrs in Shi'ite Islam.

"How may I help to prepare for Muharram this year?" Ismail asked deferentially.

Seizing on an opportunity to line his pockets, Mohsin answered quickly. "We always need financial contributions to defray expenses incurred by the parade. You know, banners must be made, food has to be prepared, there are many costs. If you could offer a small gift to the mosque, I will be glad to convey it there for you. Your generosity will be most welcome, and will surely be rewarded by Allah."

Ismail was a bit surprised. His understanding was that everyone provided their own banners and that food was donated from the community. Nonetheless, he was happy to provide whatever the clergy asked, and immediately gave a substantial sum for Mohsin to take back to the mosque.

Then he asked a favor. "Tell me again, Mullah Mohsin, the wonderful story of the martyr Husayn. No, wait one moment. I want Tahirih to be here to listen as well. She loves this story as much as I do."

The presence of Ismail's charming young wife made Mohsin's storytelling even more gratuitous, and after Tahirih had seated herself shyly beside her husband, Mohsin delightedly launched into recounting his tale to a captive audience.

"You remember," he began pompously, "that our beloved Prophet had a daughter whom he named Fatima. He loved this child dearly, and when she came of an age to be married, Muhammad prudently chose his nephew, Ali, to be her husband."

"Now Ali was very dear to the Prophet, and all good Muslims know that Muhammad, blessed be His name, designated this beloved son-in-law to be Caliph when the Prophet himself finally went to live eternally with Allah. However, to the everlasting shame of Islam," -- here Mohsin allowed his eyes to mist as he sniffed and wiped his nose on the sleeve of his robe -- "on the day our beloved Prophet passed on from this world, some of the followers acted preposterously. In great error, they selected Muhammad's uncle, Abu Bakr, to be Caliph, rather than Ali."

"When Ali learned of this, he was dismayed, but decided, in the best interests of Islam, not to challenge this erroneous decision, thinking that the wrong would soon be righted. But justice did not come immediately. Three more impostors were selected to lead the True Faith after Abu Bakr, and it was more than a decade before Ali finally became Caliph."

"The followers of Islam who accept this erroneous succession are known as Sunnis. However, Persian Muslims understand the error committed, and we scorn the four usurpers of the holy mantle of Islam. We call ourselves Shi'ite Muslims to show the difference between ourselves and the wrong thinking Sunnis."

Mohsin paused strategically, then continued. "Now Ali had sons through the Prophet's beloved daughter Fatima. Following Ali's death, his eldest son Hassan became Caliph for a short time. This beloved person was tricked into ceding the mantle of Islam to the contemptible Governor of Damascus, who immediately named his own son to be Caliph." Here Mohsin shook his head as if he could not believe that anyone could commit such a grievous sin.

"However, Ali's second son Husayn challenged this sacrilege, and in the most glorious battle in the history of Islam, Husayn heroically defended the Faith which had been ordained by Allah and established by his grandfather. He was martyred for his valiant efforts, and to this day, pious Muslims celebrate the Feast of Muharram to commemorate the eternal bravery of Husayn."

Ismail sighed softly as he listened to this oft recounted tale once again, and he thanked Mullah Mohsin for sharing it with him and his wife. He nodded to Tahirih, who excused herself and left to supervise putting the children to bed, while the men continued to talk for another hour or so. After a while, despite trying not to, Ismail began to yawn.

Mohsin did not notice and continued a one-sided diatribe in which he outlined his beliefs about education and women and foreigners and whatever else came to his mind. When Ismail finally signaled a servant to gather up the teacups, Mohsin reluctantly stood up to take his leave, but continued talking for another half hour as Ismail gently guided him toward the door.

The following morning Mohsin went to the mosque to assist with the orchestration of the parades, all the while jingling the money Ismail had given him the night before in his pocket. It did not take much thought for him to decide not to share it with the Chief Mullah.

Already, there was a lot of commotion outside the mosque, which meant that his fellow mullahs had begun to sell strategic locations in the parade formation to the wealthiest men so they could be clearly visible to the watchers. Mohsin quickly joined in, explaining where the best positions were, and offering his humble thanks for the many coins slipped into his outstretched hand.

Actually, for Mohsin, Muharram was an unpleasant experience. During the march, the men of the city beat themselves with whips while crying out in sympathy for the martyrdom of their beloved Husayn. They would strike themselves first over the right shoulder, then over then left, back and forth again and again, using whips made of long metal chains. Some also cut themselves with razors. As a mullah, Mohsin was expected to be in the forefront of the mourners, leading the self flagellation as a demonstration of piety. However, Mohsin was terrified of blood, especially his own, and he certainly did not want to create scars which would mar his smooth skin and beautiful visage. Last year he had conveniently become ill the night before the parade, but knew he could not get away with that for a second year. Well, he would have to think of something.

After a couple hours, the noise died down and Mohsin, along with some of his fellow mullahs took a break from their work. They sat idly by the side of the street and chatted about women and wealth, and how to acquire both with as little commitment as possible. Mohsin enjoyed these conversations and always had his own spicy remarks to add. The men laughed raucously, and some of the passersby wondered what the pious mullahs were finding so funny.

Meanwhile, at his stall in the bazaar, Ismail contemplated his participation in this year's parade. For a reason he could not quite grasp, he felt a special need to demonstrate his devotion to the Prophet and his grandson this year. It was as if a malignancy were growing within himself, and also within his society. Something needed to be changed, but he could not identify what it was that was so disturbing. He only knew that he was profoundly troubled.

The following day, he went to the mosque and spoke with Mullah Mohsin about where to position himself in the parade. The mullah advised him to stay near the front left area, since that was where he could best be seen by the bystanders. He accepted more coins, even though he had given the same advice to several others.

CHAPTER 6

The following day, Manizheh stopped by her daughter's home for a short visit. This child, she thought happily, was married to a very good man. Ismail was not only wealthy, but pious and thoughtful as well. Very few husbands turned out to be all three.

When she arrived, she found Tahirih talking with one of the servants and it seemed to concern a problem. However, upon seeing her mother, Tahirih immediately dismissed the servant and took her mother to the most comfortable salon in her house.

"Mother, how wonderful to see you," she said with great feeling. "Are you well? And Father? How is Aunt Azra? And her children?" She continued asking about all the family members, as was expected.

After assuring her daughter that everyone was fine, Manizheh asked what Tahirih and the servant had been discussing when she arrived.

"Well," Tahirih began, "Father recently asked Ismail to provide work for a servant who has turned out to be nothing but trouble. The servant's name is Firidun, and there is always a problem between him and someone in this household. He behaves like a bully and I think we should get rid of him, but when I said something to Ismail, he told me there was no way we could do that. Then, when I pushed the issue, Ismail became unusually angry. Eventually, I just let the matter drop, since it disturbed Ismail so much." From her own experience with trying to make suggestions to a husband about something he did not want to discuss, Manizheh advised Tahirih not to press Ismail for Firidun's dismissal. Eventually everything would work out.

However, neither woman knew the harsh reality. Firidun was Tahirih's half-brother, born to a former servant in Haji Youssef's house. Haji had determined that Ismail was the only son-in-law he could trust to keep an eye on the boy, since he did not want his own sons to know of his perfidy. So even though Tahirih was Ismail's wife, she had no idea that the hellion causing everyone so much grief in her home was in truth her father's illegitimate son.

Believing that her mother always offered sound advice, Tahirih broached yet another matter which had been disturbing her. "Dearest Mother, recently I asked Ismail for permission to learn to read." Her mother looked shocked, so Tahirih hurried along. "If he allowed me to do that, I told him I could help him with his business dealings. Well, he did not appreciate my offer, and he told me that a woman does not need to know how to read or write. He ordered me never to bring the topic up again."

Manizheh did not even have to consider an answer to this problem. She, too, had very firm ideas on the education of women. "My daughter, Ismail is absolutely correct. You must leave business dealings to him. You certainly have more than enough to do raising the children and managing the household. Men are responsible for providing for their families. It is his duty to take care of you, and he does a wonderful job of it. Be thankful for what you have, and don't bother with what you don't need to know"

Out of duty, Tahirih nodded her head submissively, while within herself she felt devastated, and tears nearly sprang to her eyes. Nontheles, she forced herself to talk normally about other matters. She told her mother that Ismail was thinking about taking the oldest boy to the bazaar with him when he turned six, which was only one year away. Tahirih was concerned that the child might wander off in the bazaar and be lost or hurt. Again her mother advised her to accept her husband's decision.

"It is of utmost importance to maintain harmony," her mother reminded her. "There is only one leader in the family, and Allah has said it should be the man. So be it. Ismail is a devoted and loving father. He will surely watch over his son with a careful eye."

After her mother left, Tahirih recalled another problem within her household. Talat, a seventeen year old servant girl who had worked in Tahirih's home for three years now, had recently been acting distressed, which was highly unusual. Tahirih walked through the house looking for Talat, and to her surprise, found the servant sitting by the small pool in the garden behind the house. Normally, Talat was a very hard worker, and her sitting idly in the middle of the day was surprising.

When Talat saw her mistress approaching, she jumped to her feet and immediately apologized for her laziness.

"It is all right to rest sometimes," Tahirih assured her. "Please remain in the garden for a moment. I want to talk with you."

Talat became very nervous, which puzzled Tahirih. Thinking that the problem might be a fear of losing her job if she married, Tahirih broached the subject directly. "Talat, you are now seventeen years old. Has your family begun to look for a husband for you?" Tahirih inquired. "Your husband would be welcome to live here and work for us, so you would both be assured of employment."

Talat looked at her mistress with almost distrustful eyes, which further surprised Tahirih. She and the servant girl had always communicated well, and she thought she was doing her duty by looking out for Talat's future.

"Thank you, Mistress," Talat responded respectfully, 'but marriage is not on my mind at this time. Please allow me to return to my duties."

Tahirih knew that Talat was very shy around men and thought perhaps she had heard bad things about the marriage bed from older women like Parvin. She resolved that in the near future, she would try to tell her how wonderful that part of marriage could be, but this did not appear to be the right time. Tahirih left the girl by the pool and went back inside her house to resume supervision of dinner.

The next morning she went next door to visit her neighbor whose daughter, a long time friend of Tahirih's, was to be married soon. The husband-to-be was a wealthy landowner who lived several hundred miles away, and within her own heart, Tahirih wondered how the girl could possibly bear to move so far away from her parents and home.

"Good afternoon, Khanem," Tahirih greeted the mother, using the term of respect women used with one another. "Is Monera preparing for her wonderful day?"

"Ah, Tahirih. You are so close to having your own fifth child, yet you come to offer help to your neighbor. You are so thoughtful. Allah will bless you," answered the distraught woman. "Monera is upset right now. Please talk with her. A friend is better than a mother right now," the woman answered sorrowfully.

Puzzled, Tahirih was conducted to the bedroom where the two girls had spent many an hour giggling and playing as children. Monera was desolately packing her personal belongings. With a sigh, the mother left them alone.

After considerable prodding, Monera reluctantly confessed that she was frightened about marrying a man she had never met. "How can I move so far away?" she cried. "What if I don't like him? What if he beats me? How can I let my family know that I am in trouble? I will be all alone with no one to help me."

"But Monera, he is your father's nephew, your own cousin. Even if you have never met him, he is family. He will treat you well, I am sure. You need not be frightened."

"He is twice my age. What if I do not please him and he abandons me?"

The exchange continued for several minutes, with Tahirih trying to be comforting, and Monera reiterating her fears. Finally, Monera's mother came to the doorway and sternly told her daughter not to be foolish. She would have a chance to meet her bridegroom two days before the wedding, when he came to town with all his family. If she did not like him then, she could call the whole thing off.

Neither Monera nor Tahirih said anything. Although everyone knew that refusing a husband was formally allowed in Islam, in reality, it occurred about as often as snow fell in the desert. A young girl did not defy her family on so important a matter. But at least it put an end to the talk about the upcoming marriage, and the conversation changed to less emotional topics.

"My butcher promised me enough meat to feed all our guests," the mother said. "Now he is saying that his suppliers won't give him what he needs and he has to coordinate with others from far away to get enough for me. He is trying to charge me a lot more money for his supposed inconvenience." She was obviously near her wit's end as she tried to tie up all the loose ends for her daughter's wedding.

"Are you talking about the one whose shop is two blocks from here?" Tahirih asked. "I know him. Actually, I discharged him recently because his meat was bad. I found another butcher who will treat you much better, I am sure. I will give you his name."

"Oh, thank you, Tahirih Khanem. It will be a great burden off my shoulders. Everything else is taken care of, I think. My mother-in-law is lending me some of her servants and the house is cleaned and almost ready. My husband has made necessary arrangements with the mullah for the service. If it rains we have provisions for celebrating indoors. The food was my only remaining concern. We are having relatives come from other cities, so they will be staying with us for several days. Actually, some are coming tomorrow. I need to be sure their rooms are ready." With that the mother again left the young women alone.

"Monera, do not be frightened," Tahirih implored. "I know that you do not know your husband-to-be, but your family does. They have your best interests at heart. Your father knows his nephew and has selected him as the best candidate of the many who have come to him asking for you in marriage, just as my father did. It will be all right."

Monera smiled tentatively and thanked Tahirih for her comforting words as Tahirih took her leave.

It was late afternoon by the time Tahirih returned to her own home. Expecting her husband back anytime, she checked on meal preparations, then cut some flowers from the garden to put in the dining room.

By that time, the twins had awakened and were crying to be fed. Her heart filled with joy as she observed her children. All of them were healthy, thanks be to Allah. Husayn was a handful, but so were all five year olds, especially boys. For a moment she wondered what made boys and girls so different to raise. Somehow girls were brought up to be obedient, while boys were allowed to talk back and even be aggressive towards their mothers. She did not approve of this, but it did not seem to bother Ismail. It was the way he had been brought up. Now his mother obeyed him, rather than the other way around. Tahirih wasn't sure she wanted it to be the same between herself and her son when he became older.

For once, she did not hear Ismail arrive home, remove his outdoor shoes, and walk to the back of the house to find his wife.

She was still playing with the twins, singing them silly songs while she tickled the bottoms of their feet.

Ismail watched for a little while before making his presence known. Her gentleness was always comforting, and it was a few minutes before he cleared his throat to announce his presence.

"Good evening, Tahirih Khanem." He greeted his wife formally, to show both respect and love. "Have the children behaved themselves today?"

Startled at the unexpected voice, she nearly knocked over a vase on the table. "Oh, I am so sorry, Ismail. I did not hear you come in." Quickly but awkwardly, she rose to her feet and called to Parvin to come get the children.

Ismail sat down on the couch and began talking about his day. On this particular evening, they were not expecting any company and they both looked forward to a quiet time by themselves.

"Young Abbas came to talk with me today," Ismail began. Abbas was a protégé whom Ismail had taken under his wing several years before, and he was now nearing thirty. "Although he did not say so directly, of course, I believe he wants to enter into some sort of partnership with me. He hinted he could do the buying, which would relieve me from so much travel. He claims to have found some new strains of tea from northern India which he believes would mix very well with our Persian teas. It is something for me to think about."

Tahirih was amazed to hear that her husband would even consider taking on a partner. He never relied on anyone else to do what he could do for himself, and she knew very well that he certainly did not want to share his profits. She answered cautiously.

"Dearest Ismail, you know how much I miss you when you are away on your buying trips. For me, it would be a gift from Allah to have someone else doing that for you. But are you sure you can rely on Abbas's judgment? What does he know about the tea business?"

Ismail was amused by her caution. "Not a great deal yet," he agreed. "He is still learning. Today he told me that he knew some people who recently came back from visiting England." He paused briefly while Parvin brought in a bowl of fruit. "While there," he continued, "they were served a tea from India that they had never tasted before. They brought some back to Shiraz, and he let me try a little this afternoon. Indeed, it is good."

Tahirih was not convinced. "Just because he may have found a new kind of tea does that mean he knows how to negotiate properly. Can he be relied upon to procure the tea, have it delivered and assure the price? It would be a great disaster for you if shipments did not come in as you expected."

Again Ismail chuckled at his wife's concern for his business's well being. "I am only considering the possibility, dear Wife. Abbas and I will have many more discussions before I agree to allow him to negotiate on my behalf."

Parvin came to the doorway to announce that supper was ready. With the main repast served at noon, supper was a light meal, and because there was no company coming this evening, they enjoyed a leisurely time as Tahirih provided an account of her visit next door. Ismail told her that he had met the groom's father several years before when he traveled to the west.

"I don't remember the groom himself, but his father was a fine man," he commented. "As I recall, his house was the center of all activities in that village. I remember that he had an incredible 'open door' policy. Anyone could come for a meal any time they wanted. There was always plenty of food and an outsider's presence was never considered a burden."

Tahirih had never heard of such a thing. Extra people for dinner every day? How could a wife plan? There would be so much wasted food if one day no one came, or maybe sometimes she would have too little. It made her feel ill even to contemplate such an arrangement. She was grateful that her husband was more practical.

Following supper, they strolled around the neighborhood, and chatted about day-to-day matters. Ismail decided not to tell Tahirih of his plans to take a second wife just yet. Although he expected that she would appreciate having a companion of her own rank around the house during the day, he did know that sometimes women did not always get along when married to the same man, and he did not want to disturb her just before their next child was due.

CHAPTER 7

In Shiraz, the day of the religious parade had finally arrived, and everywhere preparations were being finalized for this wonderful day dedicated to the glory of Islam. Wives and mothers had sewn special white shirts for this day, and young boys begged their fathers to be allowed to march with them. Early in the morning the men went to their pre-assigned spots and were often disillusioned when they found that their special location had been sold to three or four other men as well.

Ali, the goldsmith, was one of those who found several others already squabbling over his place in the parade. He had brought his banners, his coins and his self-flagellating whips, along with a couple of nephews to carry it all. When he tried to insert himself into the spot he coveted, those who had already been arguing with each other turned against him in force.

"Here now, Ali! Move over to your right and more into the center. Mustafa and Manuchir arrived before you and have already taken the spot in front. You cannot crowd in there in front of all of us," the shouts began.

"But look," Ali retorted, "I have made all these wonderful banners -- do you see the red and blue and gold colors -- and they must be seen by the pious who stand along the road watching us."

The mullahs were called over to mediate, but somehow Mullah Mohsin, who had sold the locations, could not be found anywhere. Someone said that he was not feeling well and was resting until the time came for the parade to begin.

Elsewhere amid the parade organization, others were having similar disputes, but by the time the mullahs said "Go!" everyone appeared reconciled in order to preserve the good intentions of the parade. Many, however, planned to visit Mullah Mohsin the following day and demand a return of their bribe, but they would not get it. They would be told that it was too bad that mistakes had been made, but, of course, the purpose of the parade was to honor Husayn and thereby Allah, so what was most important was for Allah to know you were there, wherever you happened to be in the formation.

Ismail gave Tahirih permission to watch the parade, but forbade her to bring the children. Tahirih agreed with her husband on this point and arranged for the servants to watch them while she was gone. She, herself, had had second thoughts about the long day of standing because she was now near her eighth month, but in the end decided that she felt well enough. Her black chador, which covered her head to foot and was held closed in front by her hand, would hide her condition.

She and some neighbor women found a slightly elevated knoll beside the parade route and stood there waiting for the parade to begin. They knew that it would start several blocks away, then wind through the streets until it passed this open area. Most observers liked to be either at the beginning or the end, but Tahirih preferred being here where she could watch the parade with more ease and less crowding. The other women moved away slightly, and eventually Tahirih found herself surrounded by strangers.

She greeted the unknown woman next to her. "Is your husband marching in the parade today?"

The woman answered in a very friendly manner. "Oh, no. My husband is not here. Actually, I'm not sure why I'm here. I guess I've just heard so much about the parade of Muharram that I wanted to see it for myself."

Tahirih was astounded. The woman looked to be about her age.

"Your husband is not in the parade, yet he allowed you to attend? How is that? Is this really the first time you have been here?"

The woman laughed gently. "My husband encourages me to decide important things for myself. He knows where I am and he probably has a relative somewhere watching to be sure I'm safe. But he would not forbid me to come. That's the way he is. And no, I have never seen this parade before."

Tahirih had never heard of a woman having such freedom. She was a little appalled, but even more intrigued.

"Well, he is surely an unusual man. Although my husband is generous and very kind to me, I could not be here if he did not approve."

Tahirih was surprising herself by speaking so openly to a

stranger, but somehow she felt that this woman was someone with whom she could communicate confidentially.

"I do not remember seeing you before. Do you live nearby?" she asked boldly.

"I'm sorry," the woman said courteously. "I did not introduce myself. My name is Soraya and we do not live too far away. My husband comes from a family of merchants, carpet sellers. He has several brothers, and they procure the best carpets available, then ship them here for my husband to sell. He has a stall in the bazaar, and some of his brothers also have other storefronts in the city. One day, if you would like, I will be happy to go to the bazaar with you and we could look at his carpets."

The woman then became embarrassed. "Oh, I'm so sorry. I surely do not mean to intrude on your time. I simply meant that I would like to become better acquainted with you and hoped that we could meet again."

Tahirih was drawn to this stranger and immediately replied, "I would like that, thank you. My name is Tahirih, and my husband is also a merchant in the bazaar. Perhaps they know each other."

Suddenly the parade came into view, and both women turned to watch. The noise preceded the vision. A legion of men were marching together, chanting praises to Allah and weeping in remembrance of the heinous assassination of Husayn. Together they prayed loudly for the spread of Islam to all humanity. It was indeed a magnificent picture, with much of the adult population of Shiraz either standing along the side of the streets or marching in the parade, united in the solitary purpose of glorifying Allah through recognition of His martyr Husayn. Now Tahirih could see the banners and they were exquisite. Some had words, which she could not read, and others were portraits of Husayn, either riding proudly on horseback as a mighty warrior or kneeling humbly as a pious servant of Allah praying for victory against the evil usurper.

As the parade approached the knoll where Tahirih and Soraya stood, the noise became deafening. Cries from the men were now of actual pain more than sympathetic understanding of the martyrdom of Husayn. Tahirih could see blood splashed all over everything, even the portraits and the banners. She thought the sight was sacrilegious, not awe inspiring. Surely human blood should not desecrate the holy words of the Koran or pictures of the martyr, she thought.

After prolonged searching, she finally spotted Ismail on the far side of the column. She was proud that he had not tried to demand a special place, but had instead accepted the place he was given. Although Tahirih revered the martyr Husayn, as she did nearly everything about Islam, she believed that piety should not be demonstrated by showing off one's wealth and power, and she was grateful that her husband seemed to have the same convictions.

"There is Ismail," she pointed out to Soraya, "The one without a beard on the far side of the group."

"Ah, he is very good looking, and his countenance is that of a kind and peaceful man. You are a fortunate woman," Soraya commented.

They continued to watch. A trail of red followed the marchers and it grew more and more manifest as they proceeded along their way toward the mosque. Snowy white shirts were no longer snowy white, and smooth skins were no longer unblemished. Tears co-mingled with blood as the men mourned the death of Husayn. Ordinarily, men did not cry, certainly not in public. But this occasion was different. On this day, public crying was not only acceptable but expected.

Some of the marchers were truly crying for the beloved martyr, but many more were there for the show of it. On this day it was hard to tell who was who. The daily practice of caring for the poor and behaving honorably were the real tests of a Muslim man, but this parade did not identify such people.

Mullah Mohsin was running alongside the paraders acting like a cheerleader. Although he had reportedly been ill only an hour before, he now had the strength to encourage men to hold their banners higher, to shout louder and to show Allah the greatness of their piety. By doing this, of course, he did not have time to beat himself and draw his own blood. His role was larger than that; it was to encourage everyone else to do so. So indeed, he had found a way to avoid self mutilation for yet another year, and he was sure the same trick could be used in the future.

The women watched the paraders pass them by, then when the parade was over, Tahirih bade Soraya goodbye and rejoined the others with whom she had come to the parade. They walked slowly back toward their homes, in no great hurry to return to their pressing lives of service to husbands and children. It was not often that women were able to be away from their daily routine, and the religious parade once a year served them well as an excuse. Today they could not be faulted for lingering, for they were demonstrating piety just as their husbands were.

As they approached their homes, the women reluctantly turned in at their own doorways. Tahirih's home was the last one on the street, and by the time she entered her doorway, she was exhausted. Her feet hurt and her back was beginning to spasm. She hoped that she would find everything under control and that she could lie down quietly and rest for a while.

When she opened the door, she heard silence. Her first reaction was alarm. Where were the children? She smelled food cooking but did not see any of the servants. She hurried to the kitchen where she finally spotted Cook. Agitatedly, she asked him where everyone else was.

"Parvin thought you would need to rest when you returned home this afternoon, so she took the children away for a little while," he answered. "She will be back later this evening, and the children will have been fed. She hopes that you will rest a little while they are gone." He looked at her and saw how tired she looked. "Please rest, Khanem. Your new child will be here soon, and then you will be even busier than you are now."

Bless Parvin, Tahirih thought gratefully. She had not asked permission to do this because she knew Tahirih would consider it an inconvenience and not allow it, so had taken it upon herself to give her mistress a little free time. Now Tahirih had the house to herself for a few hours. She gladly went to her room and lay down, falling asleep immediately.

When she awoke, it was to a horrific pain in her back. She looked at the clock and saw that she had been sleeping for more than three hours. By now everyone should have returned home, but she still did not hear any noise. She tried to sit up but was jerked back by the ferocity of the pain. With absolute clarity, she knew what was happening. Her child was coming early. In a panic, she told herself that this could not be happening, but it was. She struggled again to sit up, and called desperately for help.

"Parvin, Talat, Zahreh, someone. Come help me." The pain was overwhelming, and she was beginning to lose consciousness.

When she awoke again, it was to see her newborn child dangling off the bed from a cord between her legs. She tried to reach for it, but fainted before she could get a solid grasp. Later she re-awoke, and this time forced herself to pull the baby toward her as she again began calling for help.

This time Cook heard and came to her door, but he did not dare to open it. "What do you want, Mistress?" he asked fearfully.

"Help. The baby has come," she gasped. She could say no more, as she again faded into another realm.

All the servants were gone, except his daughter Zahreh, who Cook knew would be useless in this situation. Nonetheless, he had to call her.

"Go," he commanded ferociously. "Go next door and get help. The mistress needs a woman."

This time, Zahreh did as she was told, and in a few moments Monera's mother arrived.

Assessing the situation instantly, she took full command. She cut the umbilical cord and tenderly wrapped the dead boy child in white cloths. Then she turned her attention to the poor mother who did not yet know what had happened.

"Tahirih, love, can you hear me?" Getting no answer, she soaked a cloth in cold water and gently wiped Tahireh's face. After what seemed an eternity, Tahirih flickered her eyes open.

"Why are you here?" she murmured, not immediately remembering what had happened. Then she began to wail.

"My baby, my baby!" she screamed. "No, no! It cannot be." Her hands went to her stomach, and she felt the diminished size. "Bring me my son. I must hold him. Now. I must have my son. Bring him to me."

Monera held Tahireh's hands and allowed her to continue to scream. Eventually, she spoke quietly. "Tahirih Khanem, you must be strong," her neighbor admonished gently. "It is the will of Allah that not all children live. Some are fortunate that they go immediately to Heaven and do not have to live with the cruelties of this world. Praise Allah that he has granted this blessing to your child."

Although the words were meant as comfort, they did not have that effect. Tahirih's screams fell to a whimpering, her psychic pain being far greater than her physical wounds.

"Why did I stand for so long today. I killed my child. My innocent baby is dead because of me."

The sobbing was relentless and her neighbor could do nothing to relieve the anguish.

CHAPTER 8

Mojtabeh Amuzegar, Assistant Ambassador to Russia, was preparing to attend the party at his cousin Haji Youssef's home. He knew it was a testament to his importance that Youssef had not canceled the party, even though Youssef's daughter had suffered a miscarriage only a few days before. He spoke to himself while twirling his mustache.

"Yes, Mojtabeh Amuzegar. You are important and you have done well for yourself. Not only do you have wealth, but respect as well. Truly, your cousin does himself honor by inviting you as his principal guest tonight." He brushed his hair back for the fourth time and flicked unseen specks from his clothes. "That sharp-eyed wife of his will undoubtedly be hinting at ways to have her sons come to Tehran to enter the diplomatic service. I don't know how Youssef tolerates her. She concerns herself with matters that are meant only for men to handle, not meddling wives."

Although Mojtabeh was critical of his cousin's wife, he was quite fond of Youssef himself. He and Youssef had been not only cousins but best friends during their youth. Tonight they would have a chance to reminisce about some of the more exciting adventures they had engaged in as children. That was one nice thing, he thought, about the Muslim custom of having social gatherings separated into male and female rooms. Men could talk about things that women should not hear.

Mojtabeh continued to admire himself. At forty-seven, he maintained a healthy appearance by eating sparingly of sweets and, of course, avoiding alcohol, although that was difficult in Russia and he sometimes slipped. His fierce eyes frightened people when he found it convenient to create an atmosphere of intimidation, and his size added to the aura of great might. Measuring more than six feet, he was taller than most Persians, and his youthful passion for wrestling and weight lifting had made him very broad chested. He maintained an aloof manner with people he did not consider valuable, yet could be diplomatically engaging when the occasion called for it. For the last twenty-two of his forty-seven years he had been a faithful servant of his master, Nasir-al-Din, Shah of all the Persia Empires. Somehow, he had always felt that his duties were such that he could not marry, despite the efforts of many mothers of beautiful young women to convince him otherwise.

He added a few final touches to his appearance, before calling for his horse. Although Persian etiquette normally would have required that an out-of-town visitor stay with relatives, his situation was different because he was in Shiraz for the purpose of pursuing official court business. Indeed, he needed to be free to follow up on an investigation of various groups who had been making trouble for the Shah in Shiraz.

Mojtabeh arrived at Youssef's home fashionably late. He noted that thirty or so guests had already arrived at the well kept estate by the time he rode up on his magnificent black stallion. He was pleased to see that many of the party goers were men he had wanted to talk with, including several mullahs and some important bazaaris. It appeared that Youssef had, as usual, done a good job of selecting the right people for his social gathering.

As he dismounted, he heard Youssef's booming voice. "My dearest cousin Mojtabeh. How honored we are to have you with us tonight! Nabil, take his horse and be sure to cool it properly before stabling." The servant hurried to fulfill his master's wishes, as Youssef continued. "Now, Mojtabeh, come in and join our humble gathering. Soon Shahjari will arrive. You remember him, I am sure, the most famous reciter of poetry in all of Persia."

Mojtabeh nodded his head to indicate that he knew the fame of the old man, as Youssef resumed the greeting. "Tonight he is going to remind us of the exploits of Rustam. I recall from the days of our childhood how much you and I liked to pretend we were Rustam and his foes. You always seemed to win our battles, if memory serves me."

Mojtabeh let out his calculated laugh and nodded politely to several guests as he entered Youssef's house. Inside, he was pleased to note that Manizheh was not only cordial tonight, but also seemed to know her place. As soon as she had greeted him properly, she retired from the presence of the men and busied herself with kitchen duties.

Mojtabeh circulated among the guests comfortably, choosing not to put on his usual air of superiority. As had been his plan, he was soon talking with people from whom he had hoped to pump valuable information.

"Mullah Reza, how is your family?" he greeted a clergyman whom he had encountered several times before. "Is your eldest son well? I recall that he fell from a horse last summer and broke his leg. Is he able to walk now?"

Clearly honored that such a distinguished person would remember this incident, the mullah replied, "He is fine. Allah's will be done," and gave a slight bow to the Assistant Ambassador. A few minutes later, Mojtabeh brought the conversation around to his particular interest, slyly mentioning that he had heard of some miscreants voicing anti-Shah sentiments in Shiraz. "Have you heard about this?" he asked a group of guests.

Responses came from many at the same time. One man spoke angrily of a group of troublemakers who did not want railroads to be built, and another had heard of some ruffians complaining that the Shah wanted to create a new kind of police force that would have more power than the local gendarmes. These complaints were common throughout Persia, Mojtabeh knew, and indeed the Shah had specifically directed him to assess the magnitude of resistance to both of these issues. After an hour of circulating, Mojtabeh learned that the bazaaris were more comfortable with the idea of building a railroad, since that would make business development more viable, and the mullahs liked having a strong police presence to enforce clerical mandates such as attendance at mosque every week and the suppression of heresy. Mojtabeh was satisfied that in southern Persia, at least, the Shah's policies would not be overwhelmingly opposed by the two largest social forces in the country, the businessmen and the clergy.

When their host came to announce the arrival of Shahjari, he joined everyone else in arranging themselves on pillows scattered around the living room. Discussion of current day politics was abandoned in favor of listening to stories from the past. Hidden behind heavy drapes, the women also listened raptly to the wonderful stories about the greatness of their Persian heritage as Shahjari recited from the <u>Shah</u> <u>Nameh</u>, which meant <u>Letter</u> <u>of</u> <u>the</u> <u>Kings</u>. This was one of the longest epic poems ever written, much longer than the <u>Iliad</u> or the <u>Odyssey</u> and had been composed a thousand years before the people who were listening that night had been born. It recounted the exploits of Rustam in the early shrouds of Persian empirical history, and despite having been recited thousands of times, the <u>Shah</u> <u>Nameh</u> still captivated hearts and illumined imaginations. For the next hour and a half, Shahjari held the unswerving attention of the guests as he told of the feats of Rustam, the mightiest of all Persian warriors.

"This was a man whose strength was beyond imagining, and the mention of whose name struck terror into the heart of anyone who called him enemy," Shahjari began. He went on to narrate verse after verse, finally getting to the part of the story all his listeners wanted to hear, even though it was so sad. It described the battle where Rustam had fought with a younger man whose strength, to everyone's astonishment, very nearly equaled that of Rustam himself. After a fierce struggle, Rustam finally prevailed and slew his challenger, only to learn later that it was his own long lost son whom he had killed. Shahjari's audience was in tears as the end brought silence to all.

When the recitation was finished and adulations for Shahjari's gift of storytelling sufficiently acknowledged, the guests prepared for dancing. The sound of the lutes brought to mind nightingales in the garden, and the drums beat rhythmically, calling the men to dance provocatively while watchers clapped and whistled. Violins sang in the background as Mojtabeh Amuzegar was among the first to enter the circle of clappers, his fingers snapping and his feet moving first one direction, then another, while his hips swayed in circles. His eyes fixed on certain people in the crowd, commanding them to observe and appreciate his abilities. Other men joined him in the circle, and the noise level grew as raucous laughter began.

Tahirih's husband Ismail sat on the fringes, sipping tea and watching. He was barely able to maintain his composure as he contemplated his lost son and his wife who was so distraught that she had not yet left her room. Much of the talk going on around him was idle, with no lasting importance other than a way to pass time at a party.

"Look at Omar -- he is a tree in the wind," remarked one guest. "His movements are more intricate than those of a belly dancer."

That brought laughter and raised tea cups.

"And Mustafa -- he can't get his feet to go the right direction. His body goes back and forth and his feet go side to side."

The men continued to comment on those performing, but declined invitations to join the group in the circle.

"We would rather talk about you than have you talk about us," they laughed.

When not watching the dancing, they discussed the poetry of Persia's beloved poet, Omar Khayyam. Although most could not read, they had heard it often and many had memorized his famous quatrains.

> Wake! For Morning in the Bowl of Night
>
> Has flung the Stone that puts the stars to flight:
>
> And Lo! The Hunter of the East has caught
>
> The Sultan's Turret in a Noose of Light."

quoted one person, while another responded with

> "Here with a Loaf of Bread beneath the Bough,
>
> A Flask of Wine, a Book of Verse - and Thou
>
> Beside me singing in the Wilderness -
>
> And Wilderness is Paradise enow."

"Ah, but my favorite is this," pronounced Ismail, finally joining in to the conversation.

> "The Moving Finger writes; and having writ.
>
> Moves on: nor all thy Piety nor Wit
>
> Shall lure it back to cancel half a line.
>
> Nor all thy Tears wash out a Word of it."

"Yes, that is undoubtedly the best verse," other men agreed, paying deference to a man who had just lost a son.

Mojtabeh had finally tired of dancing and come to join the men sitting on the sidelines.

"What masterly topics have you been discussing?" he inquired.

The men laughed and shifted themselves so that Mojtabeh might have the most comfortable cushion.

"We have been deciding who is the best dancer tonight, and we have all nominated you," answered one man jokingly. "But then again, we might consider little Saeed." The group chuckled at the reference to Haji Youssef's seven year old grandson who had sneaked into the party and bounced up and down with the dancers until one of them had caught him up and carried him to another room where one of the women whisked him off to bed.

Having learned what he wanted for the Shah, Mojtabeh now studiously avoided serious discussion and instead encouraged bazaar gossip. One of the men in the group described a transaction he had completed the previous day.

"He came in from one of the villages a few miles outside Shiraz, wearing a coat so old that I think it may have belonged to a descendant of Hud."

The men chortled at this reference to the ancient prophet of the Koran who had warned the people of his time of impending doom if they did not obey the laws of Allah.

"And he approached my stall so cautiously that I thought I might need to go away so that he would be comfortable looking at my carpets. Finally he became bold enough to begin negotiating, but it was difficult even for me to figure out just which carpet he really wanted. But when we finished up, he had gotten one of my best carpets at a price far lower than I would have considered for anyone else. So tell me, who is the country bumpkin and who the crafty merchant?"

Everyone in the gathering laughed as they recalled similar incidents of feeling sorry for someone, just to find themselves totally outdone at their own game. More food was put out, and the group broke up as the men went to sample new delicacies.

"Haji Youssef, I think you have married the best pastry maker in all of Shiraz," declared one guest. The others agreed instantly, and the quality and abundance of the food then became the topic of prolonged praise, as did the presence of Shahjari, whom many had tried to have come to their own parties but few had secured. Eventually some of the guests began their farewells, gathered their wives from rooms at the other side of the house, and left for home. Now Ismail, who wanted to expand his tea enterprise beyond the confines of Shiraz, saw an opportunity to broach a discussion with Mojtabeh.

"Mojtabeh Agha," he began, "if I may have a moment of your time." Finding a subject that he thought would interest the Assistant Ambassador, he continued, "I have traveled widely in Persia but have never been to Russia. I have heard stories of gold covered domes and beautiful architecture. Is this true?"

"Yes, as a matter of fact," Mojtabeh answered pleasantly, "I have photographs of some of the buildings in Moscow, and they are indeed as beautiful as you have heard. I need to leave right now, but perhaps tomorrow you could come to my hotel and I will show them to you. This business of photography is an amazing way to preserve what our eyes think they see but don't always remember precisely."

Ismail was amazed to have been invited to speak alone with the Assistant Ambassador at his residence, but he was even more shocked to hear the man openly admit to possessing photographs. The local clergy decried picture taking as an abomination. Ismail had heard, however, that the Shah regularly posed for pictures, and even allowed his wives to have their images captured on film, so perhaps they were not so evil as he had been led to believe.

"My most gracious thanks, Mojtabeh Agha," he hurriedly replied. "I would be most honored to share some of your precious time, if it would not be too great an inconvenience to you." The men agreed on a time for meeting the following day, then Mojtabeh mounted his stallion for the ride home. Although some other guests offered to ride with him for protection, he waved them away, saying that he would be unharmed in their safe city. Actually, he wanted to be alone to contemplate the information he had picked up during the evening, and also to think about how to contrive to meet again with a particular woman he had briefly seen through a doorway.

A bachelor with no intention of ever changing that situation, the diplomat enjoyed brief encounters here and there, although he was never serious about any dalliance. When he occasionally saw a woman who particularly attracted him, he would put his charm into full action, and just this evening he had seen such a woman. It turned out that she was a recent widow who was related to Youssef's wife. How convenient, he thought purposefully to himself.

CHAPTER 9

After the last guest left, the monumental cleanup began with Manizheh directing the servants. "Tonight we will just put the food away. Tomorrow morning we will do the cleaning." She glanced over at her recently bereaved cousin. "Ohmeed, could you see if there is any damage to furniture or carpets that needs immediate attention?"

"Of course, Manizheh Khanem. I think I noticed some sticky stuff on one of the carpets. Perhaps a servant could put a little water on it so it will be easier to clean tomorrow morning."

Manizheh knew that Ohmeed was grateful to be given something with which she could occupy herself. The following day, Manizheh planned to take the new widow to visit Tahirih. Ohmeed and Tahirih had not seen each other since Ohmeed moved far away ten years before. Now, following the sudden death of her husband, Ohmeed was desperately trying to reconstruct her life, and Tahirih was likewise at a confluence in her own existence, never having lost a baby before. Ohmeed had never lost a baby because she and her husband had never been fortunate enough to have children. However, as a recent widow, she certainly understood grief. Perhaps she and Tahirih could be a comfort to one another. Manizheh hoped so. Her poor daughter was so bereft.

"Manizheh Khanem," Ohmeed reported back, "some of the men were smoking in the large salon, and I found burns on two of your carpets. I'm afraid you will have to call in the carpet repair experts. They are too extensive for my knowledge."

"Allah be with us," Manizheh muttered disgustedly. "Youssef was furious last year when we had to repair it, and now we will have to go through that all over again. Oh, well." After half an hour she pronounced, "I think we have done what we can do tonight. Go to bed, all of you, and we will start again tomorrow morning."

The servants gratefully obeyed, and Manizheh followed Ohmeed to her sleeping quarters.

"Are you sure you will be comfortable, dearest Ohmeed? Does the bed warmer keep your sheets comfortable? Are your pillows large enough?"

Ohmeed smiled gratefully and assured Manizheh that her sleeping arrangements were perfect. Eventually, they said good night and Ohmeed closed her door.

Manizheh proceeded down the hall to her own room, where her husband was already in bed. When he heard her enter, however, he sat up and to her surprise, complimented her on a very successful evening. "Tonight we accomplished a lot," he said. "My cousin Mojtabeh seemed to enjoy himself very much, and a lot of business got discussed. By the way, the food was perfectly served, and there was plenty of it. Wife, you outdid yourself tonight."

Being complimented was so rare that it lightened Manizheh's spirits considerably, and even though she was very tired, she began reminiscing about previous parties.

"Do you remember the year our own little Saeed, now father of tonight's great dancer, got into the pastries I prepared for the New Year's celebration?" Manizheh actually started giggling. "He was about ten, as I remember. He watched while we put all the goodies into a closet with a locked door, which I thought would be a safe place. But it was one of those closets with no ceiling. The little imp found a long stick with a sharp point, and when he knew no one was around, he piled up a couple of stools and lots of pillows, climbed up on top of it all and reached down over the top with his stick and stole dozens of pastries. We finally caught him when one of the stools slipped and made so much noise falling that we finally found out what was happening."

Youssef laughed and they exchanged other stories, finally drifting off to sleep in one another's arms. Although Manizheh had shared several tidbits of gossip she had heard that night, she failed to mention the many hints she had dropped into proper ears, which she anticipated would result in recommendations for Youssef's appointment to a palace post.

The next morning Manizheh and Ohmeed went to visit Tahirih, who was just beginning to move around. The loss of her son had devastated her, not only physically, but emotionally as well. It was all she could do to dress and be civil to visitors that morning.

No one realized how terribly confused Tahirih felt. Her feelings baffled her, but she could not talk with anyone about what was going through her mind because she was so ashamed. The truth was that although she grieved for her lost baby, somehow she actually felt relieved that there was not, at this moment, one more child to demand time and attention and caring. How could this be, Tahirih wondered in bewilderment. She loved her children. How could she possibly feel relief that she did not now have one more to care for? Surely she was depraved. A good mother always found a way to cope. Her mother had, even with fourteen children. What was wrong with her, that she did not appreciate the gifts Allah gave her? She had been brought up to believe that it was a woman's duty to have lots of children, and now she was secretly grateful for her loss, painful as it was. She must be mad.

These thoughts, turning over and over in her mind, kept Tahirih's eyes on the floor when her mother and her mother's cousin arrived that morning. Tahirih dimly remembered her second cousin, who was several years older than herself. In the manner expected of her, she rallied to be a courteous hostess, directing Parvin to bring refreshments, and smiling bravely.

Looking at her daughter, Manizheh grieved, thinking that she understood what Tahirih was experiencing because she too had lost three children in childbirth. But the loss of a baby was so personal, perhaps no one else could really understand, even though they had been through it themself.

"My beloved child, Ohmeed and I are here just to be with you. If you want to talk, we will talk. If you prefer silence, we will be silent with you. Ohmeed too has recently lost someone very precious to her. Perhaps the two of you can help one another."

Tahirih raised her eyes to her mother's face and saw there love and sorrow and understanding. But not understanding for what Tahirih really felt. She tried to pretend that her grief was only for the loss of the child.

"Mother, you have watched over me for several days. Now it is time for me to get back to taking care of myself, my husband and my children. I know that you had all the work to do for the party, and I am so sorry I was not there to help. But I am better. I can walk a bit now. The midwife told me how to take care of myself, and I must begin to do as she says. My grief will always be with me, but I must not allow it to disrupt my family. They must be my first concern."

Manizheh looked carefully at her daughter but did not see what was being hidden. She answered in response to what her ears heard.

"You are right, my dear child. You must get back to the duties expected of a wife and mother. I know that your grief is great, but perhaps Ohmeed can bring you some comfort, having lost her own husband just a few weeks ago. Shared grief may be more helpful to you right now than a mother's words." With that she gently kissed her daughter and left the room.

Ohmeed had been watching the young mother, wondering how she managed all the jobs she had to do. As she and Manizheh had come into the house, the servants seemed so busy caring for the children and trying to maintain the household. With no children of her own, she did not fully understand how many directions a woman could be pulled, but she could imagine. And then to lose a child. How awful could life be? Well, life had been pretty terrible for her, as well. She hoped she could help her grieving cousin.

"Hello, Tahirih Khanem. I hope I am not intruding. You may not remember me very well, since you were a young teenager when I married and went away. But I remember some things about you. Do you recall when the man with the goats was coming down the street? You were maybe five or six years old, and one of the goats just ambled over and all of a sudden butted you down? You jumped up and ran right back over to that goat and put your head down and butted it back. Do you remember that? You had everyone on the street laughing so hard that they were still talking about it weeks later."

In spite of herself, Tahirih chuckled mildly at this old memory, and her pain eased a little.

"Ohmeed, my cousin, I am grateful that you have come to visit me. Forgive me, please, for my present state. But perhaps you can best understand my need for mourning." Not wishing to speak of her own misery just yet, she deflected the conversation. "Tell me, what has happened in your life over the last several years?"

Ohmeed understood, and answered directly. "I was older than most women when I married. At first my father wanted me to stay home to care for his second wife, who was ill, but she died when I was twenty-one years old, and then he was suddenly in a great hurry to be rid of me. He accepted an offer from a stranger who lived far away, near the Turkish border. I think he expected that if I were so distant, he would not have to remember that he did wrong by me. Within a few weeks, I was married and living nearly a thousand miles from where I had grown up. I was terribly frightened, but as it turned out, I was incredibly fortunate."

"The man my father had accepted for me turned out to be the most generous, gentle and forward thinking soul on the face of this earth. He was very wealthy, having inherited a lot of land when his father died. The farmers on his property respected him, and they worked exceptionally hard. His villages were the most prosperous in the area. My husband was willing to try new methods of crop rotation, to experiment with irrigation principles, and just try new ideas to see if they succeeded or not. Of course, he had the wealth to be able to make mistakes, which a lot of people didn't. But still, he was at least willing to try, which a lot of men are not."

"Soon after we married, I became pregnant, but after a few months I bled very badly for several days, and then I was not pregnant anymore. After that I could not conceive again, and I was afraid that my husband would send me back to my father. But do you know what he did instead?" Ohmeed stumbled over her words for a moment, then went on. "Instead of sending me back to Shiraz in disgrace, as a woman unworthy of marriage, my husband recognized my shame and tried to help me do something else so that my humiliation would be eased. He taught me to read, and after I learned that, he showed me how to write down what products he brought in from the villages, how much they were worth, and what he sold them for. Pretty soon, I was his primary aide. He trusted me with his secrets. I think he loved me very much, and my feelings toward him were such that I could not even reflect on them, they were so powerful. Never had I believed that a husband and wife could be so happy together."

"For ten years we lived together like this, until one day he became ill. He was rarely ill, and always recovered quickly, so I did not think too much about it. But he got worse. Then people nearby began dying, and we learned that another smallpox epidemic had struck. Hundreds of people from our small town died, and my husband was one of them."

Here Ohmeed stopped for a moment.

"Then I was alone, and very frightened. His family had always been kind to me, but they strongly believed that a woman had no business interfering in men's concerns. One day his brothers came and removed all my account books. The family provided money for me to live, but it was clear that I was now a dependent widow."

"I wrote to my sister in Tehran and she insisted that I come east to live with her. I have been there for two months now. A couple of weeks ago your mother invited me to Shiraz. I arrived the day of your tragedy."

Tahireh's heart broke as she heard this story. To have been loved so greatly, and then to have lost it all. Not only her husband but her independence as well. Now Ohmeed could not pursue reading and writing because she had no man to defend her. Was life always like this? But no, Tahirih understood that there were many happy times in life as well. It just all wove together somehow.

Slowly, she ventured a question. "Ohmeed Khanem, if you know how to read and write, would you consider teaching me? There are many other women, I know, who would like to learn, but no one will teach us."

Ohmeed looked alarmed. In Persia, it was against the law to teach a woman to read. She already had enough trouble; she surely did not need more.

"Oh, I don't know," she dissembled. "I really don't know enough to be able to teach anyone. And the man of the house would have to grant permission. Would your husband allow that?"

"No, I'm afraid not," Tahirih answered, hiding the despondency from her voice. "I should not have suggested it. I'm so sorry. You know, I think I might try to walk to the salon and see how the children are. I have not really been able to pay much attention to them for several days. Could you help me up?"

"Here, take my arm and rise slowly. That's the way. Your legs are still wobbly, I'm sure. Just lean on me and move very gently. Does it hurt? There, that's good."

Ohmeed continued to coax Tahirih as they moved slowly from one room to another until Manizheh saw them and rushed to assist her daughter.

"Praise Allah! You are up. Just sit on the divan and I will have Talat bring the children in to see you."

"Thank you, Mama, please do. Be sure they do not jump on me. I would probably scream, and I don't want to frighten them. What have they been told?"

"Parvin told them you were ill and did not want them to catch what you had, but that the good *jinn* would make you better soon, and then they could come and say hello."

Tahirih closed her eyes and rolled them upward at the thought that the children were being put off with more stories about the *jinn*, but there was nothing she could do about it now.

"I am ready. I want to see my precious little ones."

A few minutes later Talat came in with five year old Husayn. As the oldest, and a boy, he had demanded that he be the first to greet his mother, and Parvin had given in to him.

"Are you better, Mother?" he asked. "We have not been treated right, and we want you to take care of us again now."

"What do you mean, you have not been treated right?" Tahirih asked, immediately alarmed.

"Well, Parvin would not give us any desserts while you were not feeling well. She said we had to wait until you were better, out of respect for you. So we want you to be better so we can have our sweets again."

Tahirih smiled, relieved that nothing serious had happened.

"You can tell Parvin that I am better now, and she can give you some sweets. Go and tell her now." Which he immediately did.

"How are the babies?" she asked Talat, who was standing in the corner, waiting to summon the next oldest child.

"All your children are fine. The twins are young enough that they really did not notice your absence, I think. And sweet little Scherezade just accepted that her Mommy would not be able to take care of her for a few days. She has been very obedient. She tries so hard to please, and is such a delight to care for. Here she is now."

"Mommy, Mommy," three year old Scherezade cried when she saw her mother sitting on the divan. "I missed you. I tried to be good, but I wanted to come to your room to see you everyday. Parvin told me I couldn't, that you were sick and couldn't see me. Why couldn't you see me?" The child jumped onto the divan and tried to crawl onto her mother's lap, only to be swooped up by Talat.

"I want Mommy to hold me," the child protested, beginning to cry. "Mommeeeee!"

"Yes, my dearest love. I know you missed me and I missed you, too. But sometimes I was very sleepy, and that is why Parvin would not let you come into my room. Now I am better, and you will see me everyday. Come give me a very gentle kiss and I will give one back to you."

Mollified, the little girl walked carefully over to her mother and planted a big kiss on the waiting cheek. In return she received a hug and a kiss, and a promise that soon Mommy would be able to play with her again. The twins were then brought over, one carried by Parvin and the other by Talat. Tahirih inspected them both and was satisfied with what she saw. In her time of need, her servants had cared for her family well, and she was grateful.

"I thank you for watching over my children so well," she said, "and I will be participating more now. Tell me what is being prepared for the noontime meal. Is it what Ismail Agha likes?"

"Madam," Talat answered. "Your husband has been very concerned about you and has barely been eating while you were not feeling well. He has not been coming home at mid-day because he did not want to disturb you. If you wish, we will send a messenger to tell him you are looking forward to having him join you for dinner today."

"Well, if cooking has not already begun, I think now is a little late to start. We will wait until tomorrow. Just make something small and I will eat with the children."

Tahirih forced herself to stand up, smile and walk toward the dining area while her mother and Ohmeed saw to the children, then arranged the table. She hoped her husband would still want to be near her. She needed him very badly.

CHAPTER 10

When Ismail arrived home that evening, it was to find his wife up and around, dressed neatly and with her hair combed. Her complexion was still a bit wan, but she looked much better than the last time he had seen her, which had been just after his son was born. His son. Born dead. His anger arose again but he held it in check.

"Hello, Tahirih. How are you doing?"

"Hello, dearest Ismail. I can walk by myself now. In another day or so I should be able to take over a lot of what Parvin has been having to do." She smiled. "It is such a blessing that we have her, and all the other servants, too. They have been wonderful, haven't they?"

"Yes, of course. It is what is expected of them, so there is no reason to be unduly grateful. A servant is paid to do the work around the house."

Tahirih was surprised by the surliness of the answer, but she realized that he too was just recovering from the shock of having lost a child and she ignored his attitude.

"I asked Cook to prepare a special meal for you tonight, since you were not able to come home at noon. It should be ready soon."

"Very well, but I am not hungry. I had my noon meal with Suleiman. However, I will eat a little with you."

"Oh. Is he feeling better?" she asked, masking her disappointment that her husband did not even acknowledge her effort to return to normal functioning.

"Yes, he is convalescing nicely. He should be back at his stall in a few more weeks."

"I am so glad to hear that he is doing well, poor man." Tahirih's concern was genuine.

"After we have eaten, there is a matter I wish to discuss with you." Ismail answered. "We will go to the salon at the far end of the house where we won't be disturbed. I want you to listen carefully to what I have to say, and I certainly hope that you will be grateful, since it is for your benefit as well as mine."

Mystified, Tahirih sat down to eat with her husband. Ismail spoke about some happenings at the bazaar, and as his wife answered his concerns with insight, Ismail again began to appreciate her sagacity and common sense. He relaxed somewhat, and his anger dissipated a little. Perhaps it was not her fault that the child had come early. It was probably just the will of Allah and he should not blame her. He began to regret calling her stupid to another bazaari and he told himself that in the future, he would watch his tongue.

After the meal, they walked to the end of the house. Although earlier he had had no doubts about what he wanted to say, now he was a little shy. They sat down and Ismail started talking with a bit of hesitation. "Tahirih, we have been married for six years. Have you been satisfied with me as a husband?"

Tahirih was astounded. "Of course, Ismail. No woman could ask for a better husband than you have been to me. You are generous and kind and thoughtful, and you provide well for the children and me. The servants are all happy to be part of this household. Why would you ask such a question?"

"Well, it seems to me that perhaps you have too much to do. I know you never complain, and you always seem fresh and relaxed when I see you, but still I wonder if you are not more tired than you let on. I have decided that it is time for you to have more help around the house."

"But Ismail, there are already so many servants to manage. They can do what needs to be done. Why would I want more?"

"I was not thinking of taking on more servants. I wanted to let you know that I will be taking another wife, someone who will help you with the household management and be a companion for you. The servants are not proper company for you all day long. You need someone who is your equal in status."

Tahirih just looked at her husband, gradually seeing him fade further and further away. She was dizzy, she was falling, she was dying, or at least she wished she were. *Oh, please, let this not be true. I have failed him, and now he seeks to replace me. He will send me back to my father, and I will not have my children anymore. Please, no.* That was her last thought.

"Parvin." Ismail had to shout loudly because they were at the far corner of the house. "Parvin. Come quickly. Your mistress has fainted. Carry her to our room." Ismail was panicked. This was not at all what he had anticipated. He had fully expected that she would be happy to hear that she would be having help with all her duties as well as a suitable companion for her daytime hours. Somehow, though, he did not think it was joy that he had briefly seen in her eyes before she collapsed on the floor. Well, most men just went ahead and took another wife and brought her home, without even consulting the first wife. He had not done that. He had first spoken to her about his plans. But this was not how it was supposed to be accepted. A fainting woman? Well, he would wait until she recovered to find out why she had reacted that way.

"Allah be blessed. What has happened?" Parvin was bewildered. "Oh, Tahirih Khanem. Wake up, wake up. Ismail Agha, what caused this to happen?"

"Keep your head on your shoulders, woman," Ismail answered cantankerously. "Prepare her bed and I will carry her to the room. She has fainted. There is nothing to worry about."

Parvin rushed to the bedroom, fluffed up the pillows and got out an extra comforter. When he arrived, Ismail gently laid his wife on the bed, then left the room, still confused. Sometimes he wondered why men put up with women, but of course, they were essential to having children, eating well and having a comfortable home, so there were tradeoffs. Unfortunately, this evening had not gone so well as he had envisioned. Nonetheless, he fully intended to proceed with taking another wife, whether Tahirih fainted or not.

Leaving the house, Ismail reflected on his last business trip to Tehran. He had met with the father of his prospective bride, and they had finalized arrangements. The man was a well-to-do tea merchant in Tehran, and he would be useful as Ismail expanded his markets. Three of his daughters were already married off, and the one Ismail was taking was the fourth. She was seventeen, with long dark hair and what looked like a sweet smile.

His father-in-law-to-be had agreed that his fourth daughter could marry Ismail under certain conditions. Ismail had to provide the girl with her own separate living area, which Ismail had planned to do anyway. She was to be treated with respect and not relegated to being a servant for the first wife. Ismail agreed to this, thinking that the two women would become good friends, once they had adjusted to living in the same household. She was to be allowed to come to Tehran at least twice a year to visit her family. That would be no problem as Ismail would be traveling back and forth regularly anyway. After several hours of negotiating, the men had agreed on a wedding date in the springtime. Ismail was satisfied as he left the house to his fainted wife, and proceeded on to Madam Z's House of Pleasure for an evening of entertainment, since it would be a while before his wife could satisfy him again.

The next morning, Tahirih began to stir. She opened her eyes, then closed them for fear that she might never again see these walls. She heard Parvin's voice calling to her, then her mother's. They were asking her to come back to them, come back. She did not want to. She did not want to ever come back to what she remembered her husband saying last night. Another wife. She would be banished. Her children? How could she care for her children. By Muslim law, the husband could keep all children. She could be refused even the right to visit them. How could she live a single day without her children?

"Tahirih, listen to me. You must open your eyes. Do as I say," her mother commanded.

Obediently, Tahirih parted her eyes. Obedient. She was always obedient. First to her parents, now to her husband. She did not want to be obedient. She wanted to be left alone. "Just leave me alone!" she shouted, but no one heard since the shouting was in her head. She closed her eyes again, but her mother insisted. "My darling, look at me."

Her eyes still closed, Tahirih struggled to sit up, saying "I am not well. I need to rest. Please come when I am better."

"Tahirih, what happened last night?" her mother demanded. "Parvin said that Ismail was shouting like a madman. He was so frightened for you. What caused you to faint? What happened?"

Tahirih parted her eyes slightly, saw Parvin still standing there, and nodded to her in dismissal. Parvin left the room.

"Mother, he is going to take another wife. He told me last night that I need help to run the house. He thinks I need a companion, but I understand what he really means. He means that he is going to send me back to my father. He will take the children. I will not have my children. I will be disgraced." The anguish continued to pour out. "How can he want another wife? I have tried to be such a good wife to him. What can someone else do that I cannot?"

"Tahirih, Tahirih, my beloved. He does not mean anything of the sort," Manizheh rushed to say. "Although your father never took a second wife, most men do. It does not mean that Ismail is disappointed with you. It means that he is affluent, that he can afford to support two women and their children. It is his way of demonstrating how important he is. Be grateful that you will not have to carry the whole burden of caring for him anymore. He will always treat you well. Your father would not allow otherwise. You know that. Now come, pull yourself together. We will go down to the salon and all will be well. You'll see."

Tahirih did not see. However, for right now, she would allow the words her mother spoke to make sense. Later, when she could think better, she would consider what had happened again, and perhaps she could indeed see it in a different light. But she didn't think so. Her husband wanted another woman. She had failed him.

CHAPTER 11

The Assistant Ambassador had only one day left before he had to return to Tehran. His official assignments were completed and he had done most of his shopping. Now he had time to devote to his most pressing concern, which was to contrive a way to meet again with Manizheh's attractive cousin, Ohmeed. He sent a messenger to Youssef, asking if he could stop by in the afternoon to thank him for the party. The answer came back immediately. "Please come for tea in the early afternoon, at your convenience." Youssef sent his regrets that his wife would be away, but he would nonetheless try to be a good host in her absence.

Good, Mojtabeh thought. *Who needed Manizheh?* It was the cousin he was interested in, and perhaps it would be better if Manizheh were not there to interfere. Youssef, Mojtabeh knew, would be happy to act as intermediary. So, with great care, he made sure that his fingernails were clean and trimmed, his mustache twirled and his breath fresh.

It had rained the night before, which irritated him because his carefully selected attire would be mud spattered by the time he arrived. He briefly considered hiring a carriage, but decided against it. It would be too effeminate. He mounted his stallion and spiritedly galloped down the road toward Youssef's estate. When he arrived, his boots and pants were muddy as he had feared, but the groom at the stable wiped him clean and he looked presentable by the time he was shown inside the house.

"Mojtabeh, my cousin, welcome back," Youssef said enthusiastically. "Here, come sit by the fire. Ali, bring tea and fruit to the salon."

Youssef commanded easily, Mojtabeh, he noted. Perhaps there might be a place for him at the palace.

"So, tomorrow you leave us here in the hinterlands and go back to the great metropolis. How long will you be there before leaving for Moscow?"

"Who knows?" Mojtabeh replied cagily. "The Shah is a bit of an enigma. One never fathoms his thinking. One only obeys. I expect, however, that he will want me in Russia before they begin their Christmas celebrations, which is always an excellent time to give gifts and listen to gossip. Russians like their alcohol, so it is easy to loosen their tongues. But of course, I will go when His Majesty decides I will go."

"May your trip be safe and your dreams fulfilled," Youssef pronounced as the refreshments arrived.

"I would be pleased to convey your greetings to the family of your wife's cousin -- what was her name, the one who was visiting during your party?"

"Ohmeed Tabassi." Youssef was not surprised at his cousin's interest in the widow. He had rather suspected that she was the cause of today's visit, but he doubted that Mojtabeh would get very far with his probable intentions. Ohmeed was a very proper woman, and it seemed, a very sorrowful widow. Youssef decided that it would be fun to watch this game being played out.

"Yes, that's the one." Feigning ignorance, Mojtabeh continued. "I believe she lives with her family there in Tehran. If you give me her husband's name, I will stop to express your greetings."

"You are most kind. Her husband died a few weeks ago and she now lives with her sister. It was that smallpox epidemic. Thousands of people died, just like the last time about fifteen years ago. Glory be to Allah, this time it did not affect us quite so much here in Shiraz. Ohmeed was lucky that she herself did not contract the disease."

"Ah, it is a shame for a woman to lose her husband." Mojtabeh commiserated with all his diplomatic skill. "To be a widow at such a young age. Her sister's husband must have agreed to allow her children to be raised with his own, unless they live with her husband's family." He was probing.

"No, Mojtabeh, she has no children. When her husband died, his family took over the properties and she returned to Tehran. My youngest son will accompany her back to Tehran when she goes. He will be attending the House of Science there, beginning in two weeks."

"Really, the House of Science? Have you heard the story about how that school came to be here in Persia?"

"Well, I have heard stories. What is the one you know?"

"The buildings are located in the center of the city, not far from one of the Shah's favorite palaces, the one he calls the Sun of Architecture. His Majesty the Shah, the man to whom I shall always be most loyal, is modern in his thinking, and he imports ideas from Europe. He has attended two World Fairs, and both times he came back with concepts that have radically altered Persian society. There are plenty of people who don't like it, let me assure you. Especially the clergy. He has tried to change the power structure at the palace, putting the clergy into the role of religious advisors rather than political consultants. Believe me, that got him into deep trouble."

"Here in Shiraz, the Chief Mullah has spoken about some of these things at the mosque," Youssef answered. "The mullah was very upset."

"The Shah tries to look ahead, but the clergy don't want to lose their influence. It will be interesting to see who ends up winning. But my Shah is a very smart man, and it will be difficult for the clergy to get the best of him. Anyway, he built this House of Science and staffed it with teachers from Austria. It is his hope that someday the school will become a university, but right now the classes are in elementary medicine, engineering and military tactics.

"Well, my cousin, I am among those who believe that Persia has a history of producing poets and engineers beyond compare. Right here in Shiraz, a bunch of British engineers are trying to figure out how the minarets at our mosque sway without breaking. They have had their best minds working on it for years, and still have not figured out what Persian engineers developed seven hundred years ago. So I don't believe we need to import ideas from Europe. They need to come to Persia and learn from us."

Haji Youssef was a patriotic man, with firm beliefs.

"Perhaps it should work both ways. We can learn from them and they from us. In any case, the House of Science is the beginning of university education in Persia. Up to now all that has been available are the madresehs, which are run by the mullahs. They teach poetry and religion, but not much in the way of modern sciences. Although it's true that centuries ago Islam encouraged a lot of scientific and mathematical advancement, now Muslim thinking is less advanced than European. We are trying to open up to the positive advances, and at the same time cling to the good of the past. It is a hard line on which to maintain balance."

"I will not argue with you, my cousin. It is your job to support the Shah, and it is mine to support my family. With a lot of changes, my capacity to do my job might well be decreased, and I cannot allow that to happen.

"No, of course not. We will never argue, Youssef. We have too many years of friendship between us to allow that to happen."

They heard Manizheh returning, and with her was the widow Mojtabeh had come to see. When they entered the part of the home where the men were, Youssef called out. "How is Tahirih?" he asked. To Mojtabeh, he explained, "Tahirih feels this loss very bitterly, because she blames herself for standing at the Muharram parades for several hours, just before the child came early.

"I am so sorry to hear of this," Mojtabeh said with sincerity. "Please share my condolences with your daughter and her husband."

Manizheh came into the room. "Welcome to our home, Mojtabeh Agha," she said before answering her husband. "She is doing better, Youssef. Yesterday she was up and around a little, but last night Ismail told her that he planned to take a second wife. At first she thought he was angry with her for losing the child and she was terribly afraid that he was going to send her back to live with us, but I think now she understands that he just wants to have someone to help her manage the household and be a companion for her. I think we will soon see our happy daughter again, instead of the pitifully sorrowful thing she has been for the last week."

"Good, good. Mojtabeh came by this afternoon to thank you for all the work you did preparing for the party."

Both Youssef and Manizheh knew that was not why Mojtabeh had come. If he were going to thank anyone it would be Youssef, not Manizheh, whom he clearly did not like, but Manizheh played the game.

"We do not have a chance to see you often enough, my husband's cousin. It is an honor to have you visit us, and we hope that you will be able to return soon."

"Thank you, Manizheh Khanem. Unfortunately my job keeps me moving all the time, and I am away from my beloved Persia more than I am at home. But when I am here, I want to see my family as much as possible. Not being married, I need my siblings and cousins more than most." He added this last sentence to be sure that Ohmeed knew he was single.

"Ohmeed Khanem," he continued, finally directing his attention to the object of his visit, "I am very pleased to have met you here at Youssef's house, and I pray that you will allow me to pay you a visit in Tehran after you return so that I can be sure you are safe and well. A cousin of anyone in Youssef's family is like my own relative to me."

Ohmeed was flustered. She had just been standing there, not even formally introduced to this powerful man, the Assistant Ambassador to Russia. "Thank you, Mr. Ambassador. You are so kind," she said simply as she turned her eyes toward the table.

Sensing that that was all the response he was going to get, Mojtabeh turned to Youssef and begged his permission to leave, since he had a few more things to take care of before leaving for Tehran the next morning.

"Perhaps we will all be able to come to Tehran before you leave for Russia," Manizheh offered, laying groundwork for an invitation to the palace. "We have not been there for a long time."

"You are always welcome to stay in my home, whether I am there or not. My servants will take care of you just as they do me. You must always consider my home your own," came the suave reply from Mojtabeh

With that, he bade his cousin and the women farewell, mounted his horse with a flourish, and returned to the city of Shiraz. Who knew when he might return here. As he rode around a corner, he glanced back wistfully and his heart ached for the old days of youth and lack of responsibility. To his amazement, he thought briefly that he would like a woman to call his own. Then he shook his head disgustedly, thinking that he was becoming soft in his old age. Women were nothing but a disturbance. Diplomacy brought him plenty of problems. He didn't need to come home to it as well.

THE

PALACES

CHAPTER ONE

A couple hundred miles north of Shiraz, in the ancient Persian city of Isfahan, stood an aging royal palace. Rain had been battering the aged mud bulwarks for days while gusts of wind blustered through cracks in the walls and clods of mud were tracked everywhere, creating even more drudgery for the already overworked servants.

Masoud Mirza, the oldest son of the Shah, was having one of his renowned temper tantrums. "Habib! Where did you hide my riding crop? This infernal rain will not prevent me from going hunting whenever I want. Is my horse ready? No. I don't care if those indolent stable boys think it's raining too hard. When I say I want to ride, they *will* have my horse saddled. If not, they will pay dearly, I assure you."

The eleven year old servant boy Habib answered swiftly. "Here it is, your Highness." He had endured his master's ranting for more than a year, and by now no longer paid much attention. When it became too awful, he reminded himself that the Prince had given him employment when his father was killed by an explosion in the palace kitchen the previous spring. So thanks to the Prince's kindness, Habib enjoyed daily shelter and food, which many others did not.

The Prince continued to complain about how miserable life was when it did not match his will. "I intended to go hunting with the architect Parvizian this afternoon so we can talk without tale-bearing ears listening. But that chicken is afraid to go out in this rain. Why must the summers be so hot and the winters so cold? Can we not have some moderation? Where is my hat? HABIB!"

In keeping with long established custom, Masoud, on behalf of the royal family, skimmed a substantial portion of building costs off any new construction in Isfahan, and no architect ever dared refuse. The Prince had been looking forward with great glee to discussing just how much he could get from this new project, since his own finances were becoming rather lean from his excesses. He had specifically selected Parvizian to head up the construction project because of the man's prior satisfactory involvement in such arrangements. Now, because of the rain, that scheme would have to wait for another time. Changing his mind about hunting, the Prince came up with an alternative source of amusement for himself.

"Well, if I can't go hunting, Habib, then tell that Mullah Siyyid Ashraf to come to my palace. And remember to insist that he enter by the side doorway."

Masoud smiled with that sly expression he always got when he knew he was insulting the Chief Mullah of the largest mosque in Isfahan. The side entrance was where animals were kept and it usually smelled terrible. Although he considered himself a religious man, Masoud detested the clergy, most of whom he found ignorant and foolish. Consequently, he delighted in humiliating them whenever possible. Even though Ashraf was entitled to call himself Siyyid because he was directly descended from the Holy Prophet Muhammad, Masoud nonetheless considered him far beneath the royal family in social standing, and he enjoyed letting him know it whenever possible.

"And when he arrives, inform me, then wait half an hour before you officially notify me."

Habib did as instructed, and he also left the mullah waiting in a room where there were no seats. When finally conducted to Masoud's presence, the religious leader complained vehemently about the arrogance of servants.

"Attendants have become insubordinate," he spluttered. "Really, Your Highness, that boy needs a good whipping. He did not offer me a towel to dry my face, and he just went off and left me standing there with no chair. He must be reminded that I am the Chief Mullah in Isfahan, worthy of great respect."

Masoud smiled inwardly as he replied, "Dear Mullah Ashraf, I profoundly thank you for coming out in such bad weather. The boy's impertinence will be appropriately punished. Of course, disrespect to the clergy will not be tolerated." He paused to assess the effect of his words. "However, I wanted to discuss a matter of great importance to me and my family, which is why I asked you to come here on such a miserable day."

It seemed that the quasi-apology had been accepted, so he continued. "As I'm sure you have heard, my beloved father," -- he almost choked as he uttered those words -- "His Majesty, the Shah of the greatest empire on earth, wishes to build a new mosque in the southern area of Isfahan. We in the royal family have always chosen to honor the Prophet Muhammad elaborately and with great reverence, and His Majesty feels that another mosque, built more exquisitely than any other in the city, will be a fitting way to express his love for Islam and his reverence for the Prophet. Tell me, Most Honorable One, precisely where should such a mosque be erected, and how many workers can you contribute to the completion of this noble project?"

The mullah answered deftly, competently covering his revulsion for the Prince and his pretentious piety. "Your Highness, there are numerous potential sites for the construction of a mosque such as your beloved father envisions." Knowing the malice between father and son, he relished repeating those same words and watching the Prince try to keep a straight face. "We in the service of Allah are most grateful for His Majesty's devoted thoughtfulness. Please allow me to consider your concerns, and I will be most happy to return soon to suggest the best possible location for such a project. And, of course, I will organize a work crew among Allah's faithful followers to build this monument to His greatness."

"Ah, I thank you, Mullah Ashraf. Now look. The rain has stopped and there is a magnificent rainbow in the sky to guide you back to your home. I look forward to your swift return to discuss this matter further."

Rather than go home, Mullah Ashraf instead returned to the mosque where he called his servant and demanded to be brought his favorite pastries. He munched ravenously while contemplating his response to the Prince.

"That arrogant creature. Who does he think he is, this undeserving puppy from a usurping family? Someday he will realize that only those who are directly descended from the Prophet deserve the authority to be leaders of the Persian empire. His great grandfather overthrew the legitimate heirs of Persian supremacy a long time ago, but this lowly family will be replaced soon enough. Then we will see who commands whom. Everyone knows that only those who wear the green turban and call themselves Siyyid are truly representatives of Allah on earth." He adjusted his headdress so that it fit more comfortably, as he continued chomping.

At another palace two hundred miles north of Isfahan, in the capital city of Tehran, Nasir-al-Din Shah, the ruler of the mighty Persian empire, or what was left of it anyway, was also contemplating his heritage and his future.

His great grandfather, the first Muhammad Shah, had established the Qajar dynasty in the late 1700's. Nasir-al-Din had, as a child, studied world history voraciously, so was well aware that at about the same time his ancestors were overthrowing a well established line of Persian rulers, the Americans were doing something similar far across the great ocean. Now, a century later, the Americans had become a world force, while the Shah ruled a shrinking empire. Although the Shah desperately wanted to re-establish Persia's might, somehow it kept slipping away.

Nasir-al-Din allowed his mind to reach back to memories of stories with which he had grown up. There had been several shahs who called themselves Muhammad and one of the first had been castrated by enemies. This event had influenced a cruel personality, and a demand of absolute subservience from anyone in his presence. One of the more renowned stories about this monarch was that once, when passing through a city in southern Persia, he commanded all subjects in that town to bow and hide their eyes so they could not look at him. A few residents refused to do so, and for that act of defiance, Muhammad Shah ordered his soldiers to enucleate the eyes of all 20,00 inhabitants of the city. That was but one of hundreds of stories told of Muhammad Shah's barbarity.

Well, the current Shah thought, despots like Muhammad were highly effective rulers. Indeed, that Muhammad had moved the capital from the western part of the country, where it had been established for centuries, to the more centralized location of Tehran and the Persian empire had become a great influence throughout the world. The most momentous decision Muhammad made, however, was to allow the Shi'ite sect of Islam to predominate over the vastly more numerous Sunni sect. Nasisr-al-Din wondered if this had been a mistake, although at the time it had been done in defiance of the Arabs who had swept in uninvited from the Arabian peninsula a thousand years before. These Arabs were Sunni Muslims, and they had forced acceptance of their new religion at the point of a sword. At that time, Zoroastrianism had been the well-established faith of Persia for centuries, and the Persians bitterly resented having their own culture defiled. Also, Persians were descended from the Aryan races, unlike the Semitic Arabs. Conversion to Islam was resolutely resisted for decades, but eventually it became the religion of Persia. The Persians maintained their defiance, however, by accepting the Shi'a version of the faith, rather than the Sunni version forced on them by the conquerors from Arabia.

Of course, the castrated Muhammad Shah had left no children. However, his successor, a distant relative named Fath Ali Shah, more than made up for his predecessor's deficiency in this area. Fath Ali reportedly spawned more than two thousand offspring throughout the Persian empire and the country was now littered with power-seeking pretenders to the throne, which certainly made life difficult for Nasir-al-Din. Well, he thought ruefully, how could he complain? He himself had already married twenty-two wives and could not identify all of his own children. The Shah prided himself on his virility, which he supposed must be an inherited trait. But he did have a significant complaint against his predecessor.

"If only Fath Ali Shah had been as mighty a ruler as he was a progenitor," he muttered to himself. "But no, he had to go and lose vast areas of the Persian empire, for which I, his grandson, must suffer greatly."

Nasir-al-Din was a bit self-indulgent in his consideration of the errors of others. It was true that much of Afghanistan had been lost to Russia during the Perso-Russian wars under Fath Ali's reign in the early 1800's. However, Nasir-al-Din himself had allowed the economic rape of his empire both by the British and the Russians, and he was, in truth, responsible for the loss of far more territory than his ancestors. But his own shortcomings were not what he was interested in musing about.

"Summon my son Kamran to me," he commanded a nearby servant.

Kamran was without question the Shah's favorite. When the
lad was only eight, his father had named him Minister of War
and Commander of the Army, and five years later proclaimed
him Governor of Tehran and ruler of the northern provinces of
Persia. Now that he was in his early twenties, Kamran thoroughly
enjoyed the power of these positions, even though he did not
exercise that power prudently. He and his older brother Masoud,
frequently rivaled each other to find ways to prove who was the
more powerful.

Kamran arrived momentarily after being summoned. "Good
afternoon, Father," he exclaimed obsequiously. "How may I serve
you?"

"My son, I wish to discuss matters of grave concern to both of
us. Come. Let us inspect the painting of my grandfather, Fath Ali
Shah, sitting astride his magnificent white horse." The painting
was located in the hallway leading to the throne room, and Nasir-
al-Din approached it with awe. "Napoleon himself gave that horse
to my grandfather as a present. Now there were two powerful
men, Napoleon and your great-grandfather. Don't ever forget that
you come from extraordinary stock."

Kamran was well aware that his ancestry was formidable.
However, he was infuriated with the injustice of lineage in the
Persia empire. Although he was clearly the Shah's favorite, that
favoritism did not confer upon him the right to rule the Persian
empire upon his father's death. Neither he nor his elder brother
Masoud had been born from royal mothers, and this quirk of
fate negated both young men as heir-apparent. Another brother,
Muzaffari Mirza, would be their father's successor because he

was born of a royal and legitimate wife. This was another reason Kamran and Masoud frequently banded together to cause as much devilment as they could, not only for Muzaffari but for anyone who happened to come to their attention.

The Shah continued speaking, ignoring the distant look in his son's eyes. "I regret that your education has been left largely to the mullahs. You know they have always been antagonistic towards our Qajar family, and I expect you have not been properly taught about your heritage. It is surely my duty to provide you with a different point of view of Persia's history, as well as the role of our family in that history."

Kamran had heard this lecture many times before, and he let his mind wander as his father's voice lulled him into a state of utter boredom.

"My father," the Shah persevered, "who was the second Muhammad Shah of the Qajar dynasty, was a great man, may his memory be forever blessed. However, his Prime Minister, that contemptible Aqazi, tried to usurp my father's power. He loved to play one group against another, and one of his favorite intrigues was to set that new religious sect, the Baha'is, against the mullahs. He would pretend to listen attentively to claims that their leader was a new prophet, which drove the clergy mad because they are absolutely convinced that Muhammad is meant to be the last prophet before the coming of the Promised Day. Then just when the Baha'is thought they had won him over, the trickster Aqazi would switch back and support the mullahs. No one ever won."

"But aren't the Baha'is heretics, Father? How could anyone believe what they say?" Kamran was amazed to hear a note of acceptance of the Baha'is in his father's voice.

Nasir-al-Din glanced at his son and decided to answer him honestly. "My son, whatever religious beliefs they may hold, heretical or not, the Baha'is that I have come in contact with are the most honorable advisors I have ever had. Over time I have learned that what they say can be relied upon, whereas the mullahs say one thing and mean another. I don't let it be known that anyone in my court is Baha'i, but several are and I trust them implicitly. I certainly wish I could say the same for the mullahs."

Kamran stared at his father in disbelief, unable to fathom that his father would have the courage to defy the mullahs that way.

The Shah noted the new look of respect and was appreciative. "Anyway," he continued, "when I became Shah in 1848, I immediately replaced Aqazi with Amir Kabir as Prime Minister. Now there was a truly great man, but he was much too far ahead of his time. He antagonized the clergy when he tried to limit their power to religious matters. I was new to the process of governing just then, and the clergy was far too powerful for me. They forced me to get rid of Amir Kabir after just two years."

"The man I appointed next was antagonistic to foreigners, which pleased the clergy greatly. Actually, he may have been correct that the British and Russians were trying to take over our economy for their own use, and they also seem interested in this stuff called oil, but I don't think that will ever come to much. I suppose, though, that I must do more to curb foreign influence in Persian politics. It just doesn't seem to be that crucial right now."

Kamran, bored by this kind of talk, tried to introduce a new topic. "You like to travel out of the country a lot, Father. Will you go to England someday, do you think?"

The Shah laughed almost disparagingly. "The mullahs were furious when I went to the World's Fair in Paris a couple of years ago and returned with ideas about how to reform the police. They actually tried to claim that having a state-operated police force would impinge on their religious control over social behavior." The Shah shook his head sadly. "And when I tried to introduce some new agricultural methods that worked well in Europe, they opposed me again. Even though thousands of our farmers starved during several years of bad crops, the mullahs say this is just the will of Allah and foreign ideas will not solve Persian problems. It is very difficult to move forward when I am thwarted at every turn."

They were interrupted by the arrival of servants carrying pressing documents, which afforded Kamran the opportunity to take leave of his father. Throughout the afternoon, he contemplated what he had just learned.

So his father deceived the clergy regarding his feelings toward Baha'is. Well, it certainly was not unusual for the Shah to deceive the clergy, Kamran thought derisively. He himself did that all the time. But it seemed that the man might actually respect those heretics, and that was a revelation. Actually, Kamran did not care much one way or the other about whose religious tenets were correct. He enjoyed a good show whenever he could create it, and the more bloodshed, the better. He went off in search of one of his brothers to plan the next excursion into the countryside to create more havoc.

CHAPTER 2

Habib had recently pleased his master, which happened rarely. One of the qualities he had developed was the ability to listen carefully to whisperings around the palace, and because he was just a child, Habib was frequently able to penetrate areas where adults would be immediately suspect. A few days earlier he had overheard a conversation between certain courtiers and some of the clergy who habitually haunted the palace. After sidling closer to hear what they were discussing, he had picked up intimations of an attempt to undermine the Prince's plans to build a mosque on the outskirts of town, which he had immediately relayed to his master. As a reward, he was given a small amount of cash and an afternoon off work.

To Habib, the time off work was far more precious than the money. He went to visit the brother of his deceased father. This uncle, who lived in an older section of Tehran, would be considered a poor man by most people's appraisal. However, in Habib's estimation, this man was wealthy beyond anyone else in wisdom, and at that moment eleven year old Habib believed himself in desperate need of guidance.

Upon arrival, Habib was received warmly, and after showing proper respect and listening to accounts of family happenings, Habib brought up his concerns.

"Always, my uncle, you give excellent advice. Just now, my soul is torn, and I desperately need your guidance. I must know, where is the duty of a child servant? As a child, of course I cannot contradict the orders of an adult, and as a servant I cannot disobey what my master tells me to do, most especially because he is a royal prince. But sometimes I am commanded to do things which the teachings of Allah forbid. I am afraid to refuse to comply with my master's wishes. What must I do?"

His uncle answered sadly. "Ah, my child, this is the question which endures throughout the ages. Whom do you obey, the man who controls your body, or Allah who controls your soul? All humans come to this choice in life, and only you can make it for yourself. Once it has been made, however, it is very difficult to later change your path. So choose wisely the first time."

To his disappointment, this was all the advice Habib was able to elicit. After several moments of silence, he broached another worry. "Whom should I trust among the clergy, since each mullah has a different answer to my questions?" he asked.

Here again his uncle sighed painfully as he tried to answer to the best of his ability. "Habib, there are those who study the word of Allah and believe they know exactly what is right. Beware those men who are too sure of themselves. His Holiness Muhammad, blessed be his soul, was privileged to have direct communication from the Almighty Allah. No one since then has had the same honor, and no other human ever will, for Muhammad was the Seal of the Prophets. I can only warn you to beware the fanatics, those who speak with absolute certainty. They are usually wrong in their thinking." His uncle paused for a moment, then added his deepest thoughts. "It is best, Habib, if you can learn to read. That way, you can study the words of the Holy Koran yourself. If you must always rely on someone else, the ideas you receive will be tainted by the needs of the person talking to you. Although the clergy is expected always to conduct themselves with honor and selflessness, my experience tells me that much too often they are dependent on the unlearned for their livelihood, so they manipulate their words to suit the immediacy of the situation and don't always recite the Holy Words of the Koran in the same manner to each listener."

The uncle blinked, took a deep breath, and continued. "Of course, this is not always true. There are some mullahs who truly behave in keeping with the principles they espouse. Always look for that quality in a religious leader, and you will probably be safe in following that man's guidance. But if there is any way you can do it, learn to read. You work for the Prince. Perhaps he could arrange for lessons in return for good service, if you request it wisely."

This suggestion astounded Habib. "But Uncle, you have never learned to read. Indeed, no one I know can read, other than the Prince himself. Why do you tell me this is so important?"

"Because it is. If you cannot read, you cannot judge the value of something for yourself. Just because I do not know how to read does not mean that I have not all my life desired this privilege more than anything. But I have never had the opportunity. You do have an opportunity because you work in the palace where people know how to do this. If possible, take advantage of your special circumstance."

They spoke of other things before Habib graciously and gratefully thanked his uncle for the time and advice given, then began his long journey back to the palace. When he returned, his head was filled with the newfound dream of being able to read the Koran for himself. Such a possibility had never occurred to him, yet he was now excited beyond words. He knew the Prince hated to be bothered with answering the lengthy documents that came to him, so surely Habib could offer himself as an aide with that onerous task. He would have to be careful, though, since the mullahs objected so strongly to non-clergy being able to read the Koran. Habib's mind began devising a scheme.

Later that evening, as he was preparing his master's night clothes and adding some extra wood to the fire in the bedroom, Habib noted that the Prince was in an exceptionally bad mood. Already Habib had been berated for things he had not done, and now the Prince was raving over a perceived slight from a landowner.

Habib waited patiently and continued to hold his master's nightrobe while Masoud flung his arms around wildly, punctuating his anger with jabs at the unseen householder. Finally he permitted Habib to put the robe over his shoulders, and he sat down to review some letters. Habib had not been given orders to prepare any special arrangements for tonight, which meant that the Prince was planning to sleep alone for once. Perhaps this would be as good a time as any to put forth his proposal.

"My lord," he began tentatively, "I know it is very cumbersome for you to have to read all the mail that comes to you each day. Could I possibly be of assistance? I mean, I would be happy to perform this irksome chore so that you would have time to devote to more important matters. I could learn to read a little, and then I could report to you what each letter contains so you could make a decision quickly. Of course, if there were any correspondence my undeserving eyes should not see, you would tell me, and I would hand it to you unopened."

Habib waited anxiously while Masoud reflected on this suggestion. At first, the audacity of it startled the Prince, but after some consideration, some benefit began to appear. It was true that Masoud hated the reading, and he would gladly turn it over to someone upon whose loyalty he could depend. This young whippersnapper owed his very survival to him, and could be easily intimidated and controlled. He decided to consider it further.

"I don't know if you could learn the complicated art of reading. Certainly I would not trust you to report honestly to me. But I will consider your suggestion. If I decide to allow it, I will watch you very closely to be sure you do not deceive me. If ever you do, I myself will beat you within a centimeter of your life. Now go and let me sleep."

"Yes, my lord. Thank you so much for your gracious consideration. I will never deceive you, I swear."

With that, Habib took his leave quickly, before something was thrown at him.

Meanwhile, Masoud had other problems to consider. His father had recently taken a new wife, and Masoud did not like her, not at all. Earlier in the day, he had been riding his horse and screaming at the wind.

"This woman, no, this snake, has married my father under false pretenses," he had bellowed. "She will be the cause of great turmoil within these palace walls. Just wait until the mighty Shah finds out what she really is."

His fury had been unabated, and still he was in such rage that he could not sleep. Perhaps the essence of it all was that one conniver recognized another and feared being outmaneuvered, but Masoud did not acknowledge this, not even to himself.

Elsewhere in the palace, however, another man was having a very different reaction to the same woman. The Shah was totally infatuated with his exquisite new wife, who spoke so softly and deferentially, and willingly did whatever he requested. He was beginning to believe that he might find more contentment in this marriage than he had expected, and such a prospect surely gladdened his embittered soul. The Shah believed that marriage should be more than a physical coupling or a means to acquire material things. In his occasionally romantic heart, he carried the notion that marriage should represent a union of spirits, and he was beginning to believe that, for once, this had happened for him, so he was unexpectedly happy.

As was Jila. She had charmed her Shah, no, her husband, completely, as had been her plan. Soon enough she would manage to have him out of her bedroom so that her lover could return. Meanwhile, she had convinced him she was the model of perfection. Indeed, she was well content with her work thus far. Her next step would be to have him make her a small gift of jewelry, and to provide her with an allowance that would enable her to see to her lover's needs adequately. Although she herself was from a wealthy family, she did not have direct access to her father's money, so she had to charm men into providing it to her. She lay languidly beside the Shah and stroked his back as she mulled over these thoughts in her mind and considered her next steps.

Soon after the marriage, she had begun to bewitch other members of the palace staff who would be required to make her plans work. The mullahs certainly had to be among her primary cohorts, she realized, so she began with them. For the most part she found this conquest to be very easy. Those silly men believed her blandishments about the importance of religious influence on the future of the Persian empire, and soon most of them were her puppets.

One mullah, however, was not so thoroughly taken with the Shah's new wife as she believed him to be. Mullah Askar was a man with a quick and critical thinking process who did not accept what his eyes saw without first running it through his very incisive mind. Neither was he accepting of all the hooplah connected with various religious ceremonies, nor was he impressed by fellow mullahs who misquoted Koranic teachings. He had been well educated at an early age, an unusual occurrence in those days, and he had read the Koran all the way through on multiple occasions. He genuinely believed in the principles of Islam, and devoted his life to living in accordance with them.

"Mullah Askar," Jila had begun in her beguiling manner the first time she met him, "it is my wish to be an informed wife who can meet her husband's needs in all matters. I know I can rely upon you to assist me whenever I ask."

This had been delivered more as a command than a request, and Mullah Askar was immediately put on guard. He also recognized fraud when he encountered it, and he believed that he had seen it very clearly in the woman who stood before him earlier that morning. However, he had courteously offered his time and experience to the Shah's most recent wife, while noting her manner and making a decision to proceed cautiously with any guidance he might provide.

Jila, who usually read people well, had not picked up on Mullah Askar's skepticism. She was sure that she had another convert and proceeded on to her next pursuit for that day.

Another person who noted Jila's seductive attempts with skepticism was Malijak, the twelve year old nephew of Amina. Amina was without question the Shah's favorite and most privileged wife. At least she had been, prior to the arrival of Jila. She had convinced the Shah to accept her nephew as her own son, since she could not have children, and the Shah had gladly obliged her. Accordingly, Malijak had known nothing but doting from the Shah and thus had become the ultimate spoiled brat.

Amina did not trust the new wife any more than Mullah Askar did, and she put Malijak to work observing Jila's daily comings and goings. Amina was not jealous of Jila as another woman in the Shah's bed. There were lots of those, and Amina had long since stopped caring. However, she did not like what she saw about Jila herself. The very protective Amina believed that her beloved Shah was being deceived, and that was something she would not tolerate. To Amina, the Shah was the leader of the mightiest empire on earth and he could not be made to look like a fool. She would strive to do whatever was necessary to protect him.

"Malijak, my beloved nephew," Amina had said one morning, "neither you nor I like the Shah's new wife. I fear that she may cause our Shah grave injury, and that worries me greatly. So this is what I want you to do." She proceeded to outline a plan for him to keep an eye on Jila every day, especially when Jila thought she was alone. Malijak found it delightful to be given such an assignment. Causing problems for other people enchanted his young ego. If he managed to please his aunt, to whom he owed his fortuitous situation, while he was harming someone else, so much the better. He listened to Amina's ideas, refined them a bit with a few of his own suggestions, and began to put them into practice immediately.

CHAPTER 3

Malijak was pouting. He wanted to go horseback riding, and had just marched all the way through the palace to the Shah's private quarters to invite his surrogate father to go with him. When he arrived, however, he was told that there was some courtier there and His Majesty might not be available for hours.

"Ridiculous," he groused angrily. "The Shah is always available to me. How dare you say someone else is more important than the Brigadier General of his Army. Perhaps," he considered, "I ought to command my troops to storm in and arrest whoever is there." Then he decided that such an action might possibly make the Shah angry, and he did not want to risk that. It was only a few days since the Shah had announced that Malijak had permission to marry one of his daughters, the pretty one, actually, and Malijak certainly did not want to jeopardize that offer. In truth, he really did not care which daughter it would be. The point was that any marriage into the royal family would result in even more power for him.

For right now, since he could not go riding with the Shah, he would see what mischief he could create. After a moment's thought, he decided to see what Jila was up to. In truth, he had come to admire Jila and believed that she could outsmart most of the palace functionaries. He found her to be cunning when she seemed so sweet, which Malijak found to be an endearing trait. Although most people in the palace were taken in by her, he saw another side to this woman, thanks to his Aunt Amina as well as his own second sense about people. Indeed, his careful spying had revealed that she had a lover, which placed enormous power in his adolescent hands. He decided to go see what she was up to this morning.

While Malijak set off to look for Jila, Mojtabeh Amuzegar, was apprising his master of his findings from the just completed trip to Shiraz. "I just returned from your lovely city, Shiraz," the Assistant Ambassador began deferentially, praising Shiraz as he did any other city he went to on official business within the Persian Empire. I have a cousin there. Through a party at his house, I learned about the feelings of the people regarding some of your recent innovations, especially the railroads and the police."

"As I had commanded," the Shah replied imperiously. "What else did you ask about?"

"Excellency," Mojtabeh warned, "there is a group called Bahai'is who have caused a lot of concern to the bazaaris in Shiraz. A number of them have been discovered, and although admonished to cease practicing heresy, they are very stubborn. Neither imprisonment nor confiscation of their property seems to deter them. Indeed, those who believe in this so-called prophet, Baha'u'llah, are willing to die for their faith. What is most astonishing is that many of the converts are former mullahs, who would be expected to know better. Somehow they have become convinced that this Baha'u'llah truly is the Manifestation of God prophesied not only in the Koran but also in the writings of Zoroaster as well as the Bible."

After giving this announcement some thought, the Shah answered decisively. "Well, Mojtabeh Agha, it seems to me that they are more of a threat to the clergy than they are to me. If someone can diminish the infernal power of these mullahs, then they will have my support. Not openly, of course. I will speak out against them once in a while, and maybe encourage a raid or two here and there, but I will not put the full force of the palace against them. At least not now. If, in the future, they become more of a danger than an asset, then I will reconsider."

"Yes, your Majesty. So you do not wish me to organize any retaliatory measures against them? What about measures against the clergy who attack them?"

"No, nothing. The more they fight each other, the less either of them will bother me. I will stay out of it until it suits me to become involved. Tell me, now, what else is happening in Shiraz."

They discussed the impact of the newly trained police force, which the Shah found very useful in maintaining order without having to mobilize his army, and also the extension of railroads. "If America can have railroads, so can we here in Persia," the Shah declared emphatically. "Just as that country is a rising power in the West, so Persia is a long established and far greater power here in this part of the workd. The hegemony of Persia shall never fade away."

Mojtabeh listened courteously and when it seemed the Shah had finished, he brought forward his own agenda. He reflected for a moment, deciding whether to promote his cousin for a political position or the son-in-law for economic gain, and ultimately decided on the son-in-law.

"Majesty, there is a tea merchant in Shiraz whose name is Ismail. Actually, his father-in-law is my cousin Youssef. Ismail wants to expand his tea business far beyond the confines of Shiraz. He plans to start by taking a second wife from the Manucheri family here in Tehran."

"Manucheri, yes, that family is well known throughout Tehran," the Shah replied, "and I'm not sure I like them. I think they have far too many political ambitions. Well, never mind about that. You say that Ismail's second wife will represent an economic marriage. That's fine. First wife for family, second for money. But why do you mention this Ismail," the Shah inquired, knowing perfectly well that Mojtabeh was relating more than a family story.

"Your Majesty, Ismail happened to mention that he would like to expand his sales area beyond his own city of Shiraz, even beyond Teheran. Indeed, he would like to sell tea to the Russians, which he contends would be very profitable to the Empire. This, of course, would require your approval, and he asked me to bring the matter to your attention."

"Selling tea to the Russians. Now, that is an interesting thought," the Shah murmured as he twirled his mustache. "I imagine that vast country would be a good market. Tell him that I will consider it."

"Thank you, Your Majesty. Now I must depart, for I have taken far too much of your precious time today. I await your instructions regarding when I shall leave for Moscow," Mojtabeh said, with a low bow.

Elsewhere, Jila was about to again inadvertently-on-purpose run into Mullah Askar, whom she had determined was one of the more powerful clerics in the palace. This mullah intrigued her because she had heard nothing but high praise for him from everyone from the Shah to the lowest of the servants. Being duplicitous by nature, she welcomed the challenge he presented to her.

She loved the game she was playing. Who else could cuckold the Shah while enjoying his total trust? She was sure that even if she were caught, he would do no more than banish her, which would fit her plans perfectly. The Shah had already bestowed several pieces of valuable jewelry upon her, and these were in her lover's custody. Together they had devised an emergency escape route to England, and from there they would travel to somewhere safe, maybe even America, where she heard the streets were paved with gold. At the most, it would be six more months, and then they would disappear. She actually did feel a little badly about hurting the Shah's feelings because he seemed so much in love with her, but there were so many other women he could have after she was gone. He would recover, she was sure.

"Mullah Askar, good morning to you, sir," she greeted warmly as she happened around a corner, smiling her most engaging smile. "The address you gave at the banquet last night was wonderful. It is so rare that women are allowed to attend such functions, and I personally thank you for encouraging my husband to invite several of his wives. It was kind and thoughtful of you."

The mullah answered with courtesy but wariness. "I am delighted that you are pleased, madam. I trust that you are well this morning."

"Thank you, I am fine, but please excuse me. I must be going. However, it is always pleasant to see you, sir."

"Likewise, Madam."

Malijak observed this interchange from a darkened corner. What was Jila up to now? Malijak believed that Mullah Askar had too many scruples, which did not mix well with being part of the palace. Why would he be meeting with the Shah's favorite wife? It was possibly just a chance encounter, although Malijak had come to understand that few occurrences involving Jila happened by chance. Possibly this high-minded mullah had hopes of influencing the Shah through his new wife. Well, that would bear watching.

As Malijak was returning to the main part of the palace, one of the Shah's servants informed him that the Shah desired his immediate presence. Delighted, the boy went straight to the suite he had left shortly before in anger.

"My Shah, you were asking for me?"

The Shah turned away from the window where he had been gazing out at the winter landscape. "Yes, boy, I am going hunting tomorrow afternoon. You will come with me and my son Muzaffari. We will go to the mountains, and in the evening you will see a show put on by the leopards I have had trained. It will be most amusing for you. Be ready to leave by one o'clock."

"Of course, Your Majesty. It is most kind of you to include me in your plans. I will be ready." Malijak waited for the Shah to invite him to stay to talk longer, but when it did not happen, he said obsequiously, "I look forward to tomorrow afternoon with all my heart. Until then, My Shah," and left.

Already the Shah's mind was on other matters. There was some land outside the city that one of the mullahs, a fellow known as Ali, had been telling the Shah was worthless for farming. Mullah Ali had dropped hints that the unfarmable land was indeed costing the palace money because of upkeep costs. Perhaps, it had been suggested, the Shah could donate the land to the clergy.

Because he was all too familiar with the cunning machinations of the clergy, the Shah had sought the impressions of others, but Mullah Ali had been a step ahead of him. He had arranged for several other mullahs as well as courtiers around the palace to support Ali's version that the land was a burden on the public treasury, and eventually the Shah heard it from so many sources that he believed it. Perhaps later that week he would tell Ali that the land would be donated to the glory of Allah. That would be good for him in the eyes of the clergy, and would save his treasury some money.

As he continued to muse, he considered how little money there seemed to be any more. Taxes were hard to come by because of droughts and smallpox epidemics, as well as the horrendous storms that kept destroying crop production. Most of the mullahs complained about expensive reforms he made to the judicial system, and some even muttered about the elaborate lifestyle he maintained. The worst complaints, though, were that he squandered vast amounts by traveling to Europe. Well, that was just too bad. They simply did not understand. The leader of the greatest empire on earth had to be accorded due respect, and that meant that he had to participate in international social events, and bring back to his own country ideas which would help move his society forward. That was his duty. If it cost money, that was just the way it was.

Well, now it was time to think about his son Muzzafari. The boy, who was now a man in his thirties, would have to take over ruling the empire when the Shah passed on. Unfortunately, to date he had exhibited very little interest in political matters and the Shah was worried about the continuity of empirical rule. Somehow he had to animate his son.

Because the young man loved to hunt, the Shah sometimes arranged sojourns into the countryside as a way to foster communication, although even that did not always work. Whenever the Shah tried to turn the discussions to matters such as the state of the economy or unrest in the bazaars, Muzaffari managed to steer the conversation back to hunting or women or some other pleasure activity. There were many stories that the young man could not pay his own bills because he was so generous with giving money away which certainly was not the way to rule an empire. There were so many things for a Shah to think about. Sometimes it became overwhelming.

When governing became too much, the Shah invariably turned to one of his wives. He decided to locate Jila and play a game of backgammon with her. She was quite good at the game and frequently could have beat him, but always lost at the last minute. The Shah appreciated this sign of submission. She was his dearest wife, next to Amina, who, of course, could never be replaced. While Jila was a companion, Amina was an advisor. One for pleasure, one for wisdom, and many others for his mood of the moment. He supposed he had twenty-six wives by now, but had actually lost count.

"Summon Her Majesty Jila to me, and prepare the backgammon board," he ordered curtly, "and bring refreshments. I wish to have figs, and also persimmons if they are ripe. My wife likes grapes. Bring us rice cookies and baklava as well."

"As you command, Master. It will happen immediately."

Several minutes went by, and the food arrived but Jila did not.

"Where is she?" the Shah demanded, becoming almost angry at what he perceived to be impertinence. After another fifteen minutes she slipped into the room, her face somewhat flushed. The Shah's anger melted immediately as she smiled at him.

"Forgive me, my husband. I was at a far end of the palace when you sent for me." She chose to remind him frequently that he was her husband more than her Shah. "I came as quickly as I heard you desired my presence."

Actually, she had been about to meet her lover, but the servant arrived just before there would have been a major fiasco. Jila was almost holding her breath for fear that the Shah might have somehow known, but it appeared he did not.

"Dearest Jila," he said, "let us play backgammon and chat for a while. Your presence soothes me and just knowing you are near brings me peace. Come, sit down and enjoy some tea and sweets.

Although truly, how you could need anything sweet I cannot imagine. There is nothing sweeter in the whole world than your presence."

"Your words are too kind, my husband. I merely do what I can to please you. I am so grateful if I succeed. It is my utmost wish." Jila uttered these false words with a smile as decorous as a virgin's on her wedding day.

Delightfully pleased with this response, the Shah inquired about his new bride's day. "Tell me, Beloved, what have you been doing to occupy yourself this morning, while I had to deal with tedious courtiers?"

Jila dissembled somewhat. "I happened to see that mullah who spoke last night at your banquet – Mullah Askar, is that his name? He seems an intelligent man. And earlier this morning I was preparing a surprise for you. Must I tell you what it is?" she asked coyly.

"Oh, my dearest one. How thoughtful you are. Yes, of course you must tell me. I cannot bear to wait." The leader of the Persian empire was worse than a six year old when it came to pleasant surprises.

"If I must, but I did not want to spoil the secret. Well, you see, I instructed the kitchen to prepare several of your favorite foods, and I also tried to arrange for you not to have any official duties tomorrow afternoon so that we could spend a few hours together. You know, it will be three months tomorrow that we have been married, so I wanted to have a special celebration." She looked at him meaningfully.

"Such a wonderful woman you are." The Shah's carnal nature took over. "Let me see. Tomorrow afternoon I am going riding in the mountains with Malijak and Muzaffari. Perhaps, though, since I don't have any plans for right now, we should put the backgammon game aside and carry through with your plan a little early."

"As you wish, my husband," and she smiled as if she meant it, while inwardly grimacing at the lost opportunity with her lover. Patience, she reminded herself. Patience will lead to future happiness.

CHAPTER 4

"Mullah Askar, how do I know what this word is?" Habib asked despondently. "You have told me that there is such a thing as a vowel sound, but no vowels are written here. Is this word bam or bom or bum?"

Grateful that his Prince had finally arranged for one of the mullahs to teach him to read, Habib was finding the endeavor much harder than he had anticipated. One dot under a line meant one letter, two dots meant another letter. When a letter was written by itself it appeared one way, whereas if it were joined with other letters, it looked different. No wonder only the mullahs knew how to read. But keeping in mind his uncle's admonishment that the world could open for him, Habib continued to struggle on. Little by little, he was learning to recognize some words. Fortunately, his teacher was very patient.

Mullah Askar chuckled. "You know what the word is by its context within the sentence, my boy. In the written language of Farsi, vowels are not written in, although sometime a hint is given by this little mark up here. Do you see it? Yes, that one. But you know what the word is according to the meaning of the whole thought. Have patience, lad. You will learn. You are doing very well, believe me."

Habib needed the encouragement. Sometimes he thought this effort was just too much, but Mullah Askar kept prodding. Because his master had gone off for several days and for once had not demanded that Habib accompany him. Habib and his teacher now met almost every day. Although he could not yet comprehend his master's correspondence, he could manage some of the familiar phrases from the Koran.

Finally Mullah Askar suggested that Habib rest his eyes for a few minutes, which he gratefully did as he wondered where his master might have gone. Sometimes the three brothers, his master and Kamran and Muzzafari, would go off for several days hunting or traveling or sporting somehow. Usually Habib was required to serve all of them when they did that, but this time they had taken someone else's servant. It was miserable weather outside, and Habib shuddered as he gave thanks that he did not have to be fetching firewood and keeping everyone's clothes clean and avoiding the Princes' collective anger. Now he could concentrate on learning to read, here in the dry palace with the kindly Mullah Askar. Sometimes, he thought, life was good.

Suddenly, he was summoned to the presence of the Shah's new wife, Jila Khanem. Although she seemed kind, Habib nonetheless had a disquieting feeling about her. When he asked Mullah Askar's permission to discontinue the lesson, the mullah quietly asked what Habib thought Her Majesty wanted.

"I have no idea, sir. Only once before did she send for me,

but when I got there she had changed her mind and did not want to see me after all."

"Take care, lad."

It was said so abruptly that Habib glanced at the mullah to see if there was anything else coming. No other words were said, but the look the mullah gave him was a warning, Habib was sure.

Habib made his way through the dark halls to the room where he had been told to go. When he arrived, no one else was there, so he waited until he heard a soft voice behind him.

"Habib, I wish you to do me a favor."

Habib turned toward the windows where the voice had come from, and there she was. She must have been there all along, waiting behind the curtains. Why had she hidden herself? Was she waiting to see if anyone else came with him?

"Your Majesty." Habib bowed low. "How may I serve you?"

"Child, your master is the son of my husband. Whatever he does is important for the Shah to know. Therefore I expect you to keep me aware of any plans he may make so I can act as an intermediary and help ease the way between him and his father."

Act as a spy on his own master? What was she thinking of?

"Your Majesty, my master always informs his father if he is going away or planning a special event. I do not understand what you want."

Apparently the brat understood her perfectly, which was not what Jila had expected.

"I was concerned that there might not always be good communication between the Shah and the Prince, so I was trying to help. However, if there is no problem, that is wonderful. Never mind what I have said."

"It is so good of you to be concerned about my master. Certainly I will let you know if there is any way you can help."

"Very well, go now, child."

Without a set schedule for the day, Habib decided to stop at the kitchen to visit and perhaps get some of the cook's best offerings. On the way, he pondered what that meeting had been all about. Surely the woman knew that a servant would never tattle on his master, and that business about facilitating communication was obviously a thinly veiled threat about something, but what? What was his master doing that required her surveillance? Or was she just being nosy and trying to control things that she had no business interfering with? Habib had always had to keep a sharp eye out to protect his master, and now here was one more direction to watch. Sometimes it was a lot for a young boy to keep up with.

In the kitchen, Habib was greeted by one of the cooks who had worked alongside Habib's father prior to the explosion which had orphaned Habib the year before.

"Habib, lad. So good of you to come down to see us. Now that you are a servant in higher places, we don't enjoy much of your company. What brings you here today?"

For an instant, Habib regretted returning to the site of his father's death. He quivered involuntarily as he remembered that horrible eruption caused by one of the other kitchen worker's smuggling some gunpowder from the armory. Just when he was trying to stash it in a cubbyhole, Habib's father had unwittingly struck a match nearby. Habib had been in a corner peeling carrots when the horrible conflagration occurred, and he had turned to witness his father burning before his eyes.

Fighting to regain control over himself, Habib forced himself to grin and answered that his stomach was telling him it was time to eat, and since his master was away for a few days, he had decided to come directly to the source of all good things.

Laughing, the cook ladled out a little of the stew and handed him the bowl. "And what keeps you busy these days, my boy?"

"Everything." He decided not to mention that he was learning to read, since the workers in the kitchen would undoubtedly think he was aspiring way above himself. "Today is too rainy and cold to be going outside for anything, so I thought I would come back and say hello to old friends."

"Very kind of you, lad. So what is the gossip from where you hear it?"

This might be dangerous. Habib's job was to collect gossip, not pass it on to other servants. "Nothing much, really. How about down here?"

"Oh, there is always something else filtering through down here. We are hearing that the Shah really likes his new bride, and might not take any more. That would be remarkable. But you know, he is getting older. Maybe keeping so many wives in line is getting to him, and he has finally decided that enough is enough. Who knows?"

"Really? No more wives?" Habib was astonished. Royal weddings were always so glamorous, and not having any more to look forward to would certainly put a damper on the palace. "That would be sad," he said mournfully. After finishing two bowls of

the cook's bounty, he knew he had to be on his way. "Well, thank
you for dipping the stew. It was delicious," he said gratefully.

"It was your father who taught me to cook. May Allah bless
his soul."

As he returned to the Prince's quarters, Habib reflected that
when Allah took one gift, He gave another. Although his beloved
father had been killed, Habib was consequentially now embarking
on an adventure that would never have been available to him if the
Prince had not taken him in. Who could ever have thought that
little Habib might someday learn to read?

Wanting to make the most of his time when he did not have
to serve the Prince night and day, Habib curled up on the window
seat for the best source of light. It was a little cold there, so he
pulled the curtain around him for warmth. He was sounding out
the words and letters in his head, making no sound, when he heard
a voice. He peeked around the curtain and saw that it was Jila.
Instantly he drew back as he heard someone answering her. In his
brief glimpse, however, Habib was able to establish that he did not
recognize the man with Her Majesty.

"The Prince is gone for a few days." It was the man's voice.
"That degenerate loves to make other people's lives miserable,
but today we will be able to return the favor. My brother is now
destitute because that bastard confiscated his lands. Do you know
why? Because my brother protested when a bunch of the Prince's
hooligans rode through his fields at harvest time and destroyed
nearly all of his crops."

"My beloved," came the soothing response, "in a few months
we shall be gone from this palace and everyone and everything

here. Now let us look for what we came for. You are quite sure that no one will be coming in?"

"No, Jila. The boy was down in the kitchen a few minutes ago yapping with the people who used to work with his father. I have someone posted in the hall to warn us if he is seen returning. Let us look quickly and get out of here."

They searched for some time. At one point they came within inches of Habib's spot behind the curtain, but turned away to a nearby table to open a box in which the Prince kept some papers. They leafed through this container, but found nothing.

"He must have taken it with him. Never mind, I do not have to have it. Now that I have seen his living quarters. I can carry out my plans even without that document."

Habib remained in the window for some time to be sure they were gone, then cautiously climbed down and went to look around the apartment. Nothing appeared to be disturbed, so they must have put it all back very carefully. He tried to discern what might have brought them here, but could not think of anything. He was more familiar with his master's living quarters than anyone else. What did they want that warranted such a risk? He peered down the hall and saw only cobwebs, and shadows in the dark corners.

CHAPTER 5

Assistant Ambassador Amuzegar was awaiting the Shah's call to duty, which could come at any moment now. After so many years of service, he understood that his time was one hundred per cent at the Shah's disposal. Although this way of life cost him dearly in other areas, he thoroughly enjoyed the excitement and intrigue of being a diplomat, and he had never wanted to settle down to family life. Indeed, up until now, he had believed implicitly that his success was due to his freedom to travel unfettered. But now, when he was in his mid-forties and far beyond the time of youth's folly, the mighty Mojtabeh, the invincible, long confirmed bachelor, found himself smitten. The man who made fun of his friends for their vulnerability to a woman's charms had himself been overwhelmed.

He had been to Ohmeed's sister's home twice now. What was almost funny, he mused as he prepared to visit again, was that Ohmeed appeared to have no interest in him. Unlike women who had pursued him for years because of his status and wealth, she remained correctly courteous but distant. He did not have the feeling that she was playing a game with him. She simply was not interested in being courted.

His clandestinely conducted investigations informed him that she had been very happy in her marriage to the farmer, which was a good sign, he believed. He also learned that she knew how to read and keep accounts and write letters. Mojtabeh found this to be an attractive quality, although most of his friends firmly believed that a woman who could read would be a danger. Nonetheless, from his point of view, a wife who could participate in correspondence would be an advantage, since he could keep in touch when he was out of the country for extensive periods of time. That would make her happy, and him too, he admitted. If he could write and she could respond, then he could maintain a closeness, despite distance and months of separation.

Continuing to consider his situation, Mojtabeh brooded upon Ohmeed's reticence. At first it had caused him considerable concern, but only until he convinced himself that, being recently widowed, she would, of course, show reluctance toward another man. Again, he found this to be a positive attribute. A woman who did not easily forget her husband was worthy of respect. Loyalty was a very important quality to a man who represented the Shah.

After several restless nights, Mojtabeh decided that he would indeed marry this woman. Yet now, ironically, the catch of every mother's dreams had to convince a hesitant woman that he would be a good marriage prospect. He smiled to himself as he contemplated that life was a joke sometimes, as he set out to make sure that in this instance the laughter would be for, not against, him.

He decided to start with the sister Parvaneh who appeared at least somewhat amenable to the idea of having Ohmeed marry again. Parvaneh appeared to appreciate Mojtabeh's stature, and through various subtle hints had given him the impression that she believed re-marriage would be in Ohmeed's best interest. Although Parveneh appeared willing to have her younger sister continue to live with her, it was apparent that she believed the ongoing dependency would become unbearable for a young woman who had, for a few years at least, been exposed to independence.

Mojtaben had scheduled a visit for an afternoon when he knew that Ohmeed would be out shopping with servants while Parvaneh remained at home. Upon arriving, he presented a magnificent array of gladiolas, irises and roses to the servant who answered the door, and was immediately taken to the formal salon where Ohmeed's sister was waiting.

"Parvaneh Khanem," he began, "diplomats usually talk in a very round about manner so as to create confusion, but this afternoon I hope to make myself very clear. What I have to say is this. Your sister has totally won my heart, even though she has made absolutely no effort to do so. In all my years, I have never felt this way, and I truly do not understand what has happened to me. All I know is that I want your sister to become my wife, waiting for me in my home when I return from His Majesty's postings. You are her sister and you know her heart. Do you believe there is any way I can achieve this dream?"

Parvaneh responded as judiciously as she knew how. "I will answer you directly, Mr. Ambassador, just as you have spoken to me. My sister has recently suffered a grievous loss. A few months ago she was a happily married woman. Today she is a disconsolate widow. You must know that she loved her husband dearly, and it has been unimaginably difficult for her to adjust to the many abrupt changes in her life. For Ohmeed, not only has she lost her beloved husband, who was everything to her, but additionally she was forced to leave the home she had shared with him as well. His family made it clear that if she continued to live in his house, her status would be totally changed. She would no longer have any say in the processes that she and her husband had discussed every day, but would instead be entirely dependent on their largesse. She knew she could not live like that, so came to live here with me, where she is at least loved and wanted. But her heart remains buried with her husband far away. Someday she will perhaps reawaken to life, but right now is too soon. As much as I would like to see Ohmeed cherished by another man," Parvaneh said while looking appraisingly at the unhappy Mojtabeh, "which I believe you would do, Mr. Ambassador, I will tell you honestly that if you push your suit right now, you will inevitably lose."

Mojtabeh sat quietly for a moment, digesting this answer. He was not used to being told no, especially by a woman, and he was pulled between insisting on what he wanted right now, and doing the wise thing, which was to wait. Finally his diplomatic side won. This was not an issue to force.

"Very well, Parvaneh Khanem. Please tell your sister that I would like to speak with her tomorrow. I will not press for a commitment, but I want her to understand what is in my heart. Such feelings have never been there before, and I am just as confused as she is, I think. We both have had big changes in our lives. Hers is a loss. Mine, hopefully, will be a gain. Somehow, I believe we can combine our situations and both go forward together."

With that, he left and Parvaneh mulled over how best to approach her sister. She had not been surprised by the Ambassador's declaration and she was determined to present his desire to her sister in the best possible light. She believed that he truly would cherish Ohmeed. He was basically a good man, Parvaneh believed, even though arrogant at times. He was also wealthy and powerful, and her sister's future would be in safe hands. By the time Ohmeed returned from her shopping excursion, Parvaneh had developed the beginnings of a plan.

In the same formal salon where the Ambassador had set forth his plea a few hours before, the two women now sipped tea and chatted about domestic matters. As they conversed, Parvaneh dropped a strategic hint here and there about Ohmeed's eventually finding another man, quickly adding that she understood her beloved sister was not yet ready to think about that sort of thing. Mostly, though, they talked about Parvaneh's children and what a blessing they were to a woman.

In her sister's loving presence, Ohmeed began to weep. Parvaneh was dumbfounded. Eventually, interrupted by mighty sobs, Ohmeed admitted that she could not have children, which until then had been a secret in her heart, known to no one but her husband. Because of this, she strongly believed that marriage would never again be appropriate for her. No man would want to marry a woman who was barren.

Parvaneh was shocked, having had no idea that her sister carried this horrendous burden. Quickly, though, she knew this provided exactly the opportunity she needed.

"Yes, of course, dearest Ohmeed, most men do want sons. But for a few men, for instance, an older man who has never wanted to get married, perhaps the idea of having children is what stopped him. Such a man might indeed be delighted to find a woman like you."

Ohmeed looked at her sister with tears still glistening in her eyes. In an instant, she understood what was going on.

"Oh, Parvaneh," she wailed, "am I such a burden that you want to marry me off to the Ambassador? I can never again love a man as I did my husband. That Mojtabeh, he is too stuffy and full of himself. Nothing anyone did would ever be right for him. I would be absolutely miserable with him, and besides, he travels all the time. How can you call yourself married to a man who is never home?"

"You are wrong, Ohmeed," her sister answered quietly. "Mojtabeh Amuzegar is a man of great emotion, and he is quite capable of loving someone other than himself. He has just never had the opportunity to do it. He always had to serve the Shah, so could not serve himself as well. But I will tell you this. I have seen him look at you, and I recognize adoration. That man loves you. Even if he has never loved anyone else, he loves you."

Ohmeed was not about to tolerate this kind of interference, even from her own sister. With as much dignity as she could muster, she rose from the divan.

"I am tired from all the shopping. I think I will go lie down for a few minutes." She abruptly left her sister sitting alone in the salon.

This was about what Parvaneh had expected. Part two of her plan would be put into action in a couple more hours, after Ohmeed had had a chance to digest what had been brought up unexpectedly. Although Parvaneh had expected resistance, she fully believed that what she was doing was in Ohmeed's best interest, and it would work out.

At supper, no word was mentioned about the afternoon's confrontation. Parvaneh joked with her husband and the children as she pretended to ignore Ohmeed's silence. But her husband noticed it, and after a while he commented.

"Ohmeed Khanem, why are you so silent? Did my wife exhaust you by making you do the shopping for her today?" He smiled as he continued to tease her. "You seem so tired that you are ignoring the delicious lamb stew. Our cook will be insulted, and maybe we won't get it again for months."

Amenably, Ohmeed put another spoonful of food into her mouth, but had trouble swallowing. "Perhaps I am becoming ill," she murmured. "I think I should not be around the children. I don't want them to catch whatever I have."

Parvaneh responded instantly. "You are not ill, my sister, but perplexed. Children, you are dismissed from the table. Go outside and play, after you give your aunt a kiss."

The children sensed that something interesting was about to take place, and delayed finishing their meal in hopes of trying to find out what it was. However, their mother shooed them out of the dining room, leaving just herself, her husband and Ohmeed. Parvaneh motioned to the servants to leave them as well.

Her husband, not knowing exactly what was going on, but understanding that something important was up, waited expectantly while his wife set up her game plan. He had been married long enough to recognize when she was determined to accomplish something, and he realized that he was part of the strategy for whatever it might be.

"Ohmeed, let us get my husband's advice on this matter."

Ohmeed's eyes blazed at her sister but she remained silent.

Parvaneh ignored this and continued. "As you are aware, Omar," she continued, addressing her husband, "our Ambassador to Russia has visited our home frequently since Ohmeed returned from Shiraz. This afternoon, while Ohmeed was out, he stopped by again and declared to me that he is very much in love with Ohmeed. He, the reserved and long established bachelor, wants to ask my sister to marry him, but is afraid of being rejected . . ."

"As well he should be," Ohmeed interrupted angrily. "He has no understanding of my heart." She arose angrily, her voice becoming strident. "My husband is still right here," she cried, beating her heart with a closed fist, "and will always be. I cannot and will not marry another man. I will find another place to live. I will even go back to my husband's family and live with them, before I will ever marry again."

" . . . and does not know what to do." Parvaneh continued calmly, motioning to her sister to sit down. "But he is a man of sensitivity, and is willing to wait until Ohmeed is ready to accept another man. He understands that she loved her husband, and is respectful of that. Indeed, he is greatly impressed by her loyalty, and finds that a remarkable asset, not a hurdle. All he wants is an opportunity to declare himself to her."

Omar understood that here was where he was to come in. "I have known Amuzegar for a long time," he stated softly, now that he knew what his wife was trying to do. "He is a sheep in wolf's clothing. He is very gentle and many a time I have seen him do things for people that they never knew about. Although he is a diplomat, he is also a very kind human being. If you have won his heart, my dear sister-in-law, it means that you are a very special woman. No one else has ever done this. He would be a kind and loving husband.

"But this is not what matters to you just now. You do not care who it is who has come to seek you. Right now no man could fill the hole in your heart that is there by Allah's bounty. But understand that Allah has created this hole so that it can be filled again. Allah is merciful, and He loves His people. Happiness and joy will come to you again. Do not be so foolish as to cast it aside. Pain and misery are a part of living, just as love and blissfulness are. They create a circle. When there is sorrow, know that contentment is there also. Right now your pain is so great that you cannot see the possibility of this ever again. But it will come. Just listen to what Mojtabeh has to say. Do not cut him off completely. For your own sake, do as I say."

To her amazement, Ohmeed was profoundly touched by Omar's gentle words. Both he and her sister had her best interests at heart, she knew. Perhaps she really was wrapping herself in misery.

"Very well, both of you," she said, finally sinking back into her chair. "I will do as you say. I thank you for your love and concern. Forgive my obstinacy. I will listen to what the Assistant Ambassador has to say, and I will try to prepare myself to hear him with an open heart."

With tears in her eyes, Parvaneh went to her sister and hugged her.

"You will not be sorry, dearest Ohmeed," Parvaneh promised. "All you need do is listen. He will not expect a commitment from you. He just wants an opportunity to express himself. I think he is even more frightened than you are, if that is possible."

Ohmeed hugged her sister is return, then turned to thank her brother-in-law.

"Omar Agha, I truly appreciate your concern for my well being, and when I heard you just now I knew that you were speaking to me as if you were my own brother. My heart has been heavy, indeed, it is still heavy and always will be filled with love for my husband. But your words helped me to understand that he would want me to find contentment again, not build a shrine to what was in the past. That was the kind of man he was. He loved life and appreciated every moment's joy. You are right, he would want me to continue to do that."

Ohmeed took leave of her sister and brother-in-law and went to her room. Parvaneh expressed her deep appreciation to Omar for his well-timed intervention. Having been married for so many years, they had come to understand without words, and even though he had not known what the specific problem was, he was able to supply exactly the right solution when the issue became more clear to him. That kind of communication was exceptional, and this particular husband and wife truly appreciated what they shared.

CHAPTER 6

When Mojtabeh returned the next day, he found a home filled with flowers, which was a good sign, he thought. He could not believe how nervous he was. Indeed, his first audience with the Shah had not filled him with such anxiety. Even dealing with the Tsar of Russia had been a breeze, compared with what lay ahead of him this afternoon. But as he entered the salon, he was dismayed not to find Ohmeed there, only her sister. Had he lost already, without even being able to put forth his plight? His diplomatic skills nearly deserted him as he hesitantly asked after the well-being of the family.

"Mojtabeh Agha, good afternoon. My husband Omar will be here shortly. He wanted to meet with you before you saw Ohmeed. He spoke on your behalf last night and has softened her reluctance to consider your suit."

Mojtabeh nearly collapsed with relief as he seated himself on the edge of the divan. He fidgeted with something on the table in front of him, and was unable to look directly at Parvaneh.

"Your home is very lovely today, with all the flowers. Is that a new vase?" he stammered. "I mean, I do not recall seeing it in this room before, but perhaps it was in the hallway. Is that where I saw it earlier?" He continued rambling until Omar arrived.

Ohmeed's brother-in-law had been watching from the doorway for a moment and was absolutely astonished to see one of his country's most important diplomats reduced to near incoherence. To ease the tension, he entered the room with a great deal of commotion.

"Mojtabeh Agha, we are honored to have you visit us today," he boisterously greeted. "Have you been served tea? Our cook is famous for these particular cookies." He picked up a delicate confection with a pair of silver tongs and placed it on a plate in front of his guest. "Have some and you will feel as if you have just entered Allah's presence. I assure it."

This warm welcome revived Mojtabeh's courage somewhat and the coloring returned to his face. Unwilling to acknowledge how foolish he felt, he graciously acknowledged Omar's reception. "It is always a pleasure to come to your home. I was with the Shah only this morning and he instructed me to send his greetings to you. I trust I find you and all your family well."

"We are well, thank you. I know that you have come to talk with Ohmeed. She was reluctant to hear your suit, but both my wife and I have, we hope, eased some of her fears. I trust that you will find her amenable to listening to what you wish to say. I will leave now and ask her to come. However, I will be nearby if you need me." The latter was said in deference to Persian cultural norms that precluded an unmarried man and woman being together in a room for more than a moment or two.

Mojtabeh knew that remembrance of the room at that moment would be forever etched into his mind. The beauty of the flowers. The scent of the tea. The comfort of the pillows against which he sat. The designs running through the carpet. The arrangement of the furniture. By the time Ohmeed entered the room, he had regained his composure as well as his equanimity. He had returned to being Mojtabeh the diplomat, putting forth a treaty for consideration by the Tsar. His negotiating skills were superb. He could accomplish anything.

He smiled dazzlingly as Ohmeed approached him and offered her quiet salutation. "Good afternoon, Mojtabeh Agha. Please be seated. Have you been served tea? I will pour you some."

"Ohmeed Khanem," he answered, "if I am allowed to be in your presence, I will never again have need of tea or food. The sight of you refreshes and gladdens my spirit. The knowledge of your nearness provides my very being with all the refreshment I will ever need. You know why I have come today. It is to ask you to be my wife, to share the rest of your life with me. I solemnly pledge to provide you with both material and spiritual happiness. Allah has brought you into my life and I believe He wishes you to remain there forever. Never before has He suffused my existence with such joy, such strength. When I think of you, I know I can move the Ural Mountains from Russia to Africa, I can transplant the Caspian Sea from the north of Tehran into the center of Europe." He noted that Ohmeed was almost smiling. "The remembrance of you gives my spirit strength to dare anything. The only fear in my soul is that I would not see you again. Then I would become nothing. I would ride into the desert and roam there until I am consumed by the wind and the heat and the loneliness. Ohmeed Khanem, I pledge my unwavering devotion to you. Will you consent to marry me?"

He waited, but now with confidence, not fear.

The answer came directly and simply.

"Mojtabeh Agha, your words are eloquent. I acknowledge that they come directly from your heart. They are not the words of a deceiver. Your feelings inspire me to hope that life does indeed renew itself. I have thought deeply about my situation and I now understand that I must either allow myself to be a part of the positiveness of life, or to dry up into nothing but a piece of flesh that breathes but does not live. I thank you and my sister and my brother-in-law for showing me this truth. At this moment my heart has not yet opened to allow me to love you, but I believe that in time it may. Love does not come bidden, but only when it wishes to enter the heart and deliver the spirit into the realm of Almighty Allah. The strength of your feelings for me will pull my own from the depths of my heart where they are now hidden from me as well as from you. I pray that you will give me time to allow this to happen. Yes, in time, I will marry you."

Mojtabeh tenderly regarded the woman seated beside him. He had won. The most important negotiation he had ever entered, and he had emerged victorious. His smile said everything that his voice at the moment could not. Gently he reached over and encircled her with his arm.

"May I kiss you, my wife-to-be?" He did not wait for an answer.

A few moments later, Ohmeed rang the bell that had been strategically placed on the table. After a few seconds, Omar and Parvaneh opened the door to the salon and entered the room, noting the joy on both faces. Mojtabeh spoke.

"My life is complete. Ohmeed has agreed to become my wife. We will wait until I return from this posting to celebrate our union. I must secure the permission of his Majesty the Shah to marry, of course, but I know that he will readily consent. I thank you, Omar Agha and Parvaneh Khanem, for allowing me to come today. Please allow me to invite you all to my home -- soon to be our home -- " he added, looking at Ohmeed with such feeling that she blushed and lowered her head, "for dinner tomorrow night. An occasion of such magnitude must be appropriately commemorated."

Omar and Parvaneh joyously accepted the invitation, and Mojtabeh left, traveling immediately to the palace to schedule a meeting with the Shah. When he arrived, the Shah was with his wife Jila, and Mojtabeh knew that he would not be welcome at such a time. He made arrangements to return in a couple of hours. Meanwhile, he decided to seek out one of the mullahs he had met at the palace to arrange for his wedding. He inquired after the whereabouts of Mullah Askar.

"He is with the boy Habib. I will show you the way," one of the functionaries at the palace offered. A few moments later, he directed, "They are there in that room."

To Mojtabeh's surprise, they had arrived at a room near Prince Masoud's quarters.

"Good afternoon, Mullah Askar." Mojtabeh nodded his head slightly at the boy with the mullah. "I see that I am interrupting you. I apologize. Perhaps I should return at another time."

"No, not at all, Excellency. Prince Masoud has asked me to teach this lad to read. He is a quick learner." Mullah Askar smiled encouragingly at Habib. "But perhaps we have been working at it too long today. Go ahead now, boy, and we will resume tomorrow."

Mojtabeh was astonished that a servant was being taught to read, but decided not to ask questions. Eventually he would learn what that was all about, but he had other things on his mind at the moment.

"How may I serve you?" the mullah politely inquired.

"Mullah Askar, I have decided to marry. I am seeking a very special mullah to perform the ceremony, and my mind immediately flew to you. Of course, I must first secure permission from His Majesty, the Shah, but I do not believe that will be a problem. When I have accomplished this, will you perform the ceremony?"

"Who is it that you wish to marry? Indeed, Mr. Assistant Ambassador, this news amazes me. I had always known you to be a diplomat who had no desire to marry. She must be a very special woman indeed."

"Ah, if you but knew." Mojtabeh's visage radiated a joy that the mullah knew was absolutely sincere. "You are correct. Marriage had never entered my head until now. Then I saw this woman, and ever since I have been in absolute turmoil. Never has there been a woman like her. Indeed, only an hour ago I secured her consent to marry me and now I have come to obtain the Shah's permission. Of course, it would ordinarily be proper to have His Majesty's consent first, but, quite honestly, I did not know whether she would agree, and did not want to look a fool to the Shah if there were to be no marriage."

Askar was amazed to notice how loose the Assistant Ambassador's tongue had become. He must truly be in love, the mullah thought to himself. Outwardly, however, he took it all in without appearing flustered.

"What is her name?"

"Ohmeed. Ohmeed Talabassi. She is from Tehran but moved to Urmieh when she married her first husband. She lived there for several years, and due to a tragedy in her life -- the loss of her beloved husband -- , she has now enriched mine. Is that not strange, Mullah Askar?"

"No, it is not," Askar replied gently. "Allah tells us to accept the burdens of life, for they are his gifts to us, did we but understand. Her terrible misfortune has opened a new chapter in her life, and also in yours. Do not question the mysteries that surround you. Live by the holy teachings that tell us to love and care for one another, and you will always be safe."

Mojtabeh looked carefully at this mullah. He was accustomed to having mullahs quote, or frequently misquote, the Koran to their own benefit. This one simply told him to accept that love was part of Allah's plan for mankind. He was now certain that he had made a wise selection of this man to perform his marriage ceremony.

"I will be posted to Russia for several months, probably within the next few days. Immediately upon my return it is my absolute desire to marry this woman. Arrangements can be made through her brother-in-law. I will give you his name, and will keep in touch with you to let you know when I will return."

"As you wish, Mr. Assistant Ambassador. I will be honored to perform this ceremony for you."

Mojtabeh then left to find out if the Shah was ready to meet with him yet.

CHAPTER 7

"Assistant Ambassador Amuzegar, come join me in celebration. The coffers of the treasury are about to be replenished again." The Shah was absolutely delighted with himself as Mojtabeh entered the suite of rooms where negotiations were generally held.

"Your Majesty, that is wonderful. Have we found a new taxation policy?" Mojtabeh internally heaved a sigh of relief to find the Shah in an expansive mood.

"No, no. Far better than that. We have found a new man of great wealth with a daughter in need of a husband," the Shah answered lightheartedly. He then looked a bit thoughtful as he added, "But this marriage, I think, will be perfunctory. She is an ugly thing, and I won't want her around very much. I will marry this one to make my administrators, who always tell me there is not enough money to pay for what I want, a little happier. It is a pity that you will not be here to enjoy the ceremony. However, you must leave for Russia by the day after tomorrow."

"As you wish, Majesty. Before I leave, however, there is a matter I must discuss with you." Mojtabeh paused, looked appraisingly at the Shah, then pushed on. "I have learned from your example that marriage can be wonderful. Indeed, your Majesty, I have found a woman with whom I will be satisfied for eternity, and I seek your permission to marry. However, I assure you that this marriage will in no way interfere with my willingness to take on any assignment you ever set before me."

"You WHAT?" the Shah roared, not believing his ears as he broke out laughing. "Ah, so we all get bitten, even the most determined among us, I see. You understand that she cannot go with you to Russia, do you not?"

"Of course, Your Majesty."

"And your desire to be with her will not cloud your thinking when you are negotiating for the welfare of the Persian Empire."

"Never, Your Majesty."

The Shah regarded his Assistant Ambassador approvingly. "I believe you, Mojtabeh. I know how single minded you can be." The Shah then looked narrowly at Mojtabeh and added, "The Ambassador, a good and faithful servant, is getting old and may wish to retire soon. You will replace him, of course. Having a wife will serve you well in a more elevated position. You have my blessing."

Although he had anticipated the Shah's acquiescence, still Mojtabeh's heart leapt in gratitude. "Thank you, Your Majesty. I will always serve you with my whole heart. Now, with your permission, I will prepare to leave for Russia. Do you have any specific instructions for me?"

"You will be given what you need in writing when you depart. May the blessings of Allah be upon you, now and always."

Mojtabeh left, and the Shah turned his mind to other matters, including his upcoming marriage. Meanwhile, unbeknownst to the marriage-contented Shah, the woman whose bed he had just left was in a fury.

"Have I not brought enough coin into his money chests?" she snarled furiously to herself. "Have I not given him everything a husband wants? I could understand that he took wives before me. But when he had me, he had everything. How can he tell me, just after he has made love to me, that he intends to take another wife? If I had had a knife, I would have stabbed him one hundred million times and ended his worthless life right then and there."

She collected herself and forced her mind to calm down, realizing that controlling herself was by far the wiser course of action. Now would be the time for her to leave, she decided. She would go in such a way that he would never find her. Yes, let him have his new wife and her money.

Jila finished dressing and packed a small suitcase with some of the diamonds and gold and emeralds he had given her. Most of the wealth he had lavished upon her over the months of their marriage was already stored at her lover's home. This, she knew, was the right time. She sniffed again at the injustice he had done her, then went to see the Shah one last time.

"Pardon me, my husband," she said deferentially, as she entered the room without knocking.

He looked up, surprised to see her again only an hour after he had left her bed. He had been concentrating on state business, but smiled broadly at the sight of his lovely wife.

"I wanted to visit my father for a few hours this evening. Do I have your permission to leave the palace?" she asked, looking at him with falsely loving eyes.

The Shah frowned slightly, not wanting to miss having this wife within calling distance. However, he relented and said a little petulantly,

"Well, if you must go, all right. But I want you waiting for me when I am ready to retire this evening."

"Of course, my husband," she said, smiling sweetly while knowing full well that he would never see her again. He thought he could cast her aside. Let him find out who was doing the casting. "Let me give you a kiss to remind you of what will be awaiting you," she added in honeyed tones.

"I need no reminding, but gladly accept your kiss." His eyes fondly traveled over her body and his thoughts raced ahead to a few hours hence.

She then backed quietly out of the room, and shuddered as she shut the door. What if her contrivance did not work? What if the Shah were somehow able to track them down. Their plans had been so carefully made, with stops planned into Turkey and then on to England. From there, they would set out for America by ship. But what if something went wrong?

Although terrified of traveling over water, she nonetheless felt safe because she would be accompanied by the man with whom she had made these plans, the object of her wildest fantasies. Just thinking of him now gave her courage, and she hurried down the steps and out the door to her waiting carriage. When she was well along the way, she gave the driver instructions to take her to an address he had not been to before.

"You did not want to go to your father's, Madam?" he inquired hesitantly, not wishing to incur the Shah's wrath by taking this wife to the wrong place.

"Take me to the address I gave you. I must meet a friend there, and will travel on to my father's later."

The coachman did as she bade, and made careful note of where he stopped. "This is the address, Madam," he politely informed her. "I shall wait to take you on when you are ready to depart."

"That will not be necessary. My friend will take me to my father's house. My father knows I will be a bit delayed, and does not expect me for another hour."

Being even more afraid of incurring Her Majesty Jila's wrath than that of the Shah, the driver reluctantly complied with her orders. On his return trip to the palace, he was waylaid, supposedly by robbers. They tied him up and transported him to a hidden grove of trees, knowing that it would be a day or two before he would be found. Their instructions had been not to kill him, but just to assure that he would not be able to report anything to the Shah for at least forty-eight hours.

The carriage arrived driverless back at the palace late that night, causing the Shah to dash to his courtyard in a state of utter panic. Investigators were immediately dispatched to the home of Jila's father, who knew nothing. He answered that he had not seen his daughter that evening, had not even known that she was expected. He, too, was terrified that his beloved daughter had been injured, and he sent out his own people to look for her. But because he had never known of her relationship with the man with whom she had absconded, he looked in all the wrong places.

By the time the driver was found, Jila and her lover were well into the mountains of Turkey. Their escape had been so perfectly planned that the Shah never learned what happened. Nor could he understand what had happened to several deeds that had disappeared from his son's living quarters, nor how it was that distant relatives of Jila's were now reclaiming their rights to several properties.

After four months, he bereavedly proclaimed her dead. The funeral he held for her was the most elaborate ever witnessed in Tehran, and he mourned for many more months. In the meantime, however, he married the ugly woman with a wealthy father. His attitude toward her was exactly the opposite of what it had been toward Jila. Soon she was banished to a far corner of the palace where he did not have to look at her ever again. His interest in governing increased in direct proportion to his decreased interest in the marriage bed. His other wives tried to comfort him, but only Amina was successful. She was a politician's wife, not a concubine, and her advice helped him continue to rule the Persian empire.

CHAPTER 8

Word of Mojtabeh Amuzegar's impending marriage spread throughout Persia, carried by the winds of rumor and sometimes anger. Families realized that their dreams of snagging the Assistant Ambassador for their daughters, however unlikely these hopes may have been, would never be realized. Many a father was adamant in his denunciation of the interloping widow, and mothers connived to change reality. Nothing worked, and fortunately for her, Ohmeed never learned how much societal unhappiness she had created.

In Shiraz, however, one family was joyous at hearing the news. Tahirih was exhilarated on behalf of the friend who had helped her past her own overwhelming grief, and Ismail instantly converted the engagement information into calculations for expansion of his business. With the Ambassador soon to be a relative by marriage -- well, perhaps there were a lot of indirect links, but still, being married to his wife's distant cousin would make the Ambassador almost a brother-in-law, he contended to himself -- he believed he would have more immediate access to the Shah's ear. His dreams of expanding his business into Russia and possibly even other countries bloomed.

He decided to visit Tehran, ostensibly to wish the couple well, and perhaps while he was there, he could finalize arrangements for his upcoming second marriage. Even though the journey involved a horseback ride of at least ten days over rugged terrain, Ismail believed that it would be well worth the effort to accomplish both personal and business ends for himself.

When he told Tahirih of his intentions, however, he could not believe her reaction.

"Ismail,' she had said in an almost demanding manner, " I wish to accompany you."

"Of course not," he retorted, astounded that she would consider such an undertaking. "How could you endure such a journey? Who would look after the children?"

His wife just laughed. "Have you forgotten, Ismail, when you were my cousin, not my husband, I used to out-gallop you at our family horse races?" When he looked confused, she clarified. "At my father's house, when we would have the summer picnics," she said. "There was a rider you could never catch. Someone wearing a hat so no one could see who it was."

Ismail's eyes widened in wonder. He remembered well. An unidentified rider would sweep past him in every race, but never stay around to claim a prize. "That was you? The one I named the White Wind because he just flew past us all and disappeared?"

She smiled again, with a bit of triumph in her eyes. "I could ride anything, even the ornery horses that threw my brothers off their backs like leaves in a windstorm. My father knew who I was, but he didn't tell anyone else for fear of being chastised for allowing his daughter to participate in boys' events."

"Well, even so," Ismail muttered as he regained his composure, " being able to ride a horse is not the only skill that enables a man to make a long journey. You must be able to sleep in strange places, eat at odd times, endure rain and strong winds. Women cannot do those things."

"Oh, don't be silly," Tahirih countered, now becoming a little angry. "Women have accompanied men all over Persia, whenever they move their families from one place to another. Of course I can manage. The servants have proved how well they can care for the children." She looked at him with combined pleading and fierce determination. "Ohmeed needs a woman to help plan her wedding. Of course she has her sister, but there is so much to do, I know she will welcome my assistance. She has become as dear as my own sister to me."

Although she was naming Ohmeed as the reason for wanting to accompany him on the trip, she actually wanted time alone with her husband, but knew she could not offer that as a reason he would accept, so instead put forth a 'woman's' reasoning.

Over the years, Ismail had learned to acquiesce in those rare instances when his wife was absolutely bent on accomplishing something. This was apparently one of those times, so he answered grumpily. "I will consider it." he conceded.

As he left for his day at the bazaar, his mind began to consider that this might actually work to his benefit.. Perhaps he could introduce his present and future wives, let them get to know one other before they actually shared the same house. Now that he believed he had his own reason, he decided to allow Tahirih to prove whether she could indeed ride all the way to Tehran, as she claimed.

Less than two weeks later, the two of them were on their way. Before departing, Tahirih left detailed instructions for each of the servants, including reminders that her mother would come over each day, and might sometimes take all or some of the children home with her. When Husayn heard of this, he was overjoyed, as he looked forward to being pampered at Grandma's house. He also began to plan how he would sweet talk his grandfather into letting him ride the big horse and maybe even sit on the back of the water buffalo as it walked in circles threshing the grain. So while the other children cried as their mother rode off, Husayn waved happily, then turned to his siblings and declared himself the man of the house until his father returned.

It had been several years since Tahirih had ridden a horse, and she soon realized that she had minimized her expectations of the discomforts they would encounter. She had not yet fully healed from childbirth, and consequently tired quickly because she was battling pain all the time. Sometimes the inns were full, and they had to ride on to the next town after nightfall, making the journey more gruesome as she imagined highway robbers and huge snakes coming out at night. Clouds of stinging insects pursued them during the daytime, and the sun was unmercifully hot.

Nonetheless, she continued to happily anticipate having an uninterrupted month with her husband. She planned that during this trip she would convince him that he did not need to take a second wife, that she could be enough for him. Although she missed her children every second, she knew they were safe and well cared for. Meanwhile, she hoped that she was actually stabilizing their lives by eliminating the possibility of future step-siblings, which she had seen cause appalling rivalry in other families. Plus she expected to have wonderful adventures which she could relate to them as bedtime stories for years to come. She might even meet the Shah and could share that inconceivable experience with her mother, who would be overwhelmed with pride.

However, the blissful reunion Tahirih had envisioned instead turned into an exhausting time of recriminations and anger. Slowly Tahirih saw her dream of securing her husband's full affection disintegrating into loss instead. She became more and more furious with herself for trying to accomplish such a foolhardy mission as transforming a grueling business trip into a second honeymoon. The more disillusioned she became, the more she snapped at Ismail when he blamed her unjustly for small transgressions, as happened all too often.

As the journey progressed, not only did Ismail discover that his wife was not always the compliant follower of his wishes he had believed her to be, but Tahirih likewise learned that Ismail could be brutal in enforcing his wishes.

On the fourth day, their pack horse pulled up lame as they were ascending a steep hill. "Now look what you've done," Ismail snapped. "All that clothing you insisted on bringing is just too much for the animal to carry. I told you not to bring so much. I'm of a mind to throw your suitcase over the edge of the trail, and let you arrive with nothing. That way you will have to stay out of my way while we are there."

Tahirih was livid. "I don't know what you are talking about, my dearly beloved, all-knowing husband," she shouted back. "I have one small suitcase with only a few changes of clothes. That's all. What is weighing the poor horse down is all the samples you brought."

They continued sniping at each other while each struggled with the lacings holding their baggage on to the horse. Tahirih felt that Ismail had lashed out at her unfairly one too many times, and she was not about to tolerate any more. She yanked her suitcase off the pack horse and tied it on her own instead, making it impossible for her to get on again and ride. Therefore, she continued to walk, while her husband mounted and rode on in stony silence. At times he trotted away, leaving her alone on the road, but eventually he would wait until she caught up again.

Two hours later, they finally arrived at an inn for the night. Tahirih herself spoke to the innkeeper. "We are very tired," she said as pleasantly as she could, "and would like your nicest room. The cost is unimportant. Perhaps you would even have two rooms," she added, glancing in feigned sympathy at Ismail, "as my husband in exhausted and needs to rest without interference tonight."

At this, Ismail jumped in and qualified his wife's words. "My wife has recently suffered some tragedies and her mind is not well. Please forgive her poor manners. Of course, we need only one room, and it does not have to be anything fancy. Also, I would like to exchange one of my horses for a better one." He then began a prolonged negotiation, deliberately leaving his exhausted wife standing while he bargained for more than an hour.

Similar incidents began to occur on a daily basis, and by the time they arrived in Tehran, they were not speaking to one another. Once there, however, in typical Persian fashion, they put aside their disputes so no one else would know, since in the society where Ismail and Tahirih lived, problems between husband and wife were never broadcast to the outside world.

Although Mojtabeh was now in Russia, he had insisted that Ismail stay at his home. Tahirih had not been expected, but when Ismail arrived with a wife in tow, Mojtabeh's servants immediately arranged for her comfort and well being. Ismail and Tahirih were shown to a large, airy room on the second floor of the Ambassador's enormous home. The sun poured in through a large window, and fresh cut flowers sweetened the air. One servant hung their clothes in a hand fashioned armoire while another informed them that a luncheon was to be held later that afternoon. Attending would be several influential merchants that Mojtabeh had contacted on Ismail's behalf, hoping to enhance business prospects for the tea merchant from Shiraz.

Tahirih looked longingly at the bed, wishing desperately to rest her aching body on the soft mattress. However, Ismail informed her curtly that she was expected to be dressed and downstairs in half an hour, which barely gave her time to wash and select suitable clothing to wear. Would her small town clothes be acceptable, or would the servants laugh at her behind her back? Her insecurities came flooding back, but Ismail had left the room and she had to deal with them on her own.

Slowly, she stepped out of her dusty clothes and walked over to the dresser where a lovely hand painted ceramic washbasin had been filled with warm water. Beside the basin lay an expensive comb and brush set. If these items were what was to be found in a guest room, then her friend Omeed would certainly have exquisite things for herself, Tahirih thought contentedly to herself.

She splashed the warm water on her face and immediately began to feel better. After sponging herself off, she reached for the brush and began stroking her hair. One hundred strokes a day, her mother had taught her. She relaxed as she counted, closing her eyes and taking in the pleasurable scents surrounding her. She inhaled the smell of the rose water in which she had bathed, the flowers filling her room, and the lemon polish that made the furniture sparkle. Everything was fresh and lovely. So, too, must she be fresh and lovely if she were to capture her husband back for herself. Two weeks of difficult travel were over. Now she and Ismail could be more like themselves, she promised herself.

CHAPTER 9

The luncheon, of course, was for men only. When Tahirih arrived downstairs, she was immediately taken to a separate area where she was served a much simpler lunch in isolation. The servants could not eat with her, of course, and her husband was with the men, so she was on her own already, she realized. Inside herself, she was grateful for the reprieve from social obligations, while at the same time she was furious with Ismail for not allowing her to rest after such an exhausting journey. Nonetheless, as she usually did, Tahirih decided to make the best of her situation, and allowed herself to relax and enjoy the unhurried, undemanding atmosphere with which she was presently surrounded.

The servants were serving both her and the larger luncheon party, so they kept coming back and forth from one room to another. As she nibbled at the delicious food presented to her, her mind began to unwind a little, and with that, so did her body. Presently, as the servants quietly came and went, she felt herself slipping into a dreamlike state. Gradually, her head began to drop, and she drifted off into that area somewhere between wakefulness and sleep, where one physically hears what is said around them, but does not immediately comprehend the meaning of the words.

Just outside the doorway, one servant was chatting with another, thinking that he was out of earshot of the lady Tahirih. "It sounds to me as if this merchant Ismail is here for more than business reasons," he whispered to his fellow worker. "From what I have picked up going in and out of that room, I think he came to Tehran to get himself a second wife, too. I heard him boasting about going to visit the girl's father tomorrow morning to finalize the marriage contract. He said he might even introduce the present wife to the new one the day after. Now wouldn't that be an interesting meeting? I sure would like to be a fly on the wall observing," the servant scoffed, as he laughed a bit raucously.

The other servant, whose voice was somewhat louder, quipped something about a man never being able to have too many wives to keep his nights warm, and they chuckled as they re-entered the room where the quasi-sleeping Tahirih still sat upright. Noting her state, they tried to clear the table without disturbing her, but one of them accidentally bumped her arm as he was removing the dishes. Immediately she returned to full consciousness, and embarrassedly apologized for nodding off.

She asked if she might sit in the garden for a little while. The servant, realizing that he might have been overheard, shamefacedly accompanied her to a bench near a flowering peach tree and brought her a small blanket to either sit on or put on her lap in case she grew cool. Tahirih felt disturbed about something, but could not identify what it was, and she wrapped the blanket around her legs, even though the afternoon was still warm.

She glanced around the garden and admired the gladiolas, which were her favorite flower, then reached up and picked a peach from a low hanging branch. As she quietly munched, she told herself that she had to begin to plan how to make the most of her time alone with Ismail. She loved him so dearly, and the thought of sharing him with another woman made her physically ill, but she could not allow him to see that. She had to be strong. She had to figure out what to do. But what could it be?

With growing trepidation, she acknowledged to herself that the society where she lived permitted a man to marry as many times as he pleased. With his growing financial power, it obviously pleased Ismail to show off by acquiring more than one wife. How could she demonstrate to him that he did not need to do that?

Despite turning the problem over and over in her mind, she could not come up with a viable answer to that question, which she realized was the most important question she had ever asked herself. She understood that if Ismail married for a second time, it would not be for love, but for power and prestige. A second wife would come from a family with business influences, and it would be a daughter that the father had had trouble marrying off.

With an electrifying shock, Tahirih realized that that was exactly her situation as well. Suddenly it came to her that Ismail might have married her for economic reasons, not for love, as he had always told her. As she sat in apparent composure, her heart precipitously fell to her stomach. If that were true, she realized, then he might also come to love another woman who lived in his house and was, Allah forbid, the mother of more children for him.

Why did he have to do this, she asked herself bitterly. Why can't I be enough for him? However, as hard as she chewed on the problem, no solution came to her.

Meanwhile, Ismail felt the luncheon was going well. There were three Tehrani businessmen there, all with connections to the palace. All three were outwardly courteous, if not directly helpful. It was obvious that they all were indebted to the Assistant Ambassador for various reasons. Ismail had learned, through mild probing, that in differing ways, Mojtabeh had helped each of them secure business deals. Now Mohtabeh had asked his protegees to help someone else, and out of courtesy, they were doing so. Nonetheless Ismail understood that this first meeting was merely preliminary, and that he would have to demonstrate his ability to produce profits which would not only fill the coffers of the palace, but line the pockets of these men as well as himself, if he wanted to secure any long term assurances from them. He was, however, quite confident that he could find a way to accomplish these multiple objectives.

The luncheon had begun on a social note, with each man discussing topics of general interest. Thus far they had been through climate, the state of road repair between Tehran and Shiraz, and the comparative beauty of city versus provincial women. The latter discussion had led to Ismail's bragging that he intended to take a second wife, this one from Tehran, and that was what the servants had overheard and repeated among themselves. From Ismail's viewpoint, he was subtly showing that he was already a successful man who should be taken seriously. He also knew that his second father-in-law was well known in Tehran, and he didn't mind doing a little name dropping to demonstrate his importance.

"So it is from a renowned family that you will be taking your second wife," one of the merchants commented. "My wife's younger brother is married to another of his daughters." The wily merchant did not add that his brother-in-law was miserably unhappy with the harpy he had been saddled with. It was, of course, none of his business to interfere in the proposed marriage of a stranger, but he chuckled inside himself as he thought of how this cocksure young fellow might be in for a bit more of a marriage than he had reckoned for.

 After three hours, the businessmen agreed to meet with Ismail later in the week to discuss more details about Ismail's proposed tea exporting enterprise. Ismail considered himself the model of deportment as he bade the men farewell, almost acting as if it were his own house from which he was sending them. Unfortunately, all three noted his conduct and none were pleased with it. It appeared to them that this man from the provinces appeared to be a little too sure of himself. Perhaps they would have to teach him a lesson about how businessmen behaved in the big city. In his own little world way down there in Shiraz, they said among themselves as they rode off, perhaps he was indeed someone of importance, but here in Tehran it was different. They agreed that they would scuttle his ambitions, even though they would outwardly appear to help as much as possible, in deference to their mentor and patron, Mojtabeh Amuzegar, whom they could not afford to alienate.

Following the luncheon, Ismail found Tahirih sitting in the garden. "Why are you all wrapped up as if it were cold?" he asked somewhat harshly. His positive sentiment about the meeting he had just concluded did not carry over to his irritation with the belligerence he felt his wife had been demonstrating ever since they left Shiraz.

"Dearest Ismail, I was just a little chilly, and the servant very kindly provided me with this blanket, so I used it. I think the chill came from my heart because I was feeling so badly about all the arguing we have done. I am so sorry that I have been difficult to get along with. It was undoubtedly the strain of traveling. I promise that I will behave much better in the future."

This unexpected apology caught Ismail by surprise, and he was heartened to believe that perhaps his real Tahirih was still somewhere there in the harridan he had been dealing with for the past several days. He decided to respond accordingly.

"Yes, Tahirih, the trip was arduous. Perhaps I, too, said some things I should not have. Let us put it behind us, and be friends again." Then he began an account of what he believed was his successful first meeting, while Tahirih listened attentively, making wise suggestions here and there, and even pointing out one or two potential hazards. By the time the servant came to announce dinner, they were almost back to the way they had been for more than seven years -- friends, confidantes and mutual advisors. Following dinner, they retired early, and for several hours that night Tahirih made a concerted effort to prove to Ismail that he had no need for any other woman, ever. She was sure that she had succeeded, since Ismail remarked several times how fulfilling he found her, and how much he loved her.

To her utter mortification, then, the next morning Ismail announced that he would accompany his first wife to the home of

Ohmeed's sister, after which he intended to proceed on to discuss final wedding arrangements concerning the second wife. He even invited Tahirih to go with him the following day to meet her new "sister", fully believing that this was a wonderful idea.

Tahirih was too shocked to respond to the invitation for the following day, so simply thanked her husband for arranging so quickly for her visit to Ohmeed. She was unusually silent as the hired carriage took them to Ohmeed's home, but Ismail did not notice. He was too full of ideas about his business and the advantages his second wife would bring him.

CHAPTER 10

Ohmeed was thrilled to have her friend visit. Although she did not need help with planning the wedding, she agreed that it had certainly made a marvelous excuse for Tahirih's accompanying her husband to Tehran. Since Ohmeed, too, was a woman who took chances and did things frowned upon by society, she understood how difficult such a journey was to arrange. Their bond of respect and friendship grew even stronger, and they chatted animatedly.

"Ohmeed, your Mojtabeh is a magnificent man, and you will be so happy. I just know you will," Tahirih said, perhaps a little too enthusiastically, as she tried to disguise her own worries through ebullience for her friend's coming bliss. "His home is so warm and inviting, and surely that is an indication of how he himself is."

It was a little strange that Tahirih had seen far more of Ohmeed's new home than Ohmeed herself had, and they laughed together over the anomaly. Tahirih talked about the beautiful view of Elburz Mountain from the upper level of the house, and then she described each of the servants she had met thus far.

"They are very efficient, and they certainly seem very kind. Except that they are all men. There are no female servants. Perhaps Mojtabeh will allow you to select a woman after you marry. "

"I am sure he will," Ohmeed agreed. "He is so accommodating. I cannot believe that no other woman has managed to snag him before this. Perhaps it is Allah's way of telling me never to give up hope, no matter how bleak life may seem."

Ohmeed's sagacious remark stung Tahirih's soul and nearly led her to confess her misery, but at the last instant she held her tongue. She should learn something from Ohmeed's bravery, she thought. Her own husband had not died, he was just expanding his family for business purposes. She would not die if she had to share him. Certainly sharing him was far better than losing him, which might happen if she made a fuss.

In that instant, she understood that she would never say anything to Ismail. If, indeed, he did take another wife, she would make the best of it and continue to be the finest wife she could. Of course, she always had her children to comfort her and prove her value. She thought longingly of them, and now wished that the journey would be over and she could be back with them again.

For the afternoon, the women went out shopping with Ohmeed's sister, whom Tahirih immediately liked. The three of them spent an idyllic several hours selecting the finest fabric for a wedding dress as well as an exquisite pair of shoes.

Although Tahirih was impressed with the variety of goods available in the Tehran bazaar, which far exceeded the more meager offerings in Shiraz, she was pleased to note that craftsmanship of silver products she saw here was definitely inferior to that in her own hometown. When Ohmeed expressed wonder and delight with the silver samovar Tahirih had chosen for her wedding present, Tahirih knew it was worth the effort she had made to bring it all the way by horseback, despite Ismail's protests.

"Now I certainly understand why people travel to Shiraz to buy silver," Ohmeed gushed enthusiastically. "Never have I seen anything so exquisite in all my life. How will I ever thank you, dearest Tahirih?"

"You won't, because no thanks are necessary," Tahirih answered with absolute certainty. "You have done far more for me than I could ever possibly express gratitude for," she added, thinking again of how she had nearly destroyed her relationship with Ismail by confronting him about taking another wife, only to be saved by Ohmeed's judicious words. This was the second time Ohmeed had saved Tahirih from herself, the first when she had briefly considered joining her baby in Allah's kingdom rather than remaining on earth to take care of the family that needed her, and now again. Twice now Ohmeed had saved her from precipitous actions that would have led to misery for so many people, and she knew she could never repay such a debt.

After depositing Tahirih at Ohmeed's sister's home, Ismail had ridden on to what appeared to be a surprisingly humble looking district of Tehran. When he initially negotiated the marriage contract, everything had taken place at the bazaar, so Ismail had never been to the residence before. Now when he arrived at the home itself, something about it just did not feel quite right. Nonetheless, at the address he had been given, he dismounted and reluctantly handed the reins of his horse over to the lad waiting for him.

Glancing around, Ismail was somewhat disappointed that the neighborhood did not appear to be particularly distinguished. The concourses leading to this area did not have a feeling of wealth and prosperity, and, like all other homes on the street, the one where he had stopped was surrounded by a wall. This, of course, was typical of Persian society, where walls cleverly hid the owner's fortune, and poor and wealthy lived side by side. Ismail's home shared the same characteristic of non distinction from the outside. Nonetheless, Ismail felt a mild frustration, as he had hoped for a more refined appearance, somehow.

However, when he was welcomed inside the walls, his feelings of disappointment evaporated. As he was led through the home and out to the gardens by an especially well dressed servant, he took in the size and number of rooms, the beauty of the carpets on the walls and the floors, the display of silver and gold trays, the intricate designs of hand carved furniture, and many other signs that he was indeed marrying into a very well-to-do family. He heaved an inward sigh of relief.

The servant conducted him to an outdoor seating area where he was temporarily left to admire the orderliness of flower arrangements and the fragrance of fruit trees, as well as the beauty of fountains shooting jets of water into the air and splashing down into pools filled with enormous goldfish. Yet another servant brought him delicate refreshments. All seemed to be well, he decided.

He heard a lute being played somewhere in the distance. Indeed, this is paradise, he thought to himself. It is what I want for my family, and in the not too distant future, I will have it. Tahirih will be very happy, and there is nothing on this earth more important to me than having Tahirih be happy. She is my everything. With this second wife, there will be less work for her to do, and she will have time to enjoy the wealth I provide for her.

In the midst of these thoughts, his future father-in-law arrived. "Welcome to my home, Ismail Agha," He roared enthusiastically, causing Ismail to wince at the loudness of his voice. "I am delighted to have you visit my humble abode, and I hope you are comfortable here in the garden. Do you see these roses over here? I cross-bred them myself until they were the exact color I wanted," he bragged. "As you see, these beauties are just beginning to bud out, and if we are fortunate, there will be an abundant supply for the wedding. Surely the ceremony will be enhanced by the beauty of their fragrance and the subtlety of their coloring."

He continued to talk incessantly, without giving Ismail an opportunity even to acknowledge his future father-in-law's thoughtfulness. Finally, the monologue ceased, and the two of them got down to negotiating final details of the marriage contract, which included a hefty sum of cash to be paid to Ismail on the wedding day, as well as assurances of multiple business opportunities in Tehran.

"I look forward to becoming a part of your esteemed family," Ismail assured the man. "You have given me many excellent ideas, not only for expansion of my tea business, but also for the future of my eldest son. Your comments about the educational opportunities available at the House of Sciences here in Tehran have provoked some serious thinking on my part. Perhaps I will enroll Husayn there in a few years."

"It will be good for you to send all of your sons there," his future father-in-law admonished. "My daughter will provide you with many sons, he added, pointedly reminding Ismail that his current wife had given him only one, and lost the second.

"Certainly, I assure you, that will be the case," Ismail replied. "The joining of our families is now but three months away, and as we agreed, I will have completed enlargement of my home so Mahvash will have her own quarters. My first wife has been prepared and will receive your daughter graciously. Actually, Tahirih is here in Tehran with me, and would like very much to meet her new sister. Would it be possible for us to visit again tomorrow so that they might become acquainted?"

His host was taken aback at this request, but recovered quickly. "It would be a most excellent idea to have them meet prior to living in the same home," he managed to say, although he certainly did not believe that. "Please come tomorrow to share our noon time meal."

They exchanged a few other pleasantries, and eventually Ismail left. Mahvash, who had been watching the interchange from the next room, shyly approached her father and expressed her joy and appreciation for his finding such a good man for her to marry. This Ismail seemed to be generous and thoughtful, as well as wealthy, she thought.

"Dearest father, I know I am a fourth daughter, and we are hard to marry off. I swear to you by Allah's blessed name that I will provide you with many grandchildren."

Her father looked at her sternly. "Mahvash, you will do far more than that," he said, with an implied threat in his voice. "You know that it is your duty to become the mother of the future leaders of Persia. Your children must rise to prominence, and you must assure that they have every opportunity to take control of every sphere of Persian society"

"Yes, father. I understand."

Her father continue to browbeat the young girl. "Indeed, you better, or you will never set foot in this house again. You heard him speak of having his present son attend the House of Science. I will not allow that to happen. Only *your* children will have that kind of opportunity. It is crucial that our family continue to encircle Persia until it is totally within our dominion."

He paused for a moment to catch his breath, then continued expressing his absolutist opinions. "My family is from the same ancestry as the Shah, as you have been all of your life. For years, now, I have planned meticulously. Finally, with this marriage, we will be in a position to regain our rightful heritage, and we shall do so. This I have sworn on my father's grave."

Again he paused, and looked at his daughter very carefully. "REMEMBER," he shouted, "the Shah's grandfather is also my grandfather. My grandmother unfortunately bore her children on the wrong side of the blanket, but that does not matter. Our family has noble blood flowing through our veins, and soon we will assert our right to rule Persia. Just be sure that you do your part."

The terrified Mahvash, who had been brought up with these delusions for as long as she could remember, assured her father that she would carry out her duty, just as all her sisters and brothers had done by likewise marrying in accordance with their father's choices.

The following morning Tahirih dressed herself with great care to accompany her husband for a meeting with the upcoming second wife. As they were preparing to leave, Ismail had told her that everything he did was for her, that she was the center of his life, and that without her, he would be nothing. Once again, Tahirih was glad she had held her tongue, and she knew that somehow everything would work out all right. Have faith in Allah, she told herself, just as you have always been taught. You will be safe.

The Manucheri house, she noted after they arrived, was impressive, and she could see why her husband wanted to be connected with the wealth that oozed from every carpet and piece of furniture. To her surprise, she was not intimidated by the girl with whom she would share her husband and her home for the rest of her life. Mahvash seemed gentle and considerate, especially toward Tahirih, whom she appeared to honor as the first wife. For the second time that day, Tahirih believed that this was not the disaster she had envisioned.

Two days later, she and Ismail began the return journey to Shiraz. When she arrived home, Tahirih's joy at being re-united with her children was unbounded. She expressed to her mother that the new wife was a lovely person, and was reminded that her mother had assured her that it would be so.

A SMALL
TOWN

CHAPTER ONE

Seventeen year old Talat awoke during the night. She lay in her bed with the covers up to her chin and her coat over the covers, but still she shivered. She understood that she could not remain in this household much longer, but she had no idea where to go. The mistress, Tahirih, although only a few years older than herself, had become a mother substitute to whom she had gone with various problems and received wise guidance. But this time, Talat had a problem about which she could not confide to the mistress. Nor did she feel that she could consult Parvin. Certainly she could not turn to her sisters, loving and kind as they were. They would not understand and would probably believe that Talat had brought the problem on herself. She was alone, and very, very afraid.

Well, she had to get up and face the day, whatever it might bring. Dawn was peeking through the windows, and Talat smiled in spite of her misery. She loved the early morning hours, when everything was so quiet. She dressed, washed her face and hands -- the mistress always insisted on that -- and went to the kitchen to help with breakfast. She was there even before Parvin this

morning, so began the preparations on her own. After starting a
fire in the oven and putting the risen bread in to bake, she called
a neighbor child and gave him a few cents from the jar beside the
door to go get some fresh yogurt. By the time Parvin came to the
kitchen half an hour later, she found everything well underway for
the morning meal.

"You certainly are an early bird this morning," she commented.
"To what do we owe this honor?"

Talat murmured that she had just awakened a little earlier than
usual.

"Well, I thank you for starting breakfast." Parvin answered.
"I think I am getting too old to begin the day so early. Hand me
that bowl and I will crack the eggs while you knead the bread for
tomorrow."

Together they worked in silence for a few moments. Finally
Talat decided to say something. "Parvin, I must speak with the
mistress this morning. I need to go visit my father for a few days
because I just got word that he is not feeling well. Do you think
she will give me permission?"

"So that is why you are up so early. You are worried, eh?
Don't be concerned about Tahirih Khanem. I will speak for you
if you like. Now, where is Cook this morning? Go find him for
me, will you? "

Talat left the bread sitting in the kneading bowl and went to
look for Cook, who was again arguing with his daughter.

"Good morning," Talat said, interrupting a severe tongue
lashing. "Parvin wanted to know what you planned to make for

the noon meal. She said the Master will be coming home to eat today."

"Yes, yes. I am coming. Try to talk some sense into this thick head, will you?" and a frustrated Cook stomped off, leaving Talat to deal with a teary Zahreh.

"I try to do. Just I forget. I no want be bad," Zahreh mumbled, and then the sobs started.

"It's all right, Zahreh. I know you try," Talat reassured the retarded child. Now let's go help Parvin with serving breakfast and getting the children fed."

Talat was feeling very guilty. There were so many people here who needed her and cared about her. How could she just leave? But she certainly could not stay, even though she still had not figured out where to go. Well, she was going to leave this afternoon, no matter what.

Ismail Agha did not come to breakfast that morning, having left early to say a special prayer at the mosque. After breakfast, Talat asked to see the mistress.

"Parvin told me your father is ill. How did you hear about it? Parvin said no one came to the door yesterday to talk with you." Tahirih felt something was wrong, but she could not identify what it was.

Talat felt trapped, but she boldly tried to make something up. "I, uh, I saw someone while I was out shopping for food yesterday, Tahirih Khanem. A man who was a neighbor when I was a child. He told me that my father had fallen from a rooftop and hurt himself. Please, Ma'am, may I go to visit him? I will try to come back as soon as possible."

"Of course you must be with your father if he is not well. I will send Firidun with you to be sure that you get there safely."

Talat panicked. "Oh no, Mistress! I mean, that would be such an inconvenience to you. I know there is a lot of pruning to be done just now with the roses and the gladiola and all the other flowers. I can go by myself. It is not far and I will be going in the afternoon while the sun is still bright. I will be safe, really, I will."

Tahirih did not understand why Talat was so reluctant to have Firidun go with her. Perhaps she was embarrassed by her father's condition. Well, she would have Firidun check tomorrow to be sure that Talat had arrived safely, and just would not tell her about it.

"As you wish, dear child. May Allah be with you and with your father." Then thinking some more about the matter, it occurred to her to ask, "Why doesn't your brother come for you? He lives with your father, doesn't he? "

Again Talat had to come up with a quick lie. "They are not aware I am going to come home, Mistress, so there would be no way for him to know to come get me. I will be all right, I promise you."

Tahirih could see that Talat was pleading with her not to ask more questions, so she let it go, even though she continued to feel uneasy.

After helping to clean up after breakfast and saying good-bye to the children and her fellow servants, Talat took a small packed bag and left. It was not until the following day when Tahirih sent Firidun to be sure she had arrived safely that they learned that Talat had never gone to her father's home.

Tahirih was frightened that something terrible had happened to the girl for whom she felt responsible, and she begged Ismail to hire people to look for her.

Ismail did, but after several days, nothing had been heard. Not even the servants' whispering networks could produce any information about where Talat had gone. It seemed that she had simply disappeared, and after three weeks, Ismail told Tahirih to hire another servant to take her place.

"But what could have happened to her, Ismail? Absolutely no one has seen her. Do you think she was frightened because I told her we would find a husband for her? You know, a few weeks ago, she was sitting by the pond one day, looking distracted. When I mentioned that if she got married her husband would be welcome to work here for us, she seemed terrified and ran back into the house. I can't believe she has just disappeared. Someone, somewhere has to have seen her. Shiraz is not that large."

Ismail suspected why she had disappeared, but did not want to share his thoughts with his wife. He had had several people combing the area and was just as mystified by Talat's ability to disappear into thin air as everyone else.

"I don't know where she is, and I don't know why she left. Perhaps she had an argument with someone in the household and they just aren't saying anything about it. Don't worry, dearest Tahirih. There is nothing to be gained by asking the same questions over and over. Obviously, she did not want us to know where she was going or why, so let's just leave it at that. She's gone."

Tahirih was amazed at her husband's attitude. This was someone who had worked for them for years, a young woman who had disappeared. Wasn't he concerned about her safety? At the same time, she had to admit he was right. Asking the same questions over and over was not producing any results, and she did not want to annoy Ismail. Still, she wondered, where could Talat have gone?

CHAPTER TWO

Talat managed to find her way to a small village about fifty miles west of Shiraz. Most of the way she had walked and picked fruits from roadside orchards for occasional insubstantial meals. Late on the fourth day she had been offered a ride in a wagon with a very talkative family. Their chattering covered her silence, and they had not asked questions when she pointed to a derelict farmhouse on the outskirts of town, and asked to be left off at the path that led to it.

During the ride, she had created a story which she prayed would sound believable. She would say that her husband had died while they were traveling from another town far away, she now had no one to turn to, and was consequently in need of work to support herself and her coming child.

It was early morning when she wandered into the village. "Allah, in your mercy, guide my steps," she prayed. "Soften someone's heart and fill his mind with a need for what I can offer. Oh, please, Blessed One, preserve my unworthy life. I carry another life within me. Allow me to protect it."

A week ago she had not even heard of this village, and now, ironically, it was to become her home. How was she going to survive? She sat down near the small bazaar and munched on a peach. The juice dribbled onto her chin and she absentmindedly wiped it away with the edge of her all encompassing chador. The chador's blackness made her look like every other female in town, and it covered her from head to toe, providing her with some warmth as well as protection from curious eyes. Because there were no buttons, she held it closed with one hand, keeping her face hidden behind its folds. No one could see who she was. But she could see others, and she watched as people came and went She also tried to listen, and some conversations were loud enough to be overheard.

"The latest nanny left two days ago. She was just a young thing, not more than thirteen, and when she came back from the bazaar one day, she said the house was cursed because of the child's deformities and she was afraid to work for Haji any more. That's the fourth servant in six months."

"Ack, such nonsense. Haji is the best of men, and he could not have fathered an evil child. The Mistress, now that is a different story. But she lost her mind after the child was born. Before that, she was a good woman to work for. I don't know what the Master will do. The house has a reputation now, and no servant will live there and take care of the child."

Talat listened in astonishment. Could this be what she had prayed for? A place where she might be needed? After hesitating only a moment, she followed the two women to see where they went. The home they approached was very large. Perhaps the headmaster of the village lived there. After a few moments of indecision, she made up her mind. She took several deep breaths and approached one of the servants she had observed talking. The woman was older and looked as if it she might be someone important in the household. Timidly, the seventeen year old unmarried mother-to-be spoke.

"Good morning, Mistress. Forgive me for interrupting you. May I speak for just a moment?"

The servant turned and saw what appeared to be a youngish woman in front of her, although it was difficult to tell behind the chador. Not recognizing the face, she peered more closely. Yes, she looked quite young Perhaps she came from one of the farms nearby.

"Good morning, child. Yes, you may speak with me. What do you want?"

Talat grew terrified. What was she going to say? She stood there mutely, her courage gone. The woman was looking at her curiously.

"Mistress," she began. "My name is Talat. I overheard you talking at the bazaar." She could not continue. Now she sounded like an eavesdropper, and she lowered her eyes as they began to fill with tears.

"Yes, go on." The voice was encouraging, not angry.

"I heard you say that there was a sick child in this household, a child that no one would take care of. I am from a large family, and have taken care of many sick children. I thought perhaps I could help."

The woman was intrigued, but also skeptical. "Who are you? Are you from one of the farms around here?"

It was time for the lie.

"No, Madam. My husband and I were traveling from Urmieh." She chose a city so far away that no one could trace her. "We were on our way to Tehran, traveling by horseback. My husband's family are shopkeepers there in Urmieh, and they had sent my husband to Tehran to take care of some business. Because much of my family lives in Tehran, I was allowed to accompany him. He had dismounted to show me a beautiful flower when suddenly a snake rose up from behind him and struck him. We were alone on the road and I could not find anyone to help in time. My husband, my source of support and my protector, died there on the road. It was a few days ago. Now I have no way to return to Urmieh, and I have no relatives here. I am hoping to find a home where I could work so I can support myself." She did not say that she was pregnant because it would have roused immediate suspicion.

The woman appraised the situation quickly. Snakes were common enough. It was possible that the girl was telling the truth, but she doubted it. News traveled quickly throughout the countryside, and no one had talked about a stranger dying from a snake bite recently. Also, it did not make sense that a young couple would be traveling alone so far from home. She had relatives in Urmieh, and she knew that it was very far away. How did this girl suddenly appear here in this village. Well, perhaps it did not matter. It was the will of Allah. They needed someone to care for the sick child, and here was someone offering to help.

"The child cannot walk, and he has no control over himself.

He needs constant care. Some people have said that he should be allowed to die because of his infirmities, but the Master would never condone that. Unfortunately for Haji, for that is how the Master calls himself, just Haji, his wife blames herself for bringing such a calamity on the house. She has shut herself away in her room for almost four years. The Master is a good man and tries to manage everything at home as well as all his farming concerns, but it is becoming too much for him. I am sure you are aware that the name Haji shows the Master's status as a man who has been to Mecca to perform his religious duties."

"Yes, I have known others who called themselves Haji. Tell me, please, what happened to the person who was caring for the child?" Talat knew that she was being very forward, but the woman seemed willing to talk about the situation.

"She quit when the mullah told her that the house had been cursed. The other servants have been filling in as best they can, but it is unsatisfactory. Someone is needed full time just to take care of the child, and that means that other duties have to be neglected."

Praise be to Allah, Talat thought to herself. In His benevolence, he has sent me a salvation. "I had a younger brother who needed the kind of care you talk about. He lived until the age of eight. I know that I could provide what the Master needs. Do you think he might consider me?"

Still wary, the servant equivocated. "He is not home right now. He will be back this afternoon. In the meantime, come in and we will see how you and the child do together. Where is your luggage and we will send a servant to bring it here."

Talat had not been ready for this question. She had to think fast.

"While I was caring for my husband, someone stole our bags. I have nothing now but what I am wearing, and this one small suitcase."

Again the older woman looked doubtful, but accepted this answer. If the girl could do the job, then other matters might not be so important. For right now, here was a timely solution to an enormous problem. Only time would tell if the solution had created yet another problem.

Once inside the house, Talat saw that neatness and order prevailed. Good. It appeared to be a well managed household. The Master sounded like a kindly person. She could stay here for a while, at least, she hoped.

"My name is Maryam," she heard the woman say. "Come to the kitchen and eat some breakfast. Do you hear that moaning? It is the child. He always makes those sounds. After you have eaten, I will show you where he sleeps."

Gratefully, Talat accepted a cup of tea and a plate of grapes. On the table there was also fresh bread and homemade butter, and a bowl of honey. She ate delicately, not wanting to appear greedy, although her starving stomach urged her to gulp it all down instantly. It was the first solid meal she had had in nearly five days. As she ate, Maryam introduced her to some other servants. There were two who worked only in the kitchen, and others whose duties included both indoor and outdoor work.

Greetings were courteous but restrained. She was a stranger and would have to work hard to be accepted, she knew. Everyone recognized that she was not from around this area, and she could see suspicion in most eyes. As in Ismail Agha's home, most of the women did not wear the chador inside the house, but put it on if they were going outside. Soon she would have to take hers off. Her clothes were loose fitting and her stomach had not yet started to get big. What would happen when her condition became more obvious? Well, she would just live from day to day, and trust in Allah's care.

She finished her breakfast and thanked Maryam. "Could you take me to the child?' she asked.

"Come this way. Because of the noise he makes, he is kept at the far end of the house. It is down this hallway."

Talat followed Maryam past a large salon and along a long corridor to a series of bedrooms. It looked as if this were the servants quarters, and in the last room was a bed with high sides all around. In it lay a child whose limbs were grotesquely deformed and whose head was twice the size it should have been. The eyes were open but not focused.

"What is his name?" she inquired with a pity that caused her voice to break.

Maryam hesitated. "He was not given a name. His mother did not believe he was human and would not name him. We just call him The Child. He was born nearly four years ago. "

Talat approached the bed and found to her surprise that she was not sickened by the sight of the boy. He was wearing a diaper which appeared to be freshly changed. She put out her hand and touched his arm. He convulsed away from the touch, but she left her hand on his arm anyway.

"Child," she said quietly, "I will care for you. You and I are both castaways on this earth. We will be together." Louder, she asked, "Does he ever leave this bed. Can he move at all by himself?"

"If we support him, he can sit up, and he tries to crawl. The Master wants him to move as much as possible so that his muscles still function a little, at least. We feed him over there." She pointed to a roughly made tray table that surrounded a child sized chair. "But he never goes out of the house."

"Are there other children?"

Again Maryam hesitated. "No. The Mistress has never had other children. For a couple of years she got up everyday and saw to the running of the house, but now she does not even do that. Her room is at the other end of the house so she does not hear him scream. We take food to her there, and once in a long while she will come to the kitchen to speak to someone. But for the most part, this is a very quiet household, with no one but the servants here. The Master does not entertain, and frequently does not even come home at night. But he always pays us and sees to it that we have whatever we need. I don't know why he keeps so many of us, since he is not interested in being here. He is a good man and I believe he feels obliged to provide work for us. He insists that the trees outside are pruned and the flowers maintained, and he always expects the house to be very neat and clean. He becomes very angry if he finds sloppiness." Maryam sighed, and continuing, added, "He has so many cares."

Talat tried to imagine what such a life would be like. No family, just servants.

"Why hasn't he ever married again?" she asked. "There could be more children." Again, Talat realized that she sounded very bold asking such a question and apologized. "I am sorry. Of course, it is none of my business."

But Maryam answered. "He did. About a year and a half after The Child was born. His second wife died in childbirth, and so did the baby. Since then, he has not wanted to take another wife."

There was nothing comforting to say. After a pause, Talat murmured, "I will take good care of his son. I have made a lot of clothing for children. Whatever old garments are around, I will fashion something for The Child to wear so that there is always something clean for him, and I will help with other chores."

"There is not much time. The child needs constant attention. Most of your time will be here in this room. You will even find yourself eating your own meals in here."

Talat could not imagine that caring for one child would be a twenty-four hour job. In the past, she had cared for several children at the same time and still had time for herself. Perhaps she was being told that whoever cared for this deformed creature was not welcome to mix with the rest of the household. Well, if that was the way it was, then she could tolerate the separation. When she left Ismail Agha's home, she knew she would be an outcast. At least here, she had food and shelter.

"I will do my best," she promised, as much to herself as to Maryam.

CHAPTER THREE

The Master came home around three o'clock that afternoon. He appeared tired as he slowly sank into a cushion in the salon.

"How is my wife, Maryam?" he inquired as he sipped at his tea.

"She is resting, Haji Agha. She was a little tired after the noon meal, and decided to sleep a bit."

Maryam hesitated a moment, assessing the timing, then decided to broach the subject of the newcomer.

"Sir, there is a young girl who came to the door this morning. She says that she has cared for children such as yours before, and she came to seek employment."

Haji looked at her in great surprise. "Someone just showed up at my door and said 'I will care for this child that no one else will go near?' That is hard to believe. Where does she come from? Is she dangerous?"

"Oh no, sir. She is very gentle, and appears to be competent. She had a great misfortune, and is now trying to make a life for herself as best she can."

"What kind of misfortune?" Haji was suspicious. Things like this did not just happen.

"She said that her husband died recently, and she is now left with no one to take care of her. She is very courteous, and has been with the child for several hours. She is able to get him to eat, and she sings softly, which seems to soothe him. From what I have seen so far, she is good with him."

"Bring her to me."

When Talat appeared, he watched her carefully.

"Have you been accepted by my wife yet?" he asked sternly.

"No, sir. I have not yet had the honor of meeting your esteemed wife. I have only been with your son. He is a very sweet child. He tries so hard to smile."

No one had ever said anything positive about his son before, not in four years. Haji softened.

"Where are you from?" he asked, a little more gently.

"From Urmieh, sir. I was married there nearly a year ago. My husband's father," she hesitated a moment, seeming to catch her thoughts, "is a shopkeeper with many contacts in Tehran. He sent my husband there to find a better source of suppliers. Perhaps Maryam has already told you what happened, that a snake bit him and he died." By now she was sniffling, almost believing her own story. "We were alone on the road and I could not find anyone to help us." With head bent, she continued. "I wish it had been me, but such is the will of Allah. The horses ran away, and while I was at a farm trying to get someone to help us, our bags were stolen. All our money is gone, and I am here in your village with no way to go back to Urmieh or on to Tehran. At least not until I am able to get word to my family about what has happened to me. I do not know how I could accomplish that."

Haji was moved by this account, although he too did not fully believe it. "Give me your family's address, and I will send a letter. In the meantime, you may stay here and live in my house. You seem to have made a bond with my son. No one else has done that."

"Thank you so much, good sir. You are very kind. I will do everything I can for the boy." She would have to make up an address and hope that the letter would never be returned to Haji. Perhaps she could assure that by offering to mail the letter herself after he wrote it.

"Has Maryam showed you where to sleep?"

"No, sir. I am sure she did not want to do that until you approved of my being here."

"Very well. Tell her to take you to the room next to The Child so you will be nearby whenever you are needed. By the way, what is your name?"

"My father named me Talat."

"Talat. It is a good name. I will write the letter, then you can tell me where to send it. Allah has brought you to my house, and I trust that you will care well for my son. Perhaps, through His mercy, you will also find your own healing."

Understanding that she was dismissed, Talat left the salon and went to find Maryam.

"The Master told me that he wants me to stay in a room near

the boy so I will be near if I am needed. Could you show me where I should go?"

"Come along." They walked down the hall. "This room will be yours. I can see that you will need more clothes. I will give you material and you can make yourself what you need. Come to the kitchen in an hour or so, and we will have food for you. The Master eats simply, but the food here is very good."

Talat thanked Maryam and looked around her new room. There was a carpet on the floor, and a bed that looked comfortable. On the table beside the bed was an oil lamp. It looked a little like the room she had had at Ismail Agha's house. She sat down on the bed and prayed to Allah, giving thanks that she had somewhere indoors to sleep that night. She prayed for strength and courage to face each new day, and to be a good servant so that she would not lose what she had miraculously found.

For the moment, the child was silent. She remained in her room, thinking and trying to rest a little. She had made up a story that people seemed to believe. What would happen when her pregnancy became obvious she did not know. But the Master seemed to be a good person. Possibly after her own child came, he would allow her to remain and take care of both her child and his.

For an instant she was consumed with anger as she considered how men controlled everything. A man was responsible for how she had come to be in this state, and another man now determined what her future would be. Eventually, however, her distress subsided, and she lay back and closed her eyes.

Unbidden, her mind began to wander, to recall things she did not want to remember. She thought of that night when someone had forced himself into her room and covered her mouth so she could not scream. He hurt her badly, and just laughed when she begged him not to do this. It was dark and although she could not see who it was, she was sure she knew. Again and again he had forced himself, and then left her when she lost consciousness.

When she had finally come to, someone was knocking on her door. It hurt so much to move that she told them she was ill. Parvin brought her tea and some breakfast, but Talat begged to be left alone. She pretended that she might have something contagious, and the other servants complied with her wishes..

All day she thought of how to end her life. First, she tried to smother herself with a pillow, but was not able to accomplish it. Then she looked around for a rope to hang herself with, but could not find anything in her room. All the knives were in the kitchen. Ultimately, she realized that she would have to wait for another time..

She had heard people say that this was what happened before babies were born. Allah forbid that she should be pregnant! It would be a stigma too much for her to bear. Her family would be disgraced. If she were not stoned in the marketplace, then she would be sent away and no one would help her.

A week later, he had come back again. Her bedroom door had no locks and she could not protect herself. Again she was asleep, and again he woke her and did the same thing. He whispered about what a slut she was, and his breath stank of undigested food. He said he was going to force her to marry him, and he would do this to her every night. She was terrified. Would she have to endure this forever? Was this what marriage was? Surely not.

Tahirih Khanem seemed so happy. No one could be happy if they had to tolerate this every night. He hurt her, again and again. Then he left.

The next day she asked Tahirih Khanem if she could have a lock on her door, but the Mistress did not understand. Talat could not say why she wanted one, and her explanation about wanting privacy sounded foolish. There was no reason to fear theft in this household. Everyone was honest and well known to everyone else. Finally she had to give up, and thereafter she moved her dresser against the door each night before she went to sleep. That had prevented him from coming back.

During the day, she would avoid being wherever her suspected attacker might be. Her fears had become so great that she was not taking care of the children properly, and the Mistress had to reprimand her on several occasions.

One afternoon, the Mistress had caught her sitting by the fountain in the yard and had said something about finding her a husband. Talat had been terrified. She could never be happy the way her Mistress seemed to be. Talat could not understand why she was being punished. She had always tried to do her duty to her employers, she worshipped Allah every day, and she always behaved decorously. She searched her memory for unholy things she might have done in her childhood, but could think of nothing that deserved this.

Two months went by, and her monthly flow did not come. She had heard that this was what happened when a woman was going to have a baby. All the blood was being saved to cover the child with a blanket until it was born. Then after nine months, all the stored up blood spurt out, draining the woman of her energy and providing a red carpet for the newborn child. Ismail Agha might banish her. Her family would surely disown her. She would be alone, totally alone.

One day Ismail Agha had found her crying in an abandoned shop down the street. He kindly asked her what was wrong and tried to comfort her. She could not answer him truthfully. He pressed and pressed until finally she confessed that it seemed as if she would have a baby in a few more months. Then she tried to explain what had happened, and, to her surprise, Ismail Agha was understanding. He told her that she would be allowed to stay in his house, and he would force the boy to marry her. That had terrified Talat even more, and she begged him not to do such a thing. She could not imagine living with the fiend who had stolen her serenity. Live with him every day for the rest of her life? Never! His stinking breath was indicative of his black heart. She hated him with every ounce of her being, and she swore she would kill herself before she would marry him.

When she said this to Ismail Agha, however, he became angry and called her ungrateful. She had to marry. She could not have a child without a husband. That was ungodly. They argued, which was not proper between a servant and a master, and she was afraid that other people would hear them.

Finally they returned to Ismail Agha's home with nothing resolved. The Master said he would not yet tell his wife about their conversation. She was just recovering from having lost her own child and could not deal with this kind of problem right now. The next day, he again tried to talk with Talat, but she continued to refuse to marry the boy. She would not even identify who he was, contending that she had never seen him and could not be sure. She knew that Ismail Agha was becoming very upset with her.

A week or so later, the Master had come to her room one afternoon when the other servants were gone shopping and his wife was resting. He had just finished his dinner and was about to return to his stall at the bazaar, but first he wanted to try again to get Talat to see reason. As her employer, he felt responsible for her. He wanted to tell her family about her situation, but she had begged him not to. For the moment he acceded to her wishes, but something had to be done.

"Talat, enough of this stubbornness. You must marry. If not this boy, whoever he is, perhaps I could find someone else who wants a second or third wife. I know many men who would be a good husband to you. All children must be born into a married household.

"Good Master," she pled, "I do not wish to leave this household. You and the Mistress have always been so good to me. Please allow me to stay. Do not send me away, I beg you. If you would so desire, the child could be brought up as your own, to replace the one you lost. I would care for it, but it could be as your own child. Perhaps it would console the heart of Tahirih Khanem."

Actually, Ismail himself had been thinking along this same line. Perhaps it was the will of Allah that his wife had lost a child and his servant was about to have one that she did not want. But a child raised in his house as his own indeed had to be his own. As a man of honor, he could not claim another man's child as his. Ismail had heard that if a woman knew several men, then each man was the father of the child. His answer was deliberate.

"Talat, if I were to raise this child as my own, then it must be mine. It would be dishonorable for me to call another man's child my own if indeed it is not."

He was about to go on, but Talat interrupted him in a terrified voice.

"Ismail Agha, just as you would raise a nephew as your own, you could raise this child as well. As if the father had died and you were accepting responsibility. Have I not heard that the Koran commands this, so no child is without a father?"

"No, Talat. You do not understand the holy words of the Koran. It is not the same. If my sister's husband died and I raised her children according to Allah's holy command, everyone would know that the father of those children had been her husband. I would be following Allah's ordination by bringing them up in the absence of their true father. But your situation is different. This child has no known father. At least you will not say who it is. I cannot call this child my own if it is not. It would be a disgrace to my wife if I did so. Nonetheless, the child exists. You must do something. Think carefully. If you wish, I will cover this child with my own creative juice, and then I will be able to honestly call it my own. I will come back to you tonight if you wish."

He left, believing that he was truly doing his duty to Allah, and in no way concerned that he was taking advantage of a young girl already immersed in misery and trouble.

Talat had been mortified. Not one man now, but two would do this to her, and the second would be her mistress' husband. She could not disgrace the woman who had always been so kind to her. She would have to figure out what to do. If indeed, there was anything to do other than kill herself. She had already tried to do that but had not succeeded. She fell on her bed and sobbed into her pillow. Quietly. She did not want any of the other servants to hear her or know of her plight.

That night the Master had come to her, and she had turned him away. The next day she had left his household, had left Shiraz, had left everything that was safe, and she had come here. But Allah had been kind. He had provided somewhere for her to live, and a job to take her mind off her own problems. The child in the room next door needed love more than anyone she had ever known, and she would give it to him.

CHAPTER FOUR

Talat walked over to where the child lay passively for the moment. She cooed to him, and he turned his head to look at her. Such huge brown eyes. They did not seem to look directly at her, but somewhere in the direction of her voice. What went on in that head, she wondered. Could he understand when people talked to him, but just not respond? How horrible that would be, she thought. To want to communicate and not be able to.

His diaper was dirty and she changed him. At first she had been afraid to move him, not knowing what the limits of his body were, and fearing that something she did might hurt him. She had been told that he cried all the time, but he was very quiet right now. Maybe he just needed someone to deal gently with him, to be there where he could see them.

"Talat," Maryam called from down the hall. "Talat, the Mistress wants to meet you."

She glanced again at the boy, then went quickly toward Maryam's voice.

"Here I am," she announced as she found Maryam. "Where shall I go?"

"Here *I* am. And *who* are you?"

The angry voice behind her startled Talat. She jumped, and was then embarrassed.

"Good day, Mistress," she greeted respectfully. "I am Talat. Your husband has hired me to watch over your son, if that meets with your approval."

"It does not! Never call that creature my son. Its very existence is a profanity. Such a millstone is beyond anyone's ability to bear.

Talat had no idea how to respond, so stood in angered silence, waiting for the mistress to continue. When a long time passed and no more was said, she tentatively ventured a question, the answer to which she greatly feared.

"Did you want me to leave, then, Madam?"

With a great sigh, the mistress of the house turned abruptly away and called over her shoulder.

"Stay with it, if you dare. You are a fool."

Talat looked at Maryam for guidance.

"It's all right. Go back and look after him. You will be allowed to stay here. She rarely comes to this part of the house, and when she does, bearing her tantrums in silence is usually best."

Gratefully, Talat returned to the boy's room, considering how different this mistress was from the kind and gentle Tahirih. Softly she said to the child," I have a name for you. I will call you Maerd'a'Khoda. Do you know what that means, little one? It means Man of God. You are blessed by Him, I think. There is something very special about you, that He has given you these problems. You will survive, and you will be important to someone someday. Now let's see if we can get you to speak instead of scream."

She talked to him quietly for the rest of the afternoon, then went to eat her dinner. The other servants briefly acknowledged her presence and even invited her to sit with them, but excluded her from conversations as they deliberately spoke of people and events of which she had no knowledge. She ate in silence, taking in as much as she could about the people in the village she had now chosen to be her home. She would eventually fit in, she believed. These people had known each other all their lives, and she was an outsider. If the situation were reversed, she would probably be as reluctant to welcome a stranger as they were. It would take time.

Indeed, time passed. A month later she still lived at Haji's, with her only companion for most of each twenty-four hour period being the boy, whom she now called Mak. The other servants had begun to relaxe with her a little, and sometimes they even offered to help if she needed assistance.

After asking many times, Talat finally secured permission from the Master to take Mak outside for a walk. The caveat was that Mak had to be completely covered so that no one would have to see him. Even though he was more than four years old, he was so small that Talat was able to carry him easily. She had begun taking him outside on every good weather day and made sure to walk on back roads where it was unlikely that she would run into neighbors. As they strolled along, she would tell him stories from her own youth. Much of his screaming had stopped, but he was not able to form words and communicate back to her, other than

through looks. She decided that he would never be able to talk, so
had learned to ease her own mind by telling him things she knew
he could not repeat.

One day, she told him why she had left her employer in
Tehran. When tears began to roll down her face, he shrieked in
terror. Together they stood on the side of the road, each absorbed
in each other's fears, until finally she dried her tears and calmed
him.

"No, no, my little Mak. Don't be frightened for me. I will
be all right. I will be here to take care of you. Are you hungry?
Here, I have brought you some cookies. You like these."

He stopped wailing and accepted the small biscuits she had
brought. She stopped beside a stream and washed her face, then
dried it with her chador. They sat for a long while, listening to
singing birds and watching squirrels gather nesting materials.
Once when she looked up she saw smoke coming from the village,
and wondered who had built a fire so large as to be seen from
where she was. Eventually they both fell asleep, and it was almost
evening by the time they awoke.

She was instantly alarmed. They had been away from the
house for several hours, far longer than ever before. She feared
the Mistress might have noticed. Although Haji's wife rarely paid
any attention to either Talat or the child, she somehow had a knack
for knowing when Talat did something wrong. Like when she had
tried to wash her clothes on a day the Mistress had declared a non-
work day. No one told her that every few months the Mistress
arbitrarily decided not to allow any work other than preparing
food for that day. On those days, the servants were forced to sit

in silence in the kitchen and think about how lucky they were to be employed by such a generous household. If anyone fell asleep, however, they lost the day's wages.

Not knowing this rule, Talat had been pouring water into the wash tub early one morning when the Mistress found her and berated her loudly in front of everyone else. Talat was fined two day's wages and banished from the servants' kitchen for a week. Another time the Mistress had insisted that all the furniture had to be taken outside into the sunshine and exposed to what she called the healing rays of Allah so that no ill fortune would come to her home. There were other incidents which had led Talat to wonder whether the Mistress was quite right in her head, but she said nothing, cared for Mak as well as she could, and avoided the Mistress as much as possible.

Now she picked Mak up and hurried back to the house, making sure to keep him well concealed from eyes that might be offended by the sight of such a misshaped child. As she rushed along, someone saw her and began whispering, but she ignored him. When she turned into the street where the Master's house was, however, her feet stopped moving and she was utterly dumbfounded by what she saw.

Ahead of her were ashes. The building she had known as home was now nothing more than charred pieces of brick. She heard Maryam call her name. "Talat, do not go inside. It is destroyed. Everything. It is destroyed. The Master is not home. He doesn't know yet. All our lives are ruined." Maryam broke into wailing, immediately joined by the other servants in a noise that rose to the heavens above.

"But how did this happen?" Talat begged from the person standing beside her. "Cook is always so careful. Where is the Mistress? Has she gone to find her husband?"

The neighbor spat on the ground. That crazy woman has gone to find her final peace, if it will be granted to her. What she did was the work of *jinn*. Who knows whether Allah will permit her into heaven for ten thousand years."

"What are you saying?" *Jinn*. Heaven. Where was the Mistress? Talat began to run into the house, still clutching the now bellowing Mak. Maryam caught her arm, nearly causing her to drop the child.

"Do not go inside," she commanded. "It is too awful. You must not see her."

"Who? Why not?" Still Talat had not grasped what had happened. Another neighbor yanked her away from the burnt-out house, and was about to strike her into silence when he saw the Master approach.

"Silence, now," the neighbor hissed. "Get behind me." Talat fearfully stepped back and covered her mouth with her hand as she saw the Master look pitifully at his home which was no more.

After several moments, he said quietly, "Explain."

No one wanted to answer. Finally, the man who had pulled Talat aside ventured an attempt to comply with Haji's command.

"Haji Agha, I do not know how to tell you. You are a man of Allah. Perhaps you can understand what we do not. There was no one home. All of your servants had gone to different places. The two women had gone shopping for food, Hassan the gardener was at the bazaar looking for a tool, and Cook was at a neighbor's house several blocks away visiting a sick friend. Only the Mistress, may Allah have mercy on her soul, was in the house."

With great pity he looked at Haji and forced himself to continue. "When Maryam came back from shopping she found that she could not get in the front door because it was blocked. She knocked for a long time and was about to try to climb the wall when I arrived. Then we smelled the smoke. Suddenly there was screaming. It was your wife, sounding as if she were fighting with the devil himself. She kept shouting 'No. Go away. Don't make me do this.' Then the flames showered up over the wall."

"Maryam and I tried to beat down the door, but by then the flames were everywhere and we could not do it. Maryam's arms are burned . . . " both Talat and the Master turned to look at Maryam. They saw that her chador was gone, and there were burns all over her body. ". . . and no one could get inside."

This was what Talat had seen from the riverside. Her own home burning, and she had not been there to help. How could she be so negligent, she berated herself. Then it occurred to her that if she had been there, the child would have perished. Allah be praised, he was saved. She looked down at him, asleep now, oblivious to the furor boiling around him. She looked back up at the Master and saw grief so overwhelming that she looked away out of respect.

"Was my wife saved?"

No one answered. He walked toward the shell of what he had called home. Someone started to block the way, then stood aside. The Master entered what was left of his house, and everyone waited. After a few seconds, they heard a cry as piteous as any of them ever wanted to hear for the rest of their lives.

"Allah, Allah. What hast Thou done?"

Then they heard sobbing, great sobbing, and eventually silence.

Under Muslim law a body must be buried within twenty-four hours of death, so Haji's primary obligation was to find the mullah. First, however, he humbly asked his neighbors if his servants who had no home nearby could spend the night in one of their houses just for that one night, and everyone found someone willing to take them in.

Everyone except Talat, who was not allowed in anyone's home with Mak. Because Talat would not abandon the child, they spent the night in a field. Fortunately, it did not rain that night, and she still had a few biscuits and a handful of raisins left. Haji assumed that everyone had found shelter when he did not find anyone in the street upon his return with the mullah. He carried what was left of his wife's charred body out of the house, and sadly gave instructions to prepare it for burial.

He spent the night sitting outside his house, refusing neighbors' pleas that he take shelter from the night. He thought of what he must now do. His home would be rebuilt, he decided, vowing that the *jinn* would not force him out of his own domicile.

Jinn. He had never believed in them, but look what had happened. How else could it be explained? His wife had burned down her own home, killing herself in agony. How else could such a thing have happened except through the influence of evil.

A haji could not disavow Allah, but this forlorn man came close to it that night. He sat and then he wandered and then he just sat and shrieked in agony. How many burdens could he bear? How many wives did he have to bury? Was Mak the cause of his wife's abandonment of reality?

No, he decided, after hours of intense pondering. Each person, both man and woman, is responsible for their own behavior. It does not matter how many trials are set in the pathway of life. Allah provides. All people must have patience and faith. His wife had not had enough faith, and her punishment for that lack of faith was deterioration into madness. But look how that affected so many other people. Does Allah punish everyone for one person's lack of faith? It was all too much to consider, and eventually he fell into a troubled sleep.

A few neighbors did not come to the funeral the next day, believing that Haji's wife was sinful because she had taken her own life. Self-destruction was forbidden by Allah, except in martyrdom. Her remains were finally buried in the village cemetery, but only after Haji threatened to withhold future donations to the mosque.

Following the internment, Haji called all of his servants together. He told them what he had decided.

"I will rebuild my house," he said. "It will take a few months. I will pay you all one month's wages in advance, and the women will need to find somewhere else to live while I complete the construction. The men will help with the labor. When it is finished, I want you all to come back into my service."

There was a collective sigh of relief as they comprehended that they would still have employment. Only Talat still had a problem. After the others had left, she timidly approached the Master and asked if she could speak with him.

"Master, may I have a moment of your time?"

"Of course, child. How is my son? I have been so preoccupied that I have not inquired after him. Where did you stay last night?"

"That is what I need to speak with you about, sir. No one would allow us stay in their home. We slept in the field. Soon, however, it will become too cold at night, and I fear for the child's health. What should we do?"

Haji glanced reflectively at the sky.

"People do not mean to be cruel, child. But they are afraid of what they do not understand. When they see something like this deformed child, they assume that Allah has determined that it is not worthy of life, so people do not deem it worthwhile either. I will be staying with my cousin who lives in the next village. He will allow you to stay there also. Wait for me here. I must be gone for an hour or so, then we will go together to his house. Have you and the child eaten today?"

"No, Master. We had some raisins and biscuits, but that is gone now."

"It is not far to my cousin's house. We will be there soon. Why is the child so quiet if he is hungry?"

"Perhaps in his own way he understands that this is a time for silence, and he is obeying."

"That is a funny thought," Haji reflected. How does he understand anything, I wonder?"

"I don't know, sir. It was just a guess on my part. Probably I am wrong."

Haji looked at Talat curiously.

CHAPTER FIVE

One and a half months later the house had been rebuilt and it even included a special living area for Talat and the child. Haji had taken to calling the child Mak, as Talat had instituted, and the rest of the household soon did the same.

For as long as she could, Talat hid her pregnancy, but eventually it showed. Maryam was the first to notice.

"So you are going to add to the size of our household, are you?" she said gently. "Do not be afraid. The Master will not make you leave."

Still, Talat had been afraid and wore the chador even inside the house. But eventually, as she neared delivery time, Haji noticed, and one day called her to his presence.

"Leave Mak in his crib," he said. "I wish to talk with you alone."

Fearfully, she prepared herself for dismissal as she thought desperately of where she could now go. Not back to Shiraz. Not to any of the neighbors around here. She had no idea. She resigned herself to the fate Allah planned for her, and went to see the Master.

"Talat, Maryam tells me you are with child. Is that true?"

By this time, she was so large that the answer was obvious. Still, she had to answer.

"Yes, Master," she said with her head bowed. She did not beg for mercy.

"You have been a part of this household for six months. Before you came, the atmosphere here was poisonous, with fear of Mak seeping into everyone's behavior every day. You have made a difference here. You arrived under very unusual circumstances, but I accepted that Allah had sent you to this house for a reason. By the way, I never received an answer to the letter I wrote to your family." Talat knew why, since she had been asked to take the letter to the post office, but had instead destroyed it. "At first I wondered about this and then accepted it as Allah's will. How old are you?"

"I have counted nearly eighteen summers, good Master."

He laughed. "And I nearly two and a half times that many."

His laughter caused Talat to look up at him. She was amazed to see that his face showed a wistfulness she had never seen before.

"How long did you plan to remain here?" he inquired.

"Oh, Haji Agha," she cried, falling awkwardly to his feet and looking up miserably. "I pray that you allow me to stay here all my life. I will care for Mak and work hard for you. If you send me away, I have nowhere to go."

In amazement, Haji looked at her. "Send you away? What ever made you think I would do that?"

"But sir, I am with child," she stammered.

"Yes."

"You will not make me leave?" Hope finally began to glimmer in her heart.

"You have become a mother to Mak. How could you even think I would ask you leave?" Suddenly he was angry. "The only good thing that has happened for my son in all his life, and you think I would destroy it? Do you have so little regard for me?"

Talat did not know what to say. She had made him upset by assuming that he would not want her if she had a child of her own. Instead, he was telling her she was valuable. In an instant, her perception of herself changed.

"Oh, my Master. If you will allow me to stay, I will always serve you faithfully. If I may make my home here, it will be the greatest blessing of my life. If I have any value to you, then I would be happy beyond belief."

"Well, Talat, you do have value to me. You have brought sunshine into a house where there was much gloom. Now you are about to have a child with no father to care for it. It is only fair that I do for you what you have done for me. I will adopt your child and bring it up as my own. If you like, I will marry you to assure that your child will have protection when I am gone."

Talat was still on the floor at his feet. Surely she had not heard what she thought she had. She looked up at him, then closed her eyes and reopened them. He was still there, still smiling warmly. He was extending his hand to help her get up. This was not possible. The Master would marry her? He was offering to take care of her child? Was Allah really so beneficent? Could this be true?

The shock caused her body to react violently. The pain in her stomach was unbelievable and she gasped.

"Haji," she tried to say, "the baby."

Then more pain, so much that she could not speak. Still he smiled at her, and it brought warmth and comfort through the agony.

"I will call for Maryam. Do not fight the pain. Just relax, as much as you can. In between the pains, breathe deeply. It will help."

He was gone, but only for a moment. She heard him say, 'Maryam, look after her well. Be sure that she comes through this with as little misery as possible.' In the background she heard Mak beginning to scream. Did he know that another child was coming into his house? Somehow she would care for them both. With Haji's help. Had he really said he would marry her? She was dreaming. No, this pain was too much. It was a nightmare. She wanted to awaken from it, but could not.

Maryam. What was she saying? She was wiping Talat's forehead and speaking soothingly. Maryam had gotten her to her feet and was slowly moving her toward her own room. Closer to the screaming Mak. Who would care for him now? The pain. It was too great. What would this child be like? No one knew. They thought the father was her beloved husband, of whom she had spoken so dearly. Talat knew that the father of this child was nothing but a brutal monster. Would the child be like that, too? Maryam was telling her to pull up her knees. So ignominious.

These thoughts zipped in and out of her head for hours. She did not know what was happening, other than the pain. Sometimes she heard Maryam, sometimes other servants. Once she thought she heard the Master asking after her. Always she heard Mak screaming, and someone angrily trying to shush him. Eventually, after what seemed to be forever, it was over. No more noise, no more pain. Yes, there was still pain, but it was different. No longer searing and unendurable. Now just throbbing. Maryam was saying something. Her baby. She was handing her a bundle. It moved. Her baby. Through the mist, Talat smiled. Her baby. Maryam said it was a girl. Girls were good. They comforted. Somehow she would take care of the baby. Help it to grow into a woman. What would life be like for this new member of humanity? Would it be easier than it had been for Talat? She would protect this child. In the background she heard Mak. She would take care of both of them.

She stayed in bed for days, at Haji's insistence. They brought both Mak and her daughter to her, and her heart filled with love and happiness. From constant fear she had miraculously moved to safety. She could not believe it.

The Master was not often home, but when he was, he came to see her. He spoke kindly of the baby girl. Gradually, Talat became stronger.

The days without her constant presence had sent Mak into a regression. When Talat was finally able to return to caring for him, he was almost as difficult as he had been when she first came. She tried to reassure him that she would always be there for him, but he howled more than ever. Between that and her daughter's crying for food and attention, Talat sometimes became overwrought and could not do anything effectively. Then she remembered how much worse her situation could have been, and her concentration was restored.

"Maryam, see how little Maryam wiggles." She had named her daughter after the woman who had shown her such kindness. "Maybe I will call her Wiggle Worm."

"I think Angel Stink is more like it. Phew. I will change her diaper while you look after Mak. Do you think he will ever quiet down again? For a while you had him so well behaved, he was almost like a normal baby."

"Yes, he will trust me again. I will make him. I am sorry he has gotten loud and distracting. I know it bothers everyone. I will try harder."

Talat meant what she said. She believed Mak's tantrums were deliberate and he knew exactly what he was doing. She hoped to teach him that there were better ways to get attention. It was hard alternating between two demanding screamers, though, and she was grateful for the assistance of Maryam.

Most of the other staff were not so helpful. They had heard that the Master had offered to marry Talat, and there was considerable rumbling about that. Discontent grew about an outsider coming in to their home and usurping the position of the Mistress. Some even began rumors that Talat had been seen outside the house just before the fire began, but that was soon squashed. Jealousy was far more prevalent than acceptance, but no one left the Master's service because the pay was too good and the work too easy. Maryam tried to shield Talat from the backbiting, but sometimes Talat heard it and was deeply wounded. Nonetheless, she went about the business of caring for Mak and tried to ignore the pettiness surrounding her.

Two months after little Maryam was born, the Master took Talat to a mullah one day and married her. Talat did not believe this really changed her status in the household. It was just a kindness from the Master to protect her and her baby in return for taking care of the son no one else would go near. That night, however, he took her into his bedroom. He was so gentle with her that she found she enjoyed what he did. To her astonishment, she began to look forward to nights, just as Tahirih had once told her she would.

CHAPTER SIX

One day a visitor came. He was a young boy, perhaps twelve years old, she thought. He was accompanying one of the Shah's sons on a hunting trip, but had been allowed to briefly visit Haji, who was a distant relative, as they passed through the village. His name was Habib, and he was telling Haji that his Master had arranged for him to learn to read.

"I visited your cousin, who is my uncle, in Tehran about a year ago," Habib said to Haji, "He told me that I should ask the Prince to allow me to act as his secretary. Although it was with considerable trepidation, I did so, and much to my astonishment he agreed. Now my duties include reviewing his mail and preparing letters for him to sign. The Prince has come to trust me, and I go everywhere with him. Which is wonderful, since it provided me an opportunity to visit you, Haji Agha."

Haji laughed and agreed that indeed it was wonderful that a young child should be able to travel so much. He asked about this trip.

"We are hunting. My Master loves to chase and shoot. Then

I am stuck with skinning and cleaning," he added ruefully. "but traveling around Persia is fun. Many months ago, we were in a village a little west of here. Some strange things had happened there." His manner became serious and he proceeded to tell of the horrible things he had heard happened to a religious group called the Baha'is.

"I was told that my master and his brother organized a group that went to several houses and killed the owners and all their families, then burned their houses down. There were also several local mullahs who helped with this depravity.

There was one family, I heard, where the wife was pregnant. They tied her to a door and tried to burn her alive while forcing her to watch them kill her daughter and her husband and her brother. Somehow, she escaped, but the next morning they found her a little way down the street begging for help. No one would go near her for fear of being treated the same way. My Master said this is the punishment heretics must expect." Habib looked ill just recounting the story.

"That is craziness, pure and simple," Haji said vehemently. "Persians murdering Persians? Why? Don't try to tell me that Allah wishes this. Never! What happened to the property of these people who were murdered?" he asked.

"The Princes and the mullahs divided it among themselves, " Habib answered.

"Yes, of course. All in the name of Allah. This is wrong, all wrong. I am sorry, Habib, because you work for one of these men. But this is not sanctionable behavior, no matter how they try to justify it. It is murder and greed, clothed in the name of Allah.

These people will be punished when they face their Maker in the end. Their punishment will be far worse than anything they have done to their fellow Persians."

Haji reflected, then added, "I have heard other stories. Here in our village there was a man we called Agha Bahrami. He was a good man. He had heard of this Baha'u'llah and came to love the teachings about Allah sending messengers to us frail humans in accordance with the needs of the times. Agha Bahrami used to say that each religion came from the same Supreme Being, who loved mankind and tried to teach us how to live together. He would tell us that all humanity is a brotherhood, and one day we would be united spiritually and politically. Persians, Ottomans, Europeans, Africans, even Chinese. Everyone."

"Then one day the mullahs went to his house and did exactly what you just said. They burned down his house, and they killed him, his family, even the servants. Because he talked about love."

When the boy was ready to leave, Haji called Talat to bid the boy farewell. Habib grinned at her kindly and apologized if his stories had caused her distress.

"I have learned," the child said, "to trust Allah with all my heart. The horrible things that happen around us are caused by us humans, not Allah. Perhaps we can influence those who do these things. At least I hope so. Well, good bye now. Thank you for your hospitality."

Where does a child gain such wisdom, Talat wondered. And such compassion. She would dwell on his words. Keep a pure heart, he had said. That was not easy. Not when you have been raped. How could it be done?

Returning to Mak, she sat him up in his crib and spoke gently. "Little one, help me learn how to forgive. Help me keep my heart a loving one, not one filled with bitterness and defeat."

Mak looked back at her and stopped crying. He kind of gurgled, like her daughter did some times.

"Your father is going away for a few weeks soon," she told Mak. "He is going to travel to Shiraz on business. We will not be going with him. We will be here by ourselves. By the time he comes back, let's see what we can show him that you have learned."

She began to pack her husband's clothes in a bag reluctantly. If she had still been a servant, his going would have had little bearing on her. But she was concerned that without him there, some of the other servants might make her existence more difficult because her status was now changed. She was not really the Mistress, but the Master had married her, and her status was different. She was not sure what she was. She would have to see and endure.

BACK TO
SHIRAZ

CHAPTER ONE

At Ismail Agha's home, the servants had stopped talking about Talat in front of the Master and Mistress, but among themselves they still discussed her disappearance in hushed tones while they prayed daily for her return.

Some mornings Firidun joined them. He was well aware that he and 'the Mistress' were half siblings, but, of course, the high and mighty Tahirih had no idea, at least not yet. Someday, though, he would find the opportunity to inform her, and he savored the expectation of watching her face fall into disbelief. Creating pain was his greatest joy.

His mind continued to grab at other miseries he had caused. He grinned gleefully as he reminisced over how he had gotten rid of that self-righteous servant girl, Talat. For weeks now he had watched the agony others in the household felt about her disappearance. Although he had no idea where she went, he knew precisely why she was gone.

Firidun also felt a stabbing anger at Ismail, who was the only one who knew that he, Firidun, the man he treated as a servant, was indeed his wife's half brother. Firidun would someday make him pay for that indulgence, just as he would his own father, Haji Youssef, who had arranged this humiliation. Firidun would never act openly. No one would know why the lightning struck, but strike it would, he promised himself solemnly.

Parvin had been telling a joke to lighten the mood, but no one seemed amused. They all sat glumly waiting for someone to say it was time to return to their chores. No one did.

It was dim-witted Zahreh who broke the silence. "I hear Master talk to mullah," she said. "Yesterday. He say he get married. Second time. We have another Mistress. Very soon."

Everyone stared at her as if she were mad, and it was her father who shushed her.   "Child of mine -- Dear Allah, what did I do to deserve this? -- I have heard your craziness for too long. This time it is too much. I will beat you until you can never walk or talk if I ever hear you say anything like that again."

"It true. I heard," Zahreh wailed, as she fled from the kitchen. She did not want to be beaten again. Maybe she could disappear too, like that nice Talat had. No one would ever find her either.

The morning mood broke and Parvin went to try to find Zahreh. Firidun inched his way outdoors, delighted to discover this piece of news. How interesting. He would think hard about how to create a disaster out of this situation. Ordinarily, he never trusted anything that stupid daughter of the cook said, but in this case she may have been correct. Ismail was wealthy, and wealthy men liked to show off by marrying several women. It would serve his 'sister' right to be put down. Although he was three years older than she, and the son of the same father, look which one got the respect, and who was treated like a servant. His anger grew into fury as he slid away to avoid his gardening duties. Someday he would find his way to Tehran. Yes, that was where he could establish his significance, let people know how important Firidun was. He would be called Firidun Agha, not Firidun the gardener, Firidun the servant.

Although his father had never openly acknowledged him, his mother, a former servant in Haji Yousself's household, had assured him over and over who he was. It was she who had urged him to seek his rightful rank within Haji Youssef's family. She had pointed out facial resemblances, and he himself noticed certain mannerisms that he had observed in both Haji Youssef and himself. His mother was the only woman he had ever respected, and he knew in his heart that whatever she said was true. Someday he would get even for the pain the great Haji Youssef had caused to both his mother and him. He would get even with everyone -- his father, his sister, Ismail, everyone who toyed with his life. He was a great man and he would triumph. Let them all find out.

He spat on the ground. Perhaps he would marry one of the Shah's daughters, become a Prince, live in luxury. He deserved it. He had been kept down for too long. It was time for people to see him for who he was, a man of intelligence and cunning and sagacity. Never again would he prune another man's trees, or plant another man's flowers. He would order these things done for himself. He looked down the street, as if searching for someone or something to take him away from this life of tribulation and bestow on him what he knew he deserved. He looked, but did not see anything. But one day he would. He knew he would.

Parvin found Zahreh under a bed in one of the lesser used guest rooms.

"Zahreh, come out. No one will hurt you. Come on, sweetheart. It is Parvin. You know I will not hit you. Come on now. There is much work to be done, and you are needed. You can help make the *zoolbieh* today, and then have a big piece for yourself."

That worked. Slowly Zahreh uncurled herself from the tight ball she had made herself into, and peeked out to see if it really was Parvin. Yes, it was. Parvin never lied to her. She never hurt her. Parvin was nice. Zahreh crawled out from under the bed and awkwardly stood up.

"Paavan," she stated flatly. Her mouth could not pronounce the name correctly. "My father, he hurt me."

"No, darling. He won't. He was just amazed by what you said. Did you really hear the Master talking about taking another wife?"

Zahreh nodded her head solemnly. She knew that this was very important news. Everything would be different. It frightened her.

"New wife no like me. Make me go away. Where I go?"

"Now don't be foolish. The Master would never let that happen. You can always stay here with us. Come along now. Let's get the house cleaned and dinner made so the Master will be happy when he comes home."

Zahreh went back to the kitchen. Her father looked at her disgustedly and threw some pots at her to scrub. Parvin began to polish the silver and copper and brass. There was so much of it, and every time it seemed she had caught up with the cleaning, it started all over again.

The newest servant, hired after it was decided that Talat was not coming back, joined her. As the senior female servant, Parvin delegated the work flow, and the new girl was content to clean the harder pieces. They did not rush, enjoying this time of being able to work repetitively, without having to think too carefully about what they were doing. The new servant and Parvin talked quietly, and eventually got around to a discussion of people in the neighborhood, which was always a favorite topic.

"You know, most of the wealthy men living around here have more than one wife. Look at Mustapha Agha. He already has three and I hear he is looking for another," Parvin declared. "So is Nasir Agha. I wonder what it would be like to be a second or third wife. Or worse yet, to be a first wife and have to watch another woman come into your home and share with you what has always been just yours. I was lucky. My husband said I was enough for him, he couldn't put up with more than one female if they were all like me." Parvin laughed as she said that.

Pensively, she thought back to her long marriage, which had ended many years before with her husband's death. That had happened while she still worked for Haji Youssef, long before she had been sent with the young bride Tahirih to be the foster mother and servant in Tahirih's new home.

Today Parvin had fewer responsibilities. Initially, she had jealously guarded her role as chief servant, but now the aches and pains of age had persuaded her that it was easier to command than to do, and she did not mind sharing her knowledge with someone new.

"If another woman does come to live here, who do you think it might be?" the new servant girl asked.

"Who knows. There are lots of young girls around here who need husbands, and Ismail Agha is an excellent catch. I'm sure he has been approached by several fathers."

They began to speculate on all the potential wives they could think of. By the time the polishing was done that day, they had narrowed the possibilities down to three whom they would like to have in the household because they would be least threatening to the Mistress, whom they all loved dearly. They would not be happy having another mistress to serve, but they understood and accepted reality. Another mistress was undoubtedly coming, and they might just as well get used to the idea.

As he went in and out of the house throughout the day, Firidun heard the chatter and considered how he might turn it to his own use. Another wife would give him a wedge against Tahirih. However, he doubted that it would be any of the local girls. Ismail was too ambitious for that. No, Ismail would look for an alliance that would serve his business needs. Since he wanted to expand to Tehran, that is probably where he would look. Firidun would keep his ear to the ground, knowing that he would hear the thunder. Thunder created lightning, enough to scorch everyone who had ever hurt him.

CHAPTER TWO

"Ismail Agha, I am so sorry to learn of your difficulties. However, there is no need for concern. Tahireh Khanem will be able to have many more children and you will soon have a second wife, as well."

This came from Suleiman, whom Ismail was pleased to find looking healthier with each visit. The injured man adjusted his pillows, then went on.

"Women do not know how to conduct their lives. That is why Allah ordered us men to take more than one wife, since they all need to be cared for. But enough of that. Tell me about your new home."

Ismail became eloquent. "I built a second floor over the entire house," he answered. "There is a bedroom for my new wife, several rooms for the children I expect her to give me, and some room for her servants." Ismail paused, then added, "The woman's name is Mahvash. She is a pretty enough girl, though not a beauty like Tahirih. The two of them met recently in Tehran, and they seemed to get along very well."

"Why on earth was your wife with you in Tehran?" Suleiman demanded.

"I decided to permit her to accompany me because her cousin is marrying Ambassador Amuzegar. The bride-to-be was very comforting to Tahirih after she lost our child. As it turned out, the time together was advantageous to us both."

Suleiman began to express disapproval over allowing a woman to travel on a business mission, but Ismail changed the subject. "Did I tell you that Mahvash's father sent his sons to the House of Science? That gave me the idea to do the same for Husayn when he gets a little older. He will need to understand how to run my business, which is about to expand to include trade with Russia. I believe the education will be good for him. It is becoming more and more important to know how to read and to keep track of everything going on. I try to keep up with the times, and even though I am not educated, I want my son to be."

Suleiman became agitated. "Be careful, my friend. Learning to read can be dangerous," he warned. "You do not want your son exposed to heresy. It is critical that he know only what you want him to be aware of. If he learns to read, then he will be exposed to evil ideas. Education is dangerous."

"Perhaps you are right, Suleiman Agha," Ismail replied. "But really, I watch my children closely. Of course, I would monitor what he learns, and temper it with my own experience. There won't be danger. But thanks for the warning. I will be careful."

This time Suleiman changed the subject. "I am sorry I was not able to come to your father-in-law's party. Was it well attended?"

"Oh, yes," Ismail laughed. "There were so many people there that the gossip got all tangled up and people were telling the same story with different endings all over the place," Ismail laughed. "Actually, that party is where the Ambassador met the woman he is going to marry. She is a widow who was visiting her cousin, Haji Youssef's wife, and the long time bachelor got his heart stolen when he wasn't looking. She is a beautiful woman, and very gentle. She will make him a good wife, I think."

"It's amazing that that fish finally got hooked," Suleiman chortled. "What else happened at the party?"

"Well, I'm afraid I did not pay a lot of attention. Tahirih had just lost my child, and I was not concentrating well. But the Ambassador kindly asked me to stop by his hotel before he left. He showed me photographs of buildings in Moscow and ... "

"Photographs, you say! Allah could strike you dead for viewing such things." This time Suleiman was truly alarmed.

"No, no," Ismail countered. "I really don't think so. I know the clergy think photographs are evil, but really, if you can not go somewhere yourself, then looking at a picture gives you an idea of what other places are like. My new father-in-law had a photo of his daughter, so I could see her features before I decided whether or not to pursue the idea of marriage to her."

"Paintings do the same job. You do not need a photograph."

"But a painting can be altered, while a photograph cannot," Ismail persisted. "What if my father-in-law showed me a painting of a beautiful woman, and on the day of our wedding I found my new wife to be an ugly old hag. Look how much grief a photograph could prevent."

"You are wrong," Suleiman persisted. "You must agree with the clergy. Photos are an abomination. I would certainly never allow one in my house."

It was just as well, then, that Ismail had not shown his friend the photo that the Ambassador had given him of the gold turreted building in Moscow. Although the gold could not actually be seen because the picture was black and white, the glint of the sun on the dome was apparent, and imagination could do the rest.

"Tell me, Suleiman Agha," he said to deflect Suleiman's outrage, "when do you expect to return to the bazaar? We miss you, and all your fellow bazaaris pray for you everyday."

"Thank you, my friend. Your visits and everyone's prayers have helped me recover much more quickly than expected. However, the physician still says I may not walk more than a few feet at a time. Just from here to my bedroom and back, he says. Soon, though, I promise to return. Within a month, perhaps, Allah willing."

"Excellent. That's wonderful news. I'll spread the word. Now what can I do to prepare for your return? Your stall has been kept neat and clean, as if you yourself were there. Is there any merchandise that I can procure on your behalf? Any bills that need to be paid? Do you need me to send someone to Tehran to buy merchandise for you?"

"You are so generous, Ismail Agha. Someone is buying supplies in Tehran this week, and my creditors will be patient. They know I have always been worthy of their trust."

"You are worthy of any man's trust. Just let me know if you need anything. Anything at all." With that, Ismail bade farewell to his fellow merchant and walked on to the mosque, where he joined several fellow worshippers for mid morning prayers. Ismail prayed that expanding his family would be as successful as expanding his business.

CHAPTER THREE

"Good afternoon, Ismail," Tahirih greeted with a warm smile. "How was your day?"

Ismail removed his outdoor shoes at the door and slipped his feet into the comfortable slippers that he wore inside the house, since Persians were always careful not to track dirt from outside onto their beautiful carpets.

"I stopped to see Suleiman," he answered, "and he sends his greetings to you. Something smells delicious. Is it Cook's special bread?"

"Better than that," Tahirih answered. "It is your favorite pastry. I asked him to make it just because I knew you would be tired tonight, and might need something to cheer you up."

"Why did you think I would be tired tonight, any more so than any other night?" he asked. His wife's intuition amazed him, since indeed he was more exhausted than usual.

"Wives just know these things," she teased, and would not say any more. Changing the subject, she asked "Do you remember the woman I met the day of the Muharram parades? Well, I ran into her again today, and she reminded me that her husband is also a merchant at the bazaar. He sells carpets. They invited us to their home whenever it is convenient for you."

This sounded promising to Ismail. It was always good to socialize with other businessmen. However, he would inquire about this new bazaari before accepting the invitation.

"What do you know of the family?" he inquired of Tahirih.

"Well, not much, actually. She seems to be a very quiet person. Her husband allowed her to go to the parades without any servants, but she was sure that someone was watching out for her to be sure she was safe. I saw her again today while I was shopping, and we just chatted for a while."

"What kind of husband is he that he does not assure his wife's protection?" Ismail asked angrily.

"She seemed to be perfectly all right at the parade," Tahirih assured him. "It was the Parade of Muharram. No one there would have hurt her. She and I just talked for a while. There did not seem to be any danger."

"Still, I would not have been happy if you had gone alone."

Husayn came rushing into the room just then, showing his parents a toy he had fashioned out of pieces of cloth and wood he had found around the house.

"See," he crowed, "see my new toy."

"Indeed, you are a very clever lad," his father said. "You will become a great builder. Go and tell Parvin we want some tea."

Husayn disappeared, and a few moments later Parvin came in carrying a tray filled with fruits and cookies. She poured the tea and left, after informing the mistress that more supplies were needed to finish the furniture polishing before the new mistress arrived.

"We will get whatever we need, Parvin. Send Firidun to that man at the bazaar I told you about last week. He should have everything we need," Tahirih answered.

Ismail was pleased to see that his wife was accepting the new situation with equanimity. It appeared that he would continue to have a pleasant household to come home to. That was good. He mentioned the House of Sciences.

"Do you think, Ismail, that this educational system will become more widespread by the time the other children are grown up?" she asked.

"Well," he answered cautiously, "many people, like Mullah Mohsin, for instance, believe that the influence the foreigners have had on our country is entirely bad. I have to agree that they are interlopers, trying to take over a lot of the sources of wealth of Persia. But one benefit, I think, is that those countries have education systems that are far more advanced than our own here in Persia. We can learn and profit from them. It is too bad that people like Mullah Mohsin are afraid that anything non-Persian is non-Muslim, so want nothing to do with it. When I stopped to see Suleiman this morning, he expressed many of the same fears. I wonder why some people are so afraid of anything new?"

Tahirih answered confidently. "Well, at one time, Muslims contributed great thinking to the world, Ismail. You have told me about some of the scientific developments that came from Islamic universities hundreds of years ago. Didn't you also tell me that there is some sort of mathematics called algebra that was created by Muslims? Just think about the great poetry that we hear recited all the time. That is from Muslims, too."

"Yes, Tahirih," Ismail responded, but those things are mainly from the Arab Muslims, not Persian. I don't know why the Persian clerics are so anti-education. I agree that it cannot be because of Islam. Islam encourages learning."

He paused for a moment, giving careful consideration to something flowing through his mind. "You know, now that we are talking like this, I am beginning to think that maybe I should develop better reading skills. Some of the quotations I hear from Mullah Mohsin sound different from time to time, as if he is embellishing them at the moment."

He continued to ruminate on this topic, then made a pronouncement to Tahirih. "I think I have been lazy," he suddenly laughed. "Relying on someone else to do what I need to learn myself has always been easier. It would be better, perhaps, if I kept my own books at the bazaar, and knew how to read invoices. Yes, I think I will do that."

Tahirih listened to her husband and marveled. She recalled that her new friend Soraya had repeatedly urged her to believe that education was important for all people. Soraya's reason had been that reading freed a person to learn about the teachings of Allah, so that each person could decide for themselves what to believe. It would no longer be necessary to rely on what mullahs spoon fed the illiterate masses. Soraya had even said that it was important to educate women because they were the ones with responsibility for raising children.

Now here was her husband, who had never had any use for education, starting to talk about its value. Indeed, Tahirih thought, the power of Allah to change the hearts of humans was surely beyond comprehension, but she said nothing to Ismail for fear of angering him. There were so many changes in her life coming, and she could not risk alienating him. He was her life, he and the children.

"Could we walk outside for a few moments?" she asked. "The smell of the roses everywhere is so lovely this time of year. The fruit trees are blossoming and they look so beautiful."

"As are you," Ismail replied.

CHAPTER FOUR

Six months later, Ismail had married Mahvash and the second wife was, by his observation, fitting into his household very well. He frequently heard both wives laughing together, and they seemed to share household responsibilities without rancor. Mahvash was also developing a satisfactory relationship with the children. Truly, Ismail believed, he had provided the companion his first wife needed, as well as the mother of more sons for himself.

As well as advancing domestic happiness, his business was also flourishing, and he was still considering further expansion to Russia. Although he had not yet been granted an interview with the Shah, he kept trying. With patience, he was sure he could win approval to trade outside Persian borders.

These thoughts filled Ismail's head as he sat in his home with an old friend whom he had not seen for years. He and Karim had been neighbors and childhood friends. When they were teenagers, Karim's father moved to a village which was located a day and a half away by horseback, so they had not seen each other for nearly twenty years. During that time, Karim had since visited Mecca, thereby entitling himself to be called Haji.

"Is your business going well, Ismail, my friend?" Haji had inquired solicitously.

"I am developing contacts in Tehran," Ismail answered with pride in his voice. "There is someone here in Shiraz whom I am considering allowing to act as my agent in the near future." He glanced happily at his new wife as she brought in a fresh plate of pastries. "Mahvash's family is in a similar business, and through them I am becoming better known, especially with representatives from the palace. Within a year or so, I hope that the Shah will allow me to begin international trading."

As they continued talking, Mahvash stood quietly in a corner and listened carefully. She smiled inwardly as she heard Ismail brag about his business acumen. Indeed, he understood business very well, but not wives, she had learned. He was oblivious to the fact that she, too, had plans to accomplish within a year, but they differed substantially from both Ismail's and the foolish Tahirih's. She was already pregnant and soon she would find or create an excuse to have Tahirih relegated to a lesser role in Ismail's life.

For the moment, however, it suited her purposes to be the compliant second wife, the new companion which her doting husband seemed to want so badly for Tahirih. Playing that role gave her a chance to learn confidences which Tahirih was beginning to exchange with her. So far nothing promising had been revealed, but the information she was looking for would come in time.

"May I get you anything else," she asked Ismail with a special smile.

" No, thank you, Wife. Not just now. There are some business matters we must discuss, so you may leave us." He returned her smile, and told himself that in a few hours he would be thoroughly enjoying her provocative lovemaking skills, which rivaled even those of the ladies at Madam Jamal's.

"Of course." Although stung by his dismissal, she managed to appear fully poised. "If I may serve you later, please call for me," she added sweetly.

She left and happened to bump into Tahirih, who was accompanying two of the children to their bedroom. Mahvash put on her warmest smile. "Are the children heading for bed?" she prompted, hoping for an opportunity to talk with Tahirih a little later.

"Yes, dear Mahvash, they are, so perhaps we will have a chance to chat for a few minutes after I have gotten them to sleep."

"That will be wonderful. I will wait for you," and Mahvash smiled triumphantly, although it appeared to be a friendly expression.

Half an hour later, they were conversing in the smaller salon, where they were near enough to hear the bell if Ismail rang it. Mahvash would, of course, answer, as was proper because she was the second, therefore more subservient, wife. Although she despised the role of being second, she used it well to show herself as a virtuous spouse, eager to serve her new husband.

Unfortunately for her, Ismail did not ring again that evening, so her strategy of showing Tahirih up did not work. Alternatively, therefore, she got Tahirih to talk about the servants. Most of them had been a bit aloof, always proper but still aloof, with Mahvash. She had expected this and was doing her best to hold her own with them, but was not so successful with them as she was with Ismail.

"Parvin seems a bit old to be doing so much,' she commented. "Had you thought of getting someone else to help her? Perhaps my servant Anyat could stay to assist, if you would like."

"That is very kind of you, but I am sure Anyat is eager to return to Tehran. Actually, we had one other servant a few months ago, but one day she just disappeared. I keep hoping that she will reappear. She was a very dear girl, and a hard worker. No one could ever find out where she went."

Tahirih paused a moment to settle her emotions   "It was strange how she just disappeared. One morning, she asked permission to go visit her sick father, but when she did not come back, we learned that her father had never been sick and she had not been to visit him. It is all a mystery, and no one has been able to solve it yet."

This story intrigued Mahvash. Although she was younger than Tahirih, she was far more sophisticated. She had heard of servants disappearing sometimes. Usually they were young girls whom the Master of the house had made pregnant, and they left because they could not face the Mistress anymore. She assumed that was what had happened here. Such a possibility had probably never occurred to Tahirih the Pure, she thought contemptuously.

"Is there anything I can do to help more around the house," she asked solicitously. "Just tell me, and I will be happy to do whatever you wish. I don't have any children, yet, so I am not tied up all the time as you are."

Just then they heard Ismail calling for Tahirih. He was actually calling, not ringing the bell, which startled both of them. "Tahirih, come quickly. I have unbelievable news," he shouted.

Tahirih ran quickly to the main salon, with Mahvash hot on her heels. Ismail looked at Tahirih joyfully and announced, "It is about Talat. She is safe and very well. "

Tahirih nearly fell on the divan, only to be caught by Mahvash, who instantly chided herself for not allowing Tahirih to collapse in front of company. "I don't understand. Where is she?" Tahirih turned quickly to Mahvash to explain, "That is the servant I was just telling you about," before looking back at Ismail expectantly with joy radiating from her every pore.

"When she left here, somehow she made her way to Zanjan, and through Allah's watchful care happened to take a position in Haji's house caring for his son. Not long after that, there was a tragic fire and Haji's wife was burned alive. He rebuilt the house and after a couple of months it became apparent that Talat was with child. Even though it was not his child, Haji was so grateful for the loving care she gave his son that he took pity on Talat and made her his wife for protection. Our Talat is now the wife of one of my oldest and dearest friends."

"Pregnant? Talat? That is impossible. It must be another Talat." Tahirih was too appalled to take in what Ismail was saying. But then she remembered how strangely Talat had been acting just before she left. She recalled that Talat had asked to have a lock for her door. Now Tahirih understood. How could she have been so heedless? Someone had been forcing himself into her room, and poor Talat was too mortified to tell the Mistress.

It must have been one of the servants. Instantly her mind flew to Firidun, whom she had never liked. Now she would definitely insist that Ismail dismiss that boy. Oh, but this dirty linen must never be aired in front of an outsider, which was how she suddenly thought of Mahvash.

"Ismail, this is too astonishing. Really, I cannot understand what has happened."

"My dear Tahirih, this is our Talat, I know it. I can see that you are overcome by the news. We will discuss it more tomorrow. Good night, now." He kissed her lightly on the cheek before turning to Mahvash. "Go along now. I will be there soon."

The men agreed to meet the following day, and after his friend left, Ismail went directly to Mahvash's room, where she took great care to fully satisfy his needs. When she believed he was absolutely content, Mahvash seductively asked, "Why do you suppose Tahirih acted so strangely? She had just been telling me about a servant who disappeared, then fortuitously, you said the woman had been found. Was Tahirih angry with the servant about something, do you think?"

"Oh, no, Mahvash," Ismail assured her. "Tahirih is very concerned about her servants, and she spent weeks sending searchers out to look for Talat. She was truly devastated when no one could find her. Actually, I think she was shocked when I said that Talat was pregnant before she left here. You see, Talat was a very circumspect young girl, not someone Tahirih would ever expect to be in such a situation."

He paused for a moment, then decided to tell Mahvash what he had never told Tahirih. "Just a few days before she ran away, Talat had told me that she had been raped, but I never told Tahirih because it would be too distressing to her. I tried to encourage Talat to marry the man who caused her to be in that disgraceful situation, but she refused. She would not tell me who he was. and then a few days later she was gone. I knew we would not see her again, but I did not have the heart to tell poor Tahirih."

Poor Tahirih, eh. We'll see about that, Mahvash thought to herself. Aloud she said, "Would you like me to tell her tomorrow? Perhaps it will be easier for her if she hears it from another woman."

Ismail felt as if a great burden had been lifted from him. "Yes, thank you so much, dearest Mahvash. I would be so grateful. I have never known how to tell her. I hoped that learning she was all right would have relieved her, but it seems to have made everything more complicated. Thank you very much for your assistance." To Mahvash's unrevealed disgust, he spent the next hour demonstrating his gratitude.

The following morning, Mahvash contrived to have servants watch the children. She asked Tahirih to go to the bazaar with her, supposedly to look for some household items. As they were walking along the street toward the bazaar, they happened to run into Soraya. Tahirih introduced the women to each other.

"Sister Mahvash, this is Soraya. Her husband has a carpet stall at the bazaar just a few avenues away from Ismail's tea business. Dearest Soraya, this is Mahvash, Ismail's new wife. Please help me welcome her to Shiraz."

Soraya smiled graciously and replied, "I am so happy to meet you, Mahvash. Welcome to our city. If you are going toward the bazaar, may I walk with you?"

"We would be delighted with your company," Tahirih immediately responded. Mahvash had another opinion, but kept it to herself. Instead, she listened closely to the conversation between Soraya and Tahirih, but picked up nothing useful for her ulterior purposes.

As they chatted, Soraya tried to include Mahvash in the discourse as much as possible. "Where were you born, Mahvash?" she inquired.

"In Tehran. My father is in the tea business there, just as Ismail Agha is here in Shiraz. That is how they knew each other, and I think it is really the reason Ismail married me. I am a fourth daughter, and you know how hard we are to get rid of." She pretended to laugh self-effacingly.

"Yes, I am also a late daughter, seventh, actually," Soraya agreed. "Fortunately, my father found a good husband for me as well. My husband does not believe in having more than one wife, though, so no other woman will be as lucky as I am."

"It is good to be happy in marriage," Mahvash intoned. "May we all be so forever." Well, at least one of us, she added to herself, with a sly look at Tahirih which no one else noticed.

Upon arrival at the bazaar, they parted company, Soraya going to find dried vegetables and the other women heading for a different area of the bazaar. Mahvash actually wanted some fine fabric to make herself new clothes, but on the way pretended to be concerned about finding kitchen kettles.

"I saw Cook using a pot that kept boiling over," she said. "Perhaps we should get something a little larger for him."

Tahirih had never noticed that the pots were inadequate, and was embarrassed that someone else should be more aware of what was going on in her kitchen than she was. She did not want to admit to not observing the problem, so agreed that it was indeed time to buy some new kitchen wares.

"Ever since the party at my father's home I have meant to replenish some of the things I lent out, but have never yet had an opportunity to do so. Let's go see what we find."

They looked at several sizes of kettles, and Mahvash insisted on purchasing the most expensive. "I will give you eighteen toman for that one," she told the merchant sharply.

"I would be honored to give you my merchandise at such a wonderful price," he answered amicably. "But for this one I must ask sixty-two toman."

"Sixty-two toman," Mahvash screamed. "Never. I will call the mullahs and tell them you are trying to rob your customers. I will have you arrested."

"Really, now Mahvash," Tahirih intervened. "Sixty-two is a little high, perhaps, but perhaps we could offer him thirty."

"Absolutely not. I will pay eighteen toman and nothing more. Give it to me, you worthless thief."

By then, others had gathered to watch. Although bargaining was expected in the bazaar, it was usually conducted in a relatively affable and respectful manner. If there were a big difference of opinion on the price, the customer would simply go to another vendor and try her luck there. But having a customer scream like this was unusual, and Tahirih was ashamed of Mahvash's behavior.

"My friend is from Tehran," she tried to explain. "Perhaps they bargain differently there." She attempted to pull Mahvash away from the stall, hoping to be able to speak to her privately, but it was no good.

"I will have that pot for eighteen toman, or I will have my husband come and teach you a good lesson about cheating customers. He is an important merchant here in the bazaar, and you should know not to treat his wife so shabbily."

By now, Tahirih was mortified and she jerked Mahvash by her chador, nearly pulling it off. "Come with me, now," she whispered loudly. Finally she got Mahvash far enough away that other customers had lost interest and returned to their own shopping.

"What was that all about?" she demanded.

"Obviously you don't know how to bargain effectively. Never mind, I forgive you. I suppose you were just showing your small town ignorance. You have to bargain with enough force that you will be taken seriously. If you are too polite, you never get anything at a decent price. For that pot, for instance, he would have come down to twenty-four toman, I am sure. With your methods, you probably would have paid more than thirty-five."

For the first time, Tahirih became angry with Ismail's second wife. Up until now, she had been enjoyable to be around, but she was now showing a new side which had to be dealt with.

"Let me tell you this, Mahvash. I am going to say it once, and only once," she said with a vehemence that made Mahvash take a step back and observe her thoughtfully. "You had better listen carefully. You will never, never again, use my husband's name to cheat a fellow merchant. Do you understand me?"

"Why, Tahirih, I was not trying to cheat anyone," Mahvash replied defensively. "I was just trying to get the best price I could, to save our husband money. You should always do the same. He works hard for his money, and it is our obligation to be sure that we spend it wisely."

"I mean it, Mahvash. Do not embarrass him again that way. Come, now, we are leaving."

Mahvash prudently decided not to pursue looking for expensive cloth that day as she followed Tahirih out of the bazaar. On the way home she tried to make up.

"I am so sorry, Tahirih, if I upset you." She tried to sound contrite. "Please let's not be angry with one another. We must get along well, if only for Ismail's sake."

"If you are concerned for Ismail's well being," Tahirih answered, "do not embarrass him among his fellow bazaaris." She looked at Mahvash, who was contriving to look so put down that she relented. "Very well, let us try to stay on good terms."

They proceeded in silence for a while, then Mahvash brought up the issue of Talat. "You know, Tahirih, last night Ismail told me something he had been reluctant to confide to you. I mean, he did not want to upset you, which is why he had not told you. It is about your servant Talat."

Tahirih whirled around and looked Mahvash squarely in the eye.

"What about Talat?" she demanded.

"Well, Ismail told me that he knew she was pregnant when she left here."

"He said WHAT?"

"I'm sorry, but that's what he told me. Talat had revealed that to him, and he tried to find out who was responsible, but she wouldn't tell him. I guess she was too embarrassed to tell you, and chose to run away instead. Anyway, I'm glad everything turned out well for her."

Tahirih pondered this information as they walked along in silence. Her husband had known why Talat was gone, and he had chosen not to tell her. She was stunned, which quickly turned to being so hurt that she could not think straight. *Oh, Ismail,* she wailed to herself. *Why couldn't you be honest with me?*

CHAPTER FIVE

"Tahirih, I am going to visit your father," Ismail called to his first wife. "Do you have any messages for your parents?"

"You are going tonight? May I come with you? I have some things to take to my mother."

"No, not tonight. We will be talking about business, and I will not be home until late. You need to stay here with the children. Is there something you want me to take to your mother?"

Tahirih thought for a moment, then answered. "No, I will take it tomorrow. However, when you return, there is something I would like to discuss with you. For now, it will wait. Please give my love to my parents."

Curious about what Tahirih wanted to talk with him about, Ismail rode the few miles to Haji Youssef's home as a happy man. Fortunately, taking a second wife had in no way damaged his relationship with his first father-in-law. He had promised Haji Youssef to care for his daughter, and he was upholding that commitment. Tahirih appeared to be satisfied with having Mahvash take over some functions of household management, and since he favored them equally with his nightly visits, there was no reason for Tahirih to complain on that account.

He was gratified to find that he was the first to arrive that evening. This was by design, since there were matters he wanted to discuss privately. Haji Youssef had invited several merchants for dinner that night, and Ismail wanted to talk with him before they all arrived. He nodded to the servant who took his horse and asked after the servant's family, learning that there was now a new child, and also that the eldest son was about to be married. He made appropriate comments, and proceeded to the front door.

When he was escorted into the house, however, he was disappointed to find that Haji Youssef was nowhere to be found. He was shown into a comfortable salon to await his host. To pass the time, he looked for the defect that was traditionally incorporated into the weaving of each Persian carpet. Although renowned for their beauty, all Persian carpets were crafted with a minor defect. This was not a lack of workmanship, but a tribute to Allah, since only He could create perfection.

He was inspecting the carpet and having a hard time finding the blemish when he noticed that someone had entered the room. He arose expectantly, then was annoyed to see that it was not his father-in-law. Instead it was a mullah from town, an older man well known as a peacemaker and mediator. Ismail had long respected this man, and although he was exasperated that his father-in-law had not yet arrived, if someone else had to show up, he was delighted that it was this particular person.

"Mullah Nasir, it is a great honor to be in your presence," he declared, rising immediately to give the mullah his seat. "I trust that you and all your family are well."

They continued to exchange pleasantries until a few others arrived, but still not Haji Youssef. Ismail was becoming concerned. His father-in-law was a stickler for propriety, and his lateness had reached the point of being insulting.

Then without warning, a servant burst into the room, and with a quick nod asked Ismail Agha to come out to the hallway. In a frightened tone, he relayed the message that he had received from another servant. "Haji Youssef did not return as expected so we sent someone to look for him. He was found in the far apricot grove, on the other side of the estate, lying on the ground. He was unconscious."

Ismail was alarmed. Haji Youssef had always enjoyed nothing but good health. "Where is he now," he demanded.

"We carried him back to the house and took him to his room. Manizheh Khanem is with him, and she begs you to come immediately."

Ismail ran to his father-in-law's room, where a distraught Manizheh was exhorting the servants to make her husband comfortable, while at the same time, she was desperately trying to get Youssef to speak to her. Ismail immediately saw that the side of Haji Youssef's face was slack, drooping unnaturally into the face of an idiot. His eyes, though, were alive with terror.

With a sinking heart, Ismail instantly knew that what he saw before him was one of Allah's cruelest fates to humans, a robust man capable of intricate thinking and activity, reduced to an uncommunicating heap of bone and flesh. Although his heart might continue to beat for years, Haji Youssef might never speak coherently again, and he would be dependent on other people to take care of his every need. Ismail's heart convulsed as he considered that he would have to tell this to Tahirih.

Right now, however, the immediate situation called for him to provide strength for Manizheh. His occasional frustrations with her were instantly put aside as he quickly went to her and gently took her hands in his.

"Mother, be at peace. Your husband will live. Call for the doctor, who will be able to ease his pain."

Eventually, Manizheh allowed herself to be taken from the room and comforted by servants and family members who had arrived as word about Haji Youssef's condition traveled quickly throughout the area. The other dinner guests had by then been notified, and Mullah Nasir came to Haji's room to offer assistance. He was relieved to find that services for the dead would not be needed. Ismail assured him that the most effective thing he could do was pass the word that Haji Youssef was still living, and the mullah complied instantly.

Meanwhile, Ismail sent a servant to his home to bring Tahirih, and then he sat beside his father-in-law's bed, trying to think of how to communicate with him. Finally an idea struck him, and he began to speak gently.

"My father-in-law, I know that you are having a hard time right now saying what is in your heart. Can you blink your eyes?"

In response, Haji blinked.

"Good." Ismail smiled and continued. "All right, now. I will ask you a question, then you blink once if you want to say yes, and twice if you want to say no. Can you do that?"

Again there was a blink. Ismail beamed reassuringly and began asking questions.

"Were you alone when this happened?'

Two blinks.

"Was a servant with you?"

One blink.

Ismail named all the servants working for Haji and kept getting two blinks, so he went through them all again, thinking he had misunderstood. Again he got two blinks with each name. Eventually he asked, "Was it someone else's servant?"

One blink. Good, there was progress.

"A neighbor's servant?"

Two blinks.

"My servant?"

He was surprised when he received one blink. He went through each of his servants until he arrived at Firidun and got one blink.

"Firidun?" he asked again to be sure. What would Firidun have been doing here, he wondered. "Was he here to see you?"

One blink.

How was he going to ask what it was about. This was becoming exhausting.

"Haji Youssef, you must be getting tired. I will go find Firidun and ask him what he knows."

Haji Youssef rolled his eyes toward the doorway, and Ismail saw that Tahirih was standing there, silently weeping.

"Tahirih," Ismail said quietly as he went and took her in his arms, "your father cannot talk right now, but he can still communicate. It will take some time, but everything will be all right."

Tahirih nodded her head in acknowledgment of what her husband had just said, but she knew that nothing was ever going to be all right again. Ismail held her gently for a moment, then suggested that she go to her mother and try to comfort her.

Tahirih still said nothing, but eventually did as her husband said. She had been standing there long enough to know that Firidun was mixed up in this somehow. Firidun, whom she had so intensely disliked and long considered strange, sometimes evil. She would find out what he had said to her father that had caused this to happen. She looked back over her shoulder and saw that her father seemed to have fallen asleep. "Sleep in peace," she said quietly. "I will find out what happened and I will avenge you, my beloved father."

Ismail stayed in the room for a few more minutes to be sure that Haji Youssef was sleeping soundly, then left to find his wife and mother-in-law. He was glad that Mahvash had not come with Tahirih. This was a time for family only. He was surprised to realize that he did not consider Mahvash family in these circumstances.

"Tahirih Khanem," he said gently as he entered the room where his mother-in-law appeared to be resting, and his wife sat quietly sobbing.

Tahirih looked up, then back at her mother. The doctor had given her a potion which had allowed her to fall into a fitful sleep.

"Let us go outside and walk for a few minutes."

Silently Tahirih arose, glancing over to the couch where her mother lay, then to the servant who was sitting nearby.

"Let me know immediately if she awakes," she ordered quietly, then accompanied Ismail outside.

"How much of the conversation did you witness?" he asked.

"Enough to know that Firidun is involved," she answered bitterly. "I have never liked him, and I believe he is the cause of Talat's leaving us. I know he is responsible for what happened to my father." She began to weep.

"What makes you believe that Firidun has anything to do with Talat's leaving?"

"Mahvash told me that you knew Talat was with child before she left. Well, a few days before she disappeared, she had come to me and asked to have a lock for her door. Now I understand why she needed it, and I will never forgive myself for ignoring her." By now she was crying without restraint. "Someone was frightening her terribly, and I am convinced it was that miserable Firidun. You must make him go away. He has never been anything but trouble."

Ismail made an immediate decision. He knew that if Tahirih confronted Firidun, the cad would reveal the secret he had been sworn to keep. Better that she heard it from her husband than from someone she hated. He sat down beside her and rocked her in his arms, trying to shush her with nonsense words. When the ferocity of her fury was spent, he spoke.

"Tahirih, this is a terrible time for you, and now I must tell you something that is going to make you feel even worse. But you must hear this from me, not anyone else. Can you listen?"

Nothing could be worse than what had happened to her father. She sat stiffly and nodded, not trusting herself to speak.

"Tahirih, do you believe that I love you? That I would never do anything deliberately to hurt you?"

She inclined her head, becoming even more frightened.

"And you know that your father is very devoted to your mother."

Where was this going? Tahirih was beginning to panic, but willed herself to stay still.

"A long time ago, your father made a mistake. He was overtaken with a young girl's beauty and charms, and he allowed her to convince him to consider taking her as a second wife." This was not what had happened, but it sounded better than saying that her father had forced himself on a helpless servant.

"This young girl had a child, but by then Haji Youssef knew he would not marry her, and he sent her away. She went back to her father's home where she had the child, but never told anyone who the father was. Except the child himself. She told him that Haji Youssef was his father, and the boy believed her."

Gradually the truth was beginning to dawn on Tahirih. Her father was also the father of Firidun, the man she despised. He was her brother. No, her half-brother. Her mother had nothing to do with that monster, but her father did. Suddenly, all the worshipful love she had felt for her father for twenty-two years drained away and left her empty. She was abandoned. The man who had raised her had betrayed her. This was worse than losing her own child. She had lost the source of her being. No, not entirely. She still had her mother. But her father was forever gone from her.

"Does Manizheh Khanem know this?" She prayed to Allah that she did not.

"No. Only I know it, and that is why Firidun has lived and worked at my home. It was a promise I made your father, to watch Firidun so that he would not cause harm to anyone."

"Not cause harm?" By now Tahirih was hysterical. "Not cause harm? He has destroyed everything around him, and you say he has not caused harm?" Somehow she got to her feet and tried to run, but her legs would not move properly. She collapsed and panted, feeling emotional pain ten times as miserable as any physical pain she had experienced during her childbirths.

Ismail caught up with her. "Tahirih Khahem," he admonished. "You must be brave, for your mother. What you say to her will be your decision, but this is not the time for you to make such an important decision. Trust me, I beg of you. Sit here and talk with me."

They sat beside the fence her father had built to keep out intruders, and for a long time, Tahirih said nothing. Her mind had gone blank as she tried to absorb all the pain that had been thrust at her. Her honored and beloved father, now an invalid. Was this punishment for what he had done? No, she did not believe in that. Allah was merciful, not a sender of punishment. These things happened to humans. They were natural, not a retribution. But her father did deserve this. He had dishonored her mother, who had always been loyal and the best wife any man could have.

Now her mother was affected by what had happened to her father. How did it all work together? She was so tired.

"Ismail, take me back to my mother. She needs my comfort. I will say nothing to her. She could not bear to hear this. Especially not now."

She stumbled to her feet, and Ismail slowly guided her to the house. By the time they arrived, she had composed her features so that the servants could not see her distress. Even if they did, they would assume it was related to her father's sudden illness. No one would know her true anguish.

"Your mother calls for you, Tahirih Khanem," a servant whispered to her as they entered the house. She went to the room where she had left her mother sleeping, and tried to smile, but it did not feel right.

Her mother did not notice. Her own heart was filled with such torment that she could not see anyone else's at the moment.

"How is he? Has he spoken yet?"

"Mother, he will be well. Ismail has devised a way to communicate with him even though he cannot speak. Right now he must rest, and so must you. I will have the servant bring you some tea, and you should also eat a little bread."

"My child, right now you must take care of me. I am so sorry. This is not as it should be. Where are you sisters and brothers?"

"Everyone is here, dearest Mother. They do not want to bother you. But if you would like, I will have them come."

Her mother nodded, and Tahirih motioned for the servant to call the others. Soon the room was filled with siblings, spouses and grandchildren. Tahirih felt it was overwhelming, but her mother drew comfort from their presence. She smiled.

"Childen, and children of my children. Your presence is a strength to me. Take care of one another and bring each other comfort. Your father, your grandfather, my husband will be well. Right now he is resting. He must have quiet. So I ask you to depart for now. I am glad that my family is so near and can be counted on when they are needed. I will let you know how he does."

There was much lamenting and consoling, and many of Tahireh's brothers and sisters did not want to leave, fearing that their mother might need them. Eventually, all but the eldest son left.

"As eldest son, I will make decisions regarding my Mother's well being," he swaggered. "I will decide what to do about my Father's affairs. I don't understand why Tahirih thinks that she should be the one in control here."

Tahirih regarded her brother skeptically, but said nothing, recalling that he had always put her down simply because he was the oldest and male, whereas she was the youngest and merely a female. However, when he began to remonstrate with her about not being notified more immediately, Ismail stepped in and reminded him that it was he, Ismail, who had first learned what happened to their father, not Tahirih. That stopped the tirade, and Tahirih was grateful for the protection her husband provided.

"Brother of my first wife, your esteemed father, Haji Youssef, has asked that no one come near him for a while, not even his

children. Please honor this request. You will be called immediately
when he is able to tolerate company."

"How do I know what you say is true?" the brother countered.
"My father has said nothing. He only blinks his eyes. You can
make up anything you want."

Ismail gave his brother-in-law a 'don't be so foolish as to
antagonize me' look, and finally the braggadocio left.

CHAPTER SIX

Tahirih's new friend Soraya heard of the sudden reversal in Haji Youssef's fortunes, as did nearly everyone in Shiraz. Soraya sent messages to Tahirih's home, not wanting to presume on her time but very desirous to show her concern.

Grateful to hear from her new friend, and because the next day was Friday, the Muslim holy day, Tahirih sent a servant to Soraya's home asking if they could meet at the mosque, where Tahirih would be praying for her father's recovery . The servant returned with the response that Soraya would not be at the mosque, but would have her home waiting for Tahirih when she was ready to come.

Knowing that she would find Soraya's home to be quiet and restful, so different from everywhere she had been in the past several days, Tahirih gratefully accepted the invitation, with Ismail's permission. Because she could not walk on the streets without being accompanied by a male relative or a servant, Firidun accompanied her first to the mosque, then to Soraya's home the next day. At Ismail's urging, she still had not said anything to him about what she knew. Although she wanted to lash out at him with all the vehemence boiling in her heart, Ismail had cautioned her to wait until they were able to learn more from Haji himself.

With bitter reluctance, she had acquiesced to her husband's counsel, and during the fifteen minutes of walking together she said not a word to Firidun. He, on the other hand, chattered like a magpie, knowing it would aggravate her. In his heart, he was delighted that his mighty father had been literally brought to his knees, and that this insolent half-sister of his was suffering so badly. However, he pretended to be filled with great regret at the sad turn of events.

Finally, after what seemed an eternity to Tahirih, they arrived at Soraya's home, and Tahirih addressed him abruptly.

"One of Soraya's servants will accompany me home. Do not wait." The words were flung back over her shoulder since she could not bear to look at him.

Just then the door opened and Soraya threw open her arms to greet her friend. "Come in, dearest Tahirih. You are most welcome in our home."

Soraya's husband was in the background, and he too greeted Tahirih circumspectly but warmly. Firidun took note that the woman had come to the door herself rather than having a servant announce Tahirih. Such belittling behavior, he thought disgustedly as he turned and left. And then for the husband to be there to greet a woman -- did these people have no pride? He turned on his heel and moved away quickly.

Tahirih was immediately drawn to the tranquility she found in Soraya's home. A servant moved quietly in the background. The decorations were tasteful, and the colors were soothing creams and rich browns, not the bright reds and peacock blues found in many Persian homes. The tea had a blend of cardamon in it, which created a wonderful aroma. Three children appeared briefly, paid their respects to the visitor, then left with a pleasant good bye to their mother. After exchanging a few pleasantries, Soraya's husband also departed, leaving the women alone.

"Soraya, your home is an oasis of comfort to me," Tahirih said from the bottom of her heart. "Your furnishings are so elegant and everything is arranged to please the eye and comfort the soul."

Soraya laughed gently and replied, "Well, perhaps that is because my soul is at peace."

"Yes, I just came from the mosque, and whenever I go there, I leave feeling comforted. Do you go to the mosque regularly? It is such a source of succor to me."

Soraya was not sure how to answer. She realized that if Tahirih chose to betray what she might tell her, everyone Soraya loved would be jeopardized. But Soraya had given this matter great thought and had also discussed it with her husband. They agreed that Tahirih could be trusted with the knowledge of their religious convictions.

"No, Tahirih, my family does not go to the mosque. But I have been taught to read and write and even to cipher. It was my husband who taught me these things, because he believes that Allah has told us that education is vital for every human being, both male and female. Do you believe that women can be educated as well as men?"

Although startled, Tahirih was overjoyed. Here was yet another woman who knew how to read. Perhaps this one would not be afraid to share her learning.

"Recently I met another woman who was also taught to read by her husband," Tahirih said with excitement beginning to squeeze itself out of her voice," but she was afraid to teach me for fear of offending the rules of our society. Truly, dearest Soraya, I want to learn to read more than anything. Could you help me?" Then as she thought about what Soraya had just said, she asked, "Did you say every human being should be educated? Why?"

Soraya answered simply and directly. "Because only when people know how to read can they choose what they want to know more about. Without the ability to read, one must accept what someone else thinks is best for them."

"But surely that is dangerous," Tahirih asserted. "If everyone knew how to read, they could learn bad things as well as good. Isn't it necessary to have someone knowledgeable decide what is proper and what is not?"

"Of course, there must be wisdom applied in what one chooses to read," Soraya answered. "But that so called wisdom should not be applied only by a select group of people who are ruled by their own prejudices, especially when those prejudices are so obviously tainted against whole groups of people, such as women. After all, women make up half the number of people in the world."

Tahirih had never considered that perspective before. Cautiously she said, "If half of us are not allowed to learn to read simply because of how we were born, indeed, that is not right. But how can such an idea ever be promoted if the controlling half of society does not want to listen?"

"It will happen because Allah wills it. He has told us that this is His new declaration to mankind. He has said that humanity is like a bird with two wings, one male and one female. If only one wing is strong and the other weak, then the bird will never be able to fly in a straight line and find its way to Allah. All people must be educated so that both wings can be properly developed."

"I have never heard that from any mullah," Tahirih replied. She looked at Soraya expectantly, willing her to continue.

"Consider for a moment," Soraya continued, "that mothers are the first source of teaching for a child. If the mother is overwhelmed by superstition, then that is what she will teach her children. Only education can overcome superstition and prejudice. Education will lead to an understanding that Allah loves all humanity and wants what is best for the development of all people."

With hope in her heart, Tahirih whispered, "Will you teach me to read? Even if my husband has forbidden it?"

"Your husband is a good man, Tahirih. If he has forbidden you, it is not out of cruelty, but out of his own ignorance. Someday he will come to understand, and then he will accept and appreciate your strength and determination."

"I never thought I had much strength," Tahirih answered. "I have always done what someone else told me because I believed that they knew better than I. However, sometimes I have surprised myself by resisting what I am told. I don't want to be belligerent, though. How do I trust myself to know what I should resist and what I should agree with?"

"Of course, you won't always do the right thing," Soraya answered. "That is now we learn, from our mistakes. But you are intelligent and incisive. You know how to balance right and wrong. Yes, of course, I will teach you to read, if you like. We can begin right now. Here, look at the Koran lying there on the table. The word on the front says Koran. Each letter has a corresponding sound. You see this first marking? That is the letter K. Then there is an R - do you see how that is written? Then the letter N. See there?"

Tahirih looked, and for the first time in her life, really saw. Soraya taught her how to recognize other letters, and how they fit together to form a word. She showed her that there were no vowels in written Persian language, but that each word was recognized in accordance with its meaning within a sentence, so in that way the reader knew how the connecting vowel should sound. They practiced a long time, until Soraya's husband came in to say that Tahirih was welcome to stay for supper if she could.

"What! It can't be that late already. Oh, I am so sorry, Soraya. I have presumed on your time for far too long. I must leave and go back to my family. I thank you for all you have done for me. Truly, my heart sings!"

Even though Soraya and her husband assured her that she would be more than welcome to stay longer, Tahirih insisted that she had to leave. She was not sure how she was going to hide her excitement from Ismail, because he would want to know what it was about. She left without being accompanied and walked all the way home before she realized that she was alone. Not being surveilled constantly was a new sensation to her, and she realized that she enjoyed it. It was so strange, she thought. In the midst of her misery, she had found a ray of hope.

When she arrived home, Ismail looked upset. He tersely asked her to come to the garden, then demanded to know why she had not been accompanied while walking outside.

"Really, Ismail, I don't need someone to come with me."

"What are you thinking? Of course you do. What would the neighbors say if they knew my wife was accosted on the street because she was alone? That would be disgraceful to me. Whenever you are outside, you will be accompanied."

"But really, Ismail, why? Have you ever heard of any woman being bothered just because she walked from one house to another by herself? When has that ever happened? Surely a servant's time can be spent more advantageously than babysitting an adult."

Ismail was furious. "You will not go outside my house unaccompanied again," he commanded.

Would Soraya's husband have reacted that way, Tahirih wondered. She didn't think so. He seemed to treat women as capable human beings, not as creatures in need of constant supervision.

She began to think about the role she played in life, and was somehow dissatisfied. She cherished being a mother, but all her other relationships were somehow tainted with being controlled. Actually, even her role as a mother was beginning to change. Little Husayn was starting to order her to do things and expecting to be obeyed. On a daily basis, he was exposed to the belief that only men could make decisions, and it was the woman's duty to comply. What was she doing wrong? Could she singlehandedly change the way children were raised in Persia? She laughed at her own impudence. But then again, if someone did not begin to do things differently, nothing would ever change.

Just then Husayn came running into the room. "Mother," he demanded, "I want to go to Omar's house to play. Parvin says she's too busy to take me. Order her to stop what she is doing and take me right now."

"Husayn, love, if Parvin says she is busy, then she is busy. You cannot expect her to neglect her household duties."

"But I am her most important duty. She must always take care of me. I have heard you tell her that taking care of the children comes before anything else."

"My dearest Husayn, taking care of you means watching out for your safety. It does not mean dropping everything whenever you want to do something. Now, enough of this. Parvin cannot take you to Omar's at this moment. Find something else to do for a while."

Husayn was astounded to hear his mother speak to him like that. He always got his way. In bewilderment, he went to find his father.

Well, you just stood up for yourself, Tahirih thought proudly to herself. Good for you. Keep it up.

A moment later she was startled to hear her husband's voice. "I am going back to the bazaar, and I will take Husayn over to his friend's home on my way. See to it that Parvin is there in two hours to bring him back home."

"Ismail, if you want to take Husayn somewhere, that is fine. But I just told him he would have to find something else to do for a while. If you take him, then you will have to find a way to get him back home." Again, she could not believe her audacity.

Just then Mahvash appeared.

"I will be happy to take your son to his friend's house," she deferentially offered. Firidun can accompany me back."

"Excellent. Thank you, Mahvash." With a very pointed look at Tahirih, Ismail left.

Tahirih was livid. She had been trying to establish discipline with her son, and here was the second wife undercutting her. "Mahvash, it is not your place to interfere. Never do that again."

"Tahirih, dearest, I was only trying to help. If little Husayn wants to go play with his friend, why shouldn't he? Just because one of the servants is too busy, apparently, to take him does not mean that he cannot go. There is always someone to do what needs to be done. This time it happened to be me."

"My whole point is that going to Omar's house was not a necessity, it was a whim. I am trying to teach my son that he cannot expect women to cater to him all the time. If he grows up thinking like that, he will be impossible. Mahvash, don't ever interfere in something like this again."

"Of course not," and Mahvash smiled sweetly as she took Husayn by the hand and went to the front door to look for Firidun.

CHAPTER SEVEN

Several days later, Tahirih was again at Soraya's house, studying a piece of correspondence. The handwriting was elegant, but still Tahirih was having difficulty understanding not only the words but also the meaning. After working on it for a long time, she sat back.

"Who is this letter from?" she asked. "It is written with such authority, as if the writer has profound knowledge beyond most people's comprehension."

"It is a letter from Baha'u'llah," Soraya answered quietly.

"Baha'u'llah? That means Glory of Allah. Who would dare to call himself that?"

"Baha'u'llah is the Promised One, the return of the twelfth Imam, the Master whom Muhammad promised would come to lead us into the Days of Perfection. Baha'u'llah is the Manifestation foretold in the Holy Bible and in the Koran."

Tahirih stared at Soraya in disbelief, then remembered that, when Soraya told her she had been taught to read, she had also mentioned that Allah instructed all people, men and women, to be literate. At the time, she knew she had never heard that concept from any Muslim source, but she had not thought further about it.

At that moment, she was not sure if she was hearing blasphemy or truth, but she knew that she was frightened beyond anything she had ever felt. If Ismail ever learned of this conversation, he would be angrier than she had ever known him in the past, she was sure.

"What do you mean. Do the mullahs believe this?" she asked tremulously.

"Well, a number of mullahs recognize Bahau'u'llah as the Prophet of God who was foretold in Muslim writings and traditions, but, of course, many mullahs do not, mainly because one of Baha'u'llah's most important teachings is that religious leaders are no longer necessary."

"Then who would teach us about Allah?" Tahirih was truly puzzled. "Even most men don't know what the Koran says. They rely on mullahs, and we women rely on the men."

"That is why Baha'u'llah says that everyone must be educated. Each person has to differentiate between truth and falsehood for himself. Or herself," she added pointedly. "All people must decide individually what is true and not true about their faith. No longer should a few be allowed to dictate what others must believe."

"Then we would no longer have mullahs?" Tahirih asked, thinking how nice it would be not to have people like Mullah Mohsin grandstanding in her home all the time. "I can't imagine that the mullahs would tolerate that."

"Indeed, most mullahs are not going to like having their profession, and thereby their power, taken away. They are certainly going to resist."

Soraya paused for a moment, to allow these thoughts to permeate Tahirih's thinking, then proceeded, openly acknowledging her religious convictions. "Tahirih, my husband and I are Baha'i. We believe with all our hearts that the teachings of Baha'u'llah are the truth, that Baha'u'llah is the Messenger Allah promised would come in the fullness of time. This promise is found in both the Koran and the Holy Bible. But most people, especially the mullahs, are terribly afraid to acknowledge Baha'u'llah's message because they fear it endangers not only their beliefs but, more importantly, their very livelihoods."

"Is that why the Jews disavow Christianity, and Christians think Muslims are heretics? Because it interrupts the established power of the religious hierarchy?" Tahirih asked.

"Well, not entirely, but that certainly is a part of it. But also, there are many Jews and Christians whose beliefs are based on their own personal interpretation of what their holy writings say, and what their long practiced traditions establish as the so-called truth. That is a significant part of the problem. People do not always understand what is written, although they are convinced they do. They misinterpret the meaning of their religious teachings, then believe and perpetuate their own errors."

"Doesn't that prove that a mullah is necessary, that only someone who has studied the teachings can explain them to the people?" Tahirih presented a common argument, and Soraya answered easily.

The founders of previous faiths -- Zoroaster, Abraham, Moses, Jesus, Muhammad -- none of these Messengers from Allah had their words recorded at the time they lived. Their teachings come

from oral tradition which was not written down until decades,
sometimes centuries, later. But the writings from Ba'ha'ullah
are His exact words, written by Himself. There does not need
to be interpretation of these writings because Baha'u'llah's entire
message to humanity is given to us in precisely His own words.

Tahirih shook her head, trying to clear it from all the tangled
feelings coursing through her mind.

Soraya went on. "I have taught you to read, and now you
can do that on your own. You amazed me by how quickly you
learned, and you do not need me to help you decipher letters
anymore. I will certainly understand if you wish to stop coming
here. Now that you know we are Baha'i, you may be endangered.
I am certain that your husband will not approve of your coming
here anymore, if you tell him we are Baha'i."

Tahirih answered with gravity and apprehension. "I have
heard Ismail speak of the Baha'is. He is very afraid of them, I
think, and he worries that they will corrupt the bazaar. Ismail
insisted that he would have nothing to do with a Baha'i merchant,
and that he would notify the authorities if he ever heard of any, so
I would not dare tell him that you are Baha'i. It would mean great
danger to you, I am afraid. Oh, you have been so kind to me, and
your husband, too. You have treated me like a sister. How would
I be repaying you if I caused you trouble now?"

"Whatever happens is always in Allah's hands," Soraya
responded. "He will protect us, and we are not afraid of exposure.
We know that someday indeed, someone will learn of our beliefs,
and will cause us trouble. We accept that, so we do not speak of
it to many people. Those who do know are trusted. But if we are

reported to the religious authorities, so be it. Perhaps that will be an opportunity to educate someone who might not have learned of the Baha'i Faith otherwise. Do not be afraid for us."

"Soraya, I must go. I don't know if I can ever return, now that I know you are Baha'i.

"Do not worry about it, dearest Tahirih.

Tahirih departed from Soraya's home, unaware that she was being observed.

The next morning she was mending a tear in the curtain from the main salon when Mahvash entered the room.

"Good morning," Mahvash said in such a way that even Tahirih heard the venom. Tahirih looked up from her needle, startled by the animosity she perceived. "I have heard that you now consort with infidels. Is that wise?"

"What do you mean?" Tahirih felt both fear and anger.

"You have been visiting the wife of that rug merchant at the bazaar. Or is it him that you have honored with your presence, if his wife is not there? Did you know that they are heretics? They are apostates, and you dishonor our husband by acknowledging their existence."

Mahvash had usually been subservient in the past. For her to speak this way verified that she felt she had acquired a great power, enough to overcome whatever strength Tahirih had developed in this house over the years. Tahirih felt a fear that shook her to her very being. She listened as Mahvash continued.

"I am being kind and warning you that our husband knows of your clandestine visits to that house. He feels betrayed. You had better have a good explanation. With that she melted back out of the room, leaving Tahirih dazed.

Tahirih went to find the twins and was relieved to see them in the care of Parvin. She looked for the other children as well, and found her daughter chasing a ball around the hallways and Husayn ordering his friend Omar to bring him a sweet from the kitchen without Cook's finding out about it. Everything appeared normal, but she had a terrible sense that nothing would ever be the same again.

"Parvin, I will feed one twin while you take care of the other," she said. "Come, my little love," she cooed as she picked up the one already changed and snuggled her face into her belly. "Is it time to eat?" She was answered with little fingers pulling her hair.

"What preparations are being made for the party on Thursday?" she asked in as normal a tone as she could manage. Ismail had invited twenty of his bazaari neighbors to a dinner party in celebration of yet another religious holiday. Actually, she suspected that his real reason for the party was that he wanted people to remember that he now had a second wife, which was a mark of his prosperity. Although her own life had been disrupted by Mahvash, still she was happy that her husband was able to demonstrate his fortune, and she wanted to be sure that this was a perfect occasion for him.

"Have the rooms all been cleaned and aired properly? You know that Firidun needs to be watched to assure that he does things properly."

Parvin shared Tahirih's low opinion of the bully, and she had no problem acknowledging it. "Every time I want something done around here, he is off somewhere doing Allah knows what, but he is never where he needs to be to help with the work. I wish Ismail Agha would get rid of him."

"So do I, Parvin. But I don't think that is likely to happen. I saw Zahreh trying to move some furniture yesterday because he was not there when he was needed. The poor girl hurt her back pushing against the sideboard in the large salon. Now she is incapacitated, just when we need more help. Oh well, we have managed before, and I imagine we will find ways to do whatever needs to be done." Tahirih laughed with a joviality she did not feel.

"Mistress, you must not take on too much for yourself. There is the problem with your father, and I know that you are also concerned about your mother's health. You must take care of yourself, or you will never be able to take care of your husband and the children and this household and everything else you try to do," the elderly servant advised.

"Well, after the party I will relax a little," Tahirih promised. "My father is doing better now. My job is to be sure that Ismail is taken care of, and everything else will work itself out. Everyone here helps me do my job, so it is really not so hard."

Tahirih then went to look for Husayn, who was still playing with Omar. Just as she found them, Ismail walked into the house unexpectedly. He spotted her and immediately ceased movement, just staring and looking like someone she had never seen before.

"What is it, my husband?" she asked with great concern. "What is so terribly wrong?"

Ismail, who had always been careful to talk about private matters in a way that no one else heard, began shouting in the middle of his house, so loudly that Tahirih jumped backward in alarm.

"You call yourself my wife. The mother of my children. Never again will you be addressed in that manner. You have mocked everything I have built up. Get out of my sight."

Tahirih stayed rooted where she was. She could not speak, and she did not move. After a moment Ismail resumed his tirade. "You blasphemer. You heretic. You destroyer of family. How did you think I would not hear of your treachery?"

His eyes blazed with fury and he raised his hand to strike her, but stopped just in time. Suddenly Parvin appeared from nowhere and enfolded the astounded Tahirih in her arms, whisking her away from her husband's fury.

"Master, please, have pity. Whatever she has done, she meant no harm." Parvin tried to bundle Tahirih away to another room out of her husband's range, but he followed.

"I trusted you, Tahirih. I have put my life in your hands. Now I learn that you go to a house where blasphemy is treated as something wonderful. What has she told you, this witch, this adulterer? What poison has she spilled into your ears so that you can bring it into my house to corrupt my life?"

Tahirih cringed at his words, then her anger grew when he began calling Soraya names. Soraya was the gentlest, kindest, most selfless person she had ever known.

"You are wrong, Ismail. Soraya and her husband are not blasphemers and they are not evil. They are honest people who believe in what they say and do. I don't know if their belief is correct or not, but I do know that they are faithful in behaving in accordance with what they claim to believe. It was only today that Soraya told me of their religious convictions. I never knew before. Then she told me that I should not return to their home because it would cause disruption for you if I were knowingly going to a Baha'i home –"

She realized that she was talking to the air. Ismail had shrunk away from her when she admitted that she had knowingly been in the company of a heretic, and had run from the house.

"Parvin," she said, turning to her trusted servant, "what will happen to me now?" She trembled uncontrollably and then looked to see Husayn standing nearby. She tried to stand with dignity but her knees gave way and Parvin had to catch her.

Husayn spoke defiantly. "What have you done to upset my Daddy? I don't like you, Mama." He turned and strode away to another room, striking his sister on the way.

"Parvin, help me to my room." Tahirih choked out the words. She saw her world crumbling and knew that she was at the very edge of a precipice with no bottom. She did not dare look down. "Help me."

Parvin guided her mistress to the room Tahirih had shared lovingly with a devoted husband for more than eight years. Parvin knew, even if the Mistress did not yet, that this would not be her room much longer. Surely Ismail would throw her out of the house that very day.

Mahvash was behind all this, Parvin was sure. That sorceress. Look what had happened to this very peaceful household ever since she came. Now she had gotten exactly what she had been conniving for, first place in Ismail's regard. Oh, she was a cunning little charlatan. Men, Parvin thought angrily. Sometimes they could not see beyond the nose on their ugly faces. Well, she would have to do whatever she could to keep her mistress safe.

She got Tahirih onto the bed, the same bed where all her children had been conceived and born. Where the last one had died. Where she had grieved for her father and slept alone while Ismail was at Madam Jamal's, and then in that slut's bed. Parvin wondered if the Mistress even knew about Madam Jamal's.

"Get out of this room. I will speak with my wife alone."

Ismail had returned and his frenzy was unabated. Parvin went to the corner, hoping to still be near if her mistress needed her. "GET OUT." The bellow could be heard throughout the house and Parvin edged out the door and slightly down the hall.

Ismail turned to his wife, who was trying to sit up. His voice became calm and cold as she had never heard it before.

"I am leaving. When I return, you will be out of this house. I have already sent Firidun to notify your mother that you will be there shortly. Parvin will go with you. The children are mine and will remain at my house. You will never again corrupt them with your words or by your behavior. I do not expect to ever lay eyes on you again. If you should happen to see me anywhere, anywhere at all, turn away because if I ever see you I will publicly condemn you as a blasphemer."

He turned on his heel and departed.

HERE,

THERE AND

SOMEWHERE

NEW

CHAPTER ONE

It had been several years since the Shah's beloved wife Jila had disappeared. Although the Shah never fully recovered from this personal loss, he maintained active involvement in public affairs as a way to use his time effectively until Allah called for him. He had married several more times, but no one brought him the comfort that Jila had, and he was a lonely, often bitter man.

Over the years, however, certain people brought him a temporary feeling of relaxation, and on this evening he was looking forward to an invigorating few hours with his Ambassador to Russia, who would be accompanied, as usual, by his lovely wife, Ohmeed.

Indeed, Mojtabeh Amuzegar had just returned from his final trip to Moscow. In the near future, the Shah decided, Mojtabeh would become a direct advisor to the court in Tehran. This was a fitting reward for so many years of dedicated service. The Shah knew that, for Mojtabeh, it would mean no more long separations from his wife of more than five years. Because both Mojtabeh and the charming Ohmeed had a way of allowing him to forget his past miseries, if only briefly, he would be glad to have them permanently in Tehran.

On this evening, Mojtabeh had asked if he might bring with him the merchant from Shiraz who had been so active in arranging valuable trade initiatives with Russia. After initially denying the bazaari permission to trade in a foreign country, the Shah had eventually granted permission three years before. Now, thanks to this Ismail, Persian tea was found not only in Moscow, but many other Russian cities as well. The Shah appreciated the significant additions to palace coffers that resulted from the efforts of this bazaari, and it was clear, the Shah reflected, that the merchant had likewise benefited from the palace's indulgence. His clothing was now in style with Tehran customs, and his second wife, who frequently accompanied him to the palace, adorned herself like a princess.

He was amused to note, as he greeted Ismail and the second wife, not only the more stylish clothing, but also Ismail's greatly improved communication skills. He recalled that when Ismail had first come to the palace, he had been almost a tongue-tied child. Now he spoke comfortably and confidently in the presence of his Shah. That wife of his, however, was a bit of a curmudgeon, not at all like the first wife, whom the Shah had liked. His Majesty eyed Mahvash skeptically as they all entered.

After initial greetings to all the visitors, the Shah turned his full attention to Mojtabeh.

"Tell me," he commanded, "how life is for you, my dear Mojtabeh, since you have permanently become a part of the Tehran landscape."

"Your Majesty," Mojtabeh murmured after a few seconds of introspective silence. "Your kindness in allowing me to remain in Tehran is appreciated beyond my poor capacity to express it." The Shah grinned as one of his most accomplished rhetoricians pretended to be at a loss for words. "For nearly thirty years I have been your servant in Moscow, and I will surely miss serving your Majesty there. Now, however, I am greatly honored that you wish me to be here in Tehran to continue my service to you. I will always give you my best advice on political matters."

Mojtabeh paused. "Regarding trade issues, however, I am less informed than I should be. To assist with that, Your Majesty, I recommend the wisdom of Ismail Agha, who has thrown wide the doors to expanded trade with Russia." He nodded approvingly in Ismail's direction. "Ismail and his lovely wife Mahvash have been to Moscow and London on several occasions to promote trade and advance the interests of the Persian empire."

Neither the Shah nor Mojtabeh thought Ismail's wife was lovely, other than in appearance. Certainly she was clever and appeared subservient when necessary. She supported Ismail in everything he did, but Mojtabeh found her to be devious in a manner that even an accomplished diplomat found annoying.

"Just last year," Mojtabeh informed the Shah, "Mahvash Khanem accompanied her husband on a trip to Moscow. This was, I believe, not even two months after giving birth to their second child. Truly that is astounding dedication to one's husband."

Mojtabeh pretended to be awed, but was in truth appalled. He could not comprehend that a woman with a newborn infant as well as a year-and-half old child would leave them in the care of servants for several months and travel hundreds of miles away. Although he was disgusted with such outrageous behavior, Mojtabeh's diplomatic training prevailed, and he spoke to Mahvash with courtesy and feigned respect.

"Mahvash Khanem, I hope you will again be able to accompany Ismail Agha on his next trip to Russia. A woman who is not only comely but wise will enable him to act in the best interests of Persia as well as himself."

Mahvash preened. "My husband is very talented and his business acumen exceeds that of anyone I know. I travel with him only because I cannot bear to be separated from his presence for a moment, but surely not because he needs me."

She thought this answer to be very astute, not only flattering to her husband, but also showing herself to be the utterly devoted wife. She was sure that Tahirih would never have come up with so quick and excellent a response. Although it angered her, she somehow could not rid herself of the instinct to compare what she did with what she thought Tahirih might have done in the same circumstance.

"Indeed, he is fortunate to have such a loving and protective wife," Mojtabeh answered blandly and looked to Ismail for his reaction. When none was forthcoming, he introduced another subject, after glancing at the Shah who appeared content to have Mojtabeh handling the direction of the conversation for the moment.

"I understand that Husayn now helps you with running the stall at the bazaar when you must be away from home."

Ismail was very proud of his eldest son, and answered with pride pouring out of his voice. "Yes, he has become quite an assistant to Abbas." He turned to the Shah to explain. "A few years ago, Your Majesty, I took a partner so that I could expand my business dealings into other cities. One day he brought an idea to me for advice, and I took him under my wing. Well, you know how one thing leads to another, and after a while I was allowing him to do some buying for me. He found some strains of a new tea in India to mix with our Persian teas, and they have become quite popular. Now he is training my eldest son Husayn in the business of business, so to speak.

"It is too bad that poor Ismail is so busy all the time," Mahvash interjected. "He would love to be able to spend more time with his sons, especially his two youngest, but he must be gone so much. My father is also a tea merchant, and they work together a great deal." She was subtly reminding her husband how much he owed to this marriage, which he had been made to understand all too often.

The Shah noted the discomfort on Ismail's face. He wanted an opinion on something that was of great interest to him and was sure that Ismail could give good advice, so he changed the direction of the conversation.

"Ismail Agha," he casually remarked, "my experienced and devoted servant Mojtabeh has mentioned to me that, as a youth, you traveled around Persia a great deal. And you, Madam," he added", nodding toward Ohmeed, "lived in the western provinces for several years, I believe. Let me inquire of both of you what you think about the notion of having a railroad traversing from

Tehran to, say, Tabriz or Urmieh in the west. And another one going south to Shiraz, perhaps. Would there be benefit to such an idea?"

Mahvash opened her mouth to begin an answer on behalf of her husband, but was silenced by a steely look from Ismail.

"Your Majesty," Ismail answered, "I know that there are some who believe railroads and modern farming methods and other ideas that are not native to Persian thinking represent satanic influence. However, I believe that increasing crop production and providing a way to get products to market in distant places will do nothing but enhance Persian economic interests. Certainly for my own tea business, it would be far better for my representative Abbas to ride a train for a day or two to inspect and choose what to purchase, rather than take weeks to go by horseback across the mountains. Once he made his selections, they could then come to market quickly. If it would be good for one merchant, then surely it would be excellent for a large number of merchants."

"Your Majesty," Ohmeed added before Mahvash could interrupt, "Ismail Agha refers to the business perspective of railroads. But there is also a personal side, I think. When I lived in Urmieh, which is nearly a thousand miles from Tehran, I missed my family terribly. There was no way for me to get home because of the distance. If railroads were to be built not only to Urmieh and Shiraz, but to many cities throughout Persia, families would not have to feel so irrevocably separated."

"Well, I don't know about that." Mahvash jumped in uninvited. "When a woman marries, she becomes a part of her husband's family. If she must leave her own, then so be it. She should not complain, but make herself useful to her husband in whatever way she can."

Ohmeed did not reply to the unsolicited remark, and to Mahvash's embarrassment, neither did anyone else, not even her husband. After a moment of silence, the Shah returned to his concern about railroads.

"As you know, the mullahs run around my palace as if they own the place. They are forever giving me advice I do not want to hear, and one mullah will say the opposite of the next. But the consensus seems to be that railroads are evil. For that reason alone," he laughed, "I think I will put my influence behind the idea."

"Your Majesty, you are the heart and soul of Persia," Mojtabeh declared vehemently. "Whatever you say will be done. It is my privilege and duty to assure that your commands are obeyed. The issue is finished. Railroads will be built wherever you deem advisable."

Mojtabeh's sentiments were echoed by all others present. Although they knew it was no longer true, they continued to adhere to the appearance of invincibility of any decision made by their Shah.

The conversation turned to other topics, and Mojtabeh let the talk wash over him. As he listened with only half an ear, he ruminated about his friend Ismail's present marriage and contrasted it with the first, which had been to Tahirih, the daughter of his cousin, Haji Youssef.

He knew that Tahirih, relegated to living with her parents because of some incident provoked by Mahvash, had devotedly cared for her father until Haji Youssef was finally taken to join Allah two summers before. His own beloved wife, Ohmeed, had remained in touch with Tahirih and her mother over the years, keeping him well informed of the situation there.

According to Ohmeed, Tahirih quickly learned the eye blinking technique her husband had established, and essentially took over the formidable task of caring for her father as her mother sank into lethargy, apparently unable to face the reality of her husband's decline.

Not only was Tahirih the one caring for her father, but she also had to manage the daily affairs of what had been a huge estate. Most of Haji Youssef's servants, believing that the house had been twice cursed -- first by Haji's illness, then by the forced return of a heretic -- had deserted one by one. Only Parvin, Tahirih's long time servant, had remained faithful, but she was now so old that she had become more of a burden than a help to Tahirih. The estate had declined in value, and now Tahirih and her mother lived in near poverty. Mojtabeh tried to send assistance, but was thwarted by Tahirih's older brother who was apparently waiting to reclaim the family property for himself when its value deteriorated to the point that no one else would want it.

Mojtabeh had eventually learned that Firidun was Tahirih's half-brother. After his father's death, Ismail insisted that Firidun move to another town, where he caused incessant trouble. He was accused of stealing from neighbors, bullying the local children, and behaving in an unseemly manner with other men's wives. No one mourned when he was knifed to death one night by a furious husband.

Firidun is not worth my thought, Mojtabeh remonstrated with himself. On the other hand, Mojtabeh had always had great respect for Tahirih. Although he understood Ismail's outrage at Tahirih's faulty judgment in befriending people who adhered to a heretical faith, nonetheless, he was saddened that this normally temperate man had banished Tahirih completely from his life for this one lapse. Aside from the religious blunder, Tahirih was a good woman who had always been a loving wife and devoted mother.

Mojtabeh's daydreaming was cut short by a sudden turn of the conversation.

"Mojtabeh," the Shah was asking him, "do you recall a few conversations we had about this group called the Baha'is? I hear that their teachings have spread into Russia and that novelist, what is his name -- Tolstoy? -- has taken quite a fancy to what they have to say. What did you hear about that while you were in Russia?"

Mojtabeh did not miss a beat and immediately answered the query with his typical non committal type response. "Tolstoy has blown hot and cold on that issue, Your Majesty. At first he wanted to investigate to see if there might be anything interesting there that he could include in his novels. He was very impressed with their teachings, and actually had a Baha'i come to live with him for a while as a teacher. I am not sure just what his attitude toward them is right now. Like most Russians, he goes back and forth with his opinions. "

Mojtabeh noted that Ismail had blanched and turned his head away from his wife when the Shah began talking about the Baha'is. Perhaps, he thought, Ismail still did have some feelings for Tahirih, and Mojtabeh resolved to press the issue at a later time.

"Baha'u'llah has been living in the Ottoman Empire for years as a prisoner of the Turkish Sultan. This has been at my direction, as you know," the Shah announced. "They are keeping him in a harsh prison in Acre, but even so, he manages to turn his jailers and even many of the city people into adherents. Do you suppose there is anything to his claim that he is The Promised One?"

The Shah was truly puzzled by the tenacity of this exile who had converted so many Persians and Turks to His teachings despite harsh retaliation against anyone who proclaimed the Faith openly. Even some of the mullahs at the palace, including Mullah Askar, who had performed the marriage ceremony for Mojtabeh and Ohmeed, had become disciples, and they had approached the Shah to try to explain the teachings.

"Absolutely not," assured Mojtabeh. "It is all trickery and smoothness of words. No one can replace Muhammad."

But the Shah wondered. Hadn't the Jews said the same when Jesus proclaimed that He was the Messenger Allah had sent to bring a new faith to the world? Hadn't the Christians discounted Muhammad in the same way?

"Your Majesty," Ismail interjected, "I see that my wife has suddenly become quite pale. I must beg your leave for us to depart; I fear that she may have become ill."

She did not look any different to anyone else in the room, and everyone understood that Ismail was finding an excuse to leave because the conversation had taken a turn that disturbed him greatly.

"Of course, Ismail Agha. Madam, I pray that you will recover quickly."

Ismail and Mahvash rose to leave, she for once not countering what her husband said.

"Your Majesty, we are humbled by your gracious permission to visit this evening. We pray for your health and well-being everyday." Mahvash nodded her agreement with the sentiments expressed by her husband,and they backed out of the room slowly, producing formal bows and curtsies as they left.

"Mojtabeh," the Shah pronounced after they had departed, "be thankful you do not have a wife such as that," and he smiled appreciatively at Ohmeed, who blushed and looked away.

"Your Majesty, she means well. However, Ismail's first wife was far more gentle. She was my cousin's daughter and even today remains Ohmeed's friend. Unfortunately, as you know, Ismail banished her when she consorted with some Baha'is several years ago. I think he might regret what he now sees as a mistake. But Mahvash seems to be truly committed to helping her husband however she can." Ever the diplomat, Mojtabeh tried to smooth over Mahvash's behavior.

"Being obnoxious does not help much, I think," muttered the Shah. They spoke of other matters for another few minutes, then Mojtabeh could see that the Shah had had enough company for the evening.

"Your Majesty, please allow us to leave now. We do not wish to tire you. There are so many matters for you to juggle all the time, and we hope that we have been able to provide some brief diversion from all your cares. I shall begin tomorrow to pursue the matter of the railroads."

As they journeyed home, Mojtabeh speculated to Ohmeed that possibly Ismail might decide to reconcile with Tahirih someday. Ohmeed shared this hope, and they agreed to encourage it subtly if they could.

CHAPTER TWO

Indeed, Ismail did miss Tahirih's gentle ways. Although Mahvash's family was useful to his business ambitions, it was becoming more and more apparent that his second wife was a very difficult woman to live with. All too often, she talked about her family's rightful place in the power structure of Persia. Somehow, she had gotten it in her head that her father not only could, but should, dictate Persian political and economic decisions, even to the Shah himself. Once or twice, Mahvash had actually said inappropriate things within the hearing of the Shah. Ismail had thus far been able to amend the flow of conversation so that her meaning was not clear, but one day she was going to say something that could totally interrupt everything he had worked for.

Far worse than her personality, however, was the fact that she clearly was not a good mother to his children. This truly disturbed him. Perhaps, he thought, he should initiate contact with Tahirih again. For quite some time now, he admitted to himself, he had been longing for the wisdom of her words.

What would her reaction be, he wondered briefly. For an instant, he thought of how he would feel if he had been abruptly expelled from someone's life, then after many years, that person reappeared. He would be furious, he imagined, and confused. But soon he began to rationalize that a woman would actually be grateful to be allowed back into the luxury of his lifestyle rather than having to endure the poverty she and her mother had been surviving in for some time now. Fleetingly, he considered that he was the cause of that poverty, but it soon slipped out of his consciousness as he considered what he could now offer her. Yes, he ultimately concluded, it was time to take her back into his life.

He would begin, he decided, by stopping by one day, unannounced. He would take a gift of some sort, perhaps some imported fabric for making curtains. No, that might not work. It would give away that he had been having someone keep a surreptitious eye on her. Otherwise, how would he know that the furnishings in the house had become threadbare? Well, then, fruit and nuts and spices. In large quantity. That would do it.

It had been half a decade since she had seen him. How would he look to her now? He had put on some weight. He realized that she hadn't, from the few times he had seen her at a distance. With all the financial changes she had faced since her father's death, maybe she did not have enough to eat. He pondered what that might be like, but could not actually imagine it.

He reflected that, in truth, his first wife had been poorly cared for of all these years. Actually, he mused, she had not been taken care of at all. No one watched out for her. Instead, it was the other way around. She had assumed responsibility first for caring for her father, and now her mother and the servant, Parvin. In addition, she had been hiring people to manage the little bit of crop production still going on at the farm and trying her best to supervise that activity.

This was the first time he had really considered life from her point of view. Always before he had exalted in knowing how difficult life was for her, which he felt was deserved since she had come so close to ruining his own. Now he wondered if it had been right to drive her into such difficult circumstances.

His fury over the Baha'i incident had long since abated. Actually, as he had come to know more about Baha'i beliefs, he found them inspiring rather than horrifying, although he still believed it would be dangerous for him to acknowledge his revised thinking openly. Covertly, though, he had, in his unceasing desire to understand the world around him, listened to fragments of conversations here and there, and had come to admire many of the principles the Baha'is stood for.

He remembered being fascinated when he heard the analysis that through the Zoroastrians, Allah had initially sent the teachings of family loyalty. Then beginning with the Jews, and expanding to Christians and later the Muslims, the degree of that allegiance had amplified first to tribal, then national loyalties. Now from this Baha'u'llah came the teaching that all mankind was one in the eyes of Allah, that humanity should be regarded as a universal brotherhood. In thinking about his interactions with the Kurds in the west, the Russians in an entirely different country, and other nationalities that he dealt with regularly, he found that there were indeed more similarities among peoples than there were differences. The concept of universality appealed to Ismail's sense of rightness.

On the other hand, in the society where he lived, Baha'i teachings were considered heresy by the clergy. The clergy controlled everything -- social mores, political power, everything. Ismail did not dare cause affront, because he reveled in the prestige he had earned by becoming Shiraz's leading entrepreneur. Acknowledging Baha'i beliefs would be too dangerous to his business and his lifestyle. His wealth grew day by day, and now he was even thinking of taking a third wife. Perhaps, though, before he seriously considered number three, he ought to see what could be done to make things right with number one.

Ismail set about working on what he considered his latest entrepreneurial enterprise, recapturing his first wife. Typically, he planned it out, stage by stage, just as if he were organizing a business deal.

First, there would be the small talk to create a relaxed atmosphere, then a gradual introduction of what he wanted to accomplish, followed up by promises of benefit to both sides. After giving careful thought to various options that might come up, he finally set a date for putting the scheme into action. Two weeks from today he would drop by her home.

CHAPTER THREE

In the shadows created by the voluminous clouds overhead, Tahirih walked wearily back to the house, hoping that today her mother was feeling a little better. When Haji Youssef suffered his stroke, her mother lost her forward-looking convictions. Now that he had passed on the next world, Manizheh barely seemed to want to survive day to day. The transformation in her mother's outlook angered Tahirih, who felt that even though she too had suffered greatly, she still had not lost hope that things might someday get better.

Tahirih was now close to thirty years old, so her mother must be nearly sixty, she conjectured, never having been told for sure. Tahirih understood that her mother did not have the strength, either physically or emotionally, to contribute to daily work at the farm. Tahirih ran everything, with doddering assistance from Parvin. Nearly everything was on Tahirih's shoulders, and it was a heavy load indeed.

During these years, her friend Soraya had been an enormous comfort to Tahirih. Not only had she continued to teach Tahirih to read, but had also added enough math lessons so that Tahirih knew when debtors were cheating her, which happened often.

Tahirih sold fruit from the orchards, wool and meat from the sheep, and grain from the vast fields. Her hard work somehow allowed her to earn enough money to keep the estate running, just as her father had directed her to do before he died. Her eldest brother initially tried to defy his father's edict, but other family members had heard their mother interpret Haji's eyeblinks two days before he died, and they forced the brother to respect their father's final wish. However, because of Tahirih's continuing contact with Soraya, her family shunned her otherwise. They offered no help with managing the estate or paying the bills.

Knowing that her mother was uncomfortable in the reduced circumstances now facing her, Tahirih tried to convince Manizheh to live with one of her other daughters. Oddly, Manizheh insisted that Tahirih needed her mother, and would not leave the estate. However, mother and daughter had bitter disagreements over Tahirih's continuing to associate with avowed heretics, but on this issue, Tahirih would not give in. She pointed out the material benefits gained by her learning to read and cipher. The spiritual benefits of her continued contact with Soraya and her family were even greater, she contended, but this argument fell on Manizheh's deaf ears. Manizheh insisted that if Tahirih would give up this craziness, her husband might hear of it and allow her back into his home.

As Tahirih approached the house, she saw her mother standing outside. That was unusual, Tahirih thought, and she hastened her steps a little. She peered ahead to see if she could discern what was the matter, and saw great agitation on her mother's face. She tried to hurry, but was so tired, she could barely get one foot in front of the other.

"Mother, what is it?" she inquired fearfully, when she finally drew near enough to converse. Perhaps something had happened to Parvin.

"You have been gone so long. Where have you been?" her mother inquired petulantly.

She sounded like little Husayn, Tahirih thought, but pushed the remembrance away, since it hurt too badly.

"I had to go to the market to buy eggs and bread. I told you before I left. Then I stopped to see Soraya for a few minutes. Is anything the matter; you look so upset?"

Her mother spat on the ground at the mention of Soraya's name.

"That woman. She is the cause of all this adversity. Why must you continue to see her?" Her mother was now furious.

"Mother, we have talked about this many times. I am sorry if it bothers you, but truly, she is one of my few comforts. Let's not argue."

"Not argue, eh? Well, let me tell you. Your husband was just here looking for you, and you were out talking to *her*."

Tahirih stopped in her tracks. "Ismail was here? Looking for me?"

"He will be back in an hour. He brought pomegranates. And dates. And other things, too. For once, we will have something pleasant to eat."

"Mother, what did he say? He vowed never to lay eyes on me again. Why was he here?"

"Come inside and get yourself into something decent looking. Come along, now. Hurry up. He will be back soon."

Tahirih allowed herself to be rushed into the house. At the closet, Manizheh pushed Tahirih aside and selected the nicest looking dress her daughter still had.

Tahirih could not imagine what this meant. Apparently, though, as she ruminated on what her mother had said, he had come in a friendly manner, if he brought gifts. Might she be allowed to see her children again? Hope arose in her heart and bubbled into her face, as she dressed with more animation.

"Mother, do you think he has come to talk about allowing me to see my babies? They are not babies now, are they? The twins are older than Husayn was when I left. Do you think it is possible that I could see them again?" She almost began to babble as excitement overtook her, and she looked desperately to find her makeup that she had not used in years.

She was still checking her appearance when she heard her mother say, "He is here. Go sit in the salon. I will have Parvin bring tea." Tahirih slipped her best shoes onto her swollen feet and almost ran to the living room. On the way, however, she paused for a moment.

"Mother, I will speak with Ismail alone. It is very important that you do not come into the room until I come to get you. Will you promise me that?"

Manizheh glared at her daughter, but acquiesced. Tahirih

went on alone to the salon, and then suddenly, there he was, looking prosperous and healthy, if a little heavier. She hardly dared to glance at him, until she noticed that he was smiling. He was saying words she could not fathom. How was she? What did he mean, how was she? What did he expect? Tears welled behind her eyes, but she refused to let them out.

"Hello, Ismail Agha," she greeted formally. "Please be seated. Parvin will bring tea." No other words would come. Not 'why are you here'. Not 'how are my children'. Not anything. She looked down at the carpet and waited.

Ismail was almost equally tongue tied, except that he had had time to anticipate this meeting. He had prepared himself emotionally, whereas Tahirih had been blindsided. He looked at his wife, and the conflicting emotions almost caused him to stumble over his words.

"Tahirih Khanem."

She noticed that he addressed her formally, as he would a respected person. It was the same way he used to address her when they lived together.

Then Ismail stopped, unable to bring any other words into thought formation.

She looked up at him, and suddenly a calm came to her, enveloping her with such radiance that she was able to smile. "This is a difficult moment for both of us, Ismail. Perhaps it is best if you just tell me why you have come." It was said forthrightly, with no bitterness or venom.

"Yes, of course. You were always able to say the right thing to make it easier for me to talk." His shoulders started to relax, and his voice lost its tension. "First, let me tell you that the children are all well. Husayn comes to the bazaar with me everyday, and he is going to be a good businessman. Scheherazade helps with taking care of the house and the younger children. She will be a very good housewife. The twins are both doing well. Everyone is healthy. The small pox that struck many homes last year did not come to mine. I was very fortunate."

Perhaps you were, Tahirih thought to herself. Here it killed the last servant who had stayed with us after my father died, so now only my mother and Parvin and I live in this huge house. But she did not say this.

He continued. "Tahirih, it is time for us to put the past where it belongs. I was very angry at one time because I believed you had betrayed me and endangered everything I worked so hard to achieve. But now we must look forward. It is time to forgive what has happened and move on."

Tahirih straightened her dress as well as her back. She would be honest with her husband as she had not been in the past.

"Ismail, you speak of moving forward. In my own way, I have been doing that already. Although the physical conditions you see here are not good," she looked around at the worn furnishings and poorly maintained physical structure of her home, "there are other dimensions to life that I have found. I have come to believe that everyday I must do three things for myself, and if I accomplish them, then I have something to look forward to for the next day. Are you interested in hearing what I have learned?"

Ismail was astounded that Tahirih spoke so forthrightly. "Indeed, please tell me," he encouraged.

"I believe that there are multiple aspects to all human beings. First, there is the physical part of all of us, that part that needs food and clothing and shelter. Obviously, that dimension of me has not been pampered as it used to be, but it has been adequately taken care of. I have met this need basically, and have learned that it is not so important as I used to think."

She paused, looking to see if he were paying attention. He seemed rapt.

"Then there is the intellectual side of a human being," she continued. "For me, I want to learn something new everyday. One day it will be how to do something, another day it will be an effort to understand why things happen as they do. In any case, each and every day I must learn something I did not know the day before."

She paused, then proceeded confidently. "In order for me to be able to take care of that part of me, I have learned to read." Now she looked directly at Ismail, but did not pause. Now I can discover more than just what I hear people say. I am finally able to discern what I myself believe, not just what someone else believes is suitable for me to know."

Ismail began to interrupt, but Tahirih pushed ahead. "Most importantly, Ismail, I have discovered that there is a spiritual side to all humans. Indeed, I firmly believe that we people are spiritual beings, not just physical creatures. The spiritual part of me needs nurturing just as much as my body needs food. Over the last few years, it has become vital to me to learn as much as I can about Allah. I no longer base what I think solely on what someone else says. I read, then I make decisions and accept responsibility for what I choose to do regarding my religious beliefs."

She glanced at him, drew a deep breath, and forged on to her conclusion. "Ismail, I truly believe that what the Baha'is teach does come from Allah. It is my comfort to believe this. I would have a very difficult time listening to the ramblings of Mullah Mohsin now without saying something to refute his poorly thought out arguments. Ismail, I have declared myself a Baha'i."

Tahirih stopped and fearfully awaited Ismail's response.

He thought for a moment, then broke into a chuckle. "Tahirih, I remember that you always tried to do what I wanted, but there was still a bit of rebelliousness in you that I used to resent. Now as I look back, I think I really admired your inquiring spirit more than I resented it. Believe it or not, I too have come to believe that reading and independent thinking is important. Actually, I have made arrangements for Husayn to attend the House of Science in Tehran beginning next year, where he will get a good education, untainted by the teachings of the clergy."

Tahirih's heart leapt, and she forgave her husband whatever he had done to her if he had truly made such provisions for her son to be educated. "Is this true, that my son will get an education? Ismail, you can never know how thrilled my heart is at this moment."

Ismail discerned that he had made progress toward his goal, and pressed his advantage. "About Mullah Mohsin. I am sorry to tell you that he died last year."

"Oh, Ismail, I am so sorry," Tahirih murmured. "I know he was important to you. What happened?"

"He involved himself a lot in rooting out what he contended was heresy, but eventually I saw that it was just a way to make himself wealthy at the expense of less fortunate people." Ismail lowered his head for a moment.

"A home owned by a Baha'i was being burned, and Mullah Mohsin was there. I am sorry, I know that is disturbing to you," Ismail acknowledged, as he saw the horror on Tahirih's face. "Mohsin ran back into the house for a third time to get one more carpet. Suddenly, his robe caught fire, and no one could put it out. The poor man suffered terrible burns, and eventually died. It was a horrible death for him."

Ismail paused before adding, "However, I had begun to learn that his thinking was not always right. Indeed, I have not relied on his judgment very much at all for the last couple of years."

Despite not liking him, Tahirih felt Mohsin's loss, and she said a silent prayer for his soul. After a moment, however, she returned to the subject that Ismail had neatly avoided answering.

"Ismail, what is it that you want of me. Why, after five years of silence, have you suddenly appeared at my house, and are conversing with me in what would probably be considered a normal manner?"

Now Ismail was more relaxed, and he answered her directly. "Tahirih, my wife, it is time for us to settle our differences. I have come to bring you home."

Just like that. Not do you want to come back to live with

me. No discussion of how she would live in the same house with the woman who had usurped her husband and her home and her children. And what about her mother, who now depended on her? She could not believe Ismail could be so thick-witted.

"Just how would that be accomplished, Ismail?" she asked, with more than a touch of sarcasm in her voice.

Ismail did not hear it. "You and your mother and Parvin could come back with me today, if you would like. Or tomorrow, if today is too sudden." He made it sound so simple.

"Have our children been told that you want me to return?" She wondered if he had told them that their mother would be coming back today, without even consulting her.

"No, not yet. I did not know when you would be able to return."

"You know, Ismail," she said, looking around her, "this is my home, too. This is where I grew up and where I have lived for the last five years. Actually, I lived in this house for more years than I lived in yours. As I tried to explain to you, I no longer blindly do whatever I am told. I don't know if you would be comfortable with me as I am now."

"Tahirih, my wife." Ismail truly spoke from his heart. "I have never stopped loving you. I have missed you more than I was ever willing to admit to myself. It seems we both have changed, and I believe our changes are in the same direction. Today we realize that life is more than just about material things. I always wanted to understand the world around me, but did not take time to consider whether it was more important to make money or to live right. Sometimes the two go together, but frequently they do not."

"If they did not, Ismail, if you had to sacrifice your wealth for your beliefs, could you do that?"

As she asked that impossible question, she suddenly recalled Soraya's story about her pregnant cousin Givih who had been massacred by a group of zealot Muslims. There had not been wealth there to sacrifice, but something far greater, life itself. Givih's life, her husband's and little girl's lives, even her brother who was not Baha'i but happened to be visiting at the wrong time. The brother who had just finished education at the House of Science.

"Oh, that would never happen," Ismail laughed. "I give to the mosque and to the poor in the street. I do what Islam teaches me. There would never be a problem."

"Ismail, perhaps you did not comprehend what I said. I believe in the teachings that Mullah Mohsin and so many others call heresy. I am Baha'i. Can you live with that?"

It took Ismail a moment to answer. "Tahirih, at one time I would have forbidden you to believe these things. But you have made it clear that you have taken on a new individuality. I cannot argue with that. Indeed, I must respect it because it demonstrates who you are. It is what I have loved most, and also become most angry with, about you."

Again he paused, then plunged forward. "If you agree not to discuss your convictions with anyone who would cause danger to me, I can accept that a woman can think independently and hold her own beliefs, even if they are contrary to those of her husband."

When he had come here today, he had no concept that he would make such a concession. What had happened? Who was this new woman, daring to bargain with him regarding his own future? He had just agreed to allow a heretic back into his home, except that he no longer believed that Baha'I teachings were heresy. Tahirih was capable of discretion, he knew. Life had just taken a very interesting turn for him, and he looked forward to it as he did his business ventures, with some apprehension, but a final certainty that it would all turn out well.

Tahirih went to find her mother. As she explained the agreement that she and Ismail had just reached, her mother expressed overwhelming joy. Tahirih merely hoped that it would all turn out as well as Ismail envisioned.

CHAPTER FOUR

Tahirih did not move back the next day. Instead, she first notified her eldest brother that the estate would now be available for his management. She then made arrangements for her mother to live with one of her sisters, believing that Manizheh would be more comfortable than in the household where Tahireh would be returning to an unknown situation. Finally, she prepared herself emotionally for a reunion with her children, not knowing what they believed of her now after five years of being influenced by Mahvash.

Three days later, she did return, and indeed the adjustment was a horrendous ordeal for her. Mahvash was condescending, and none of her old servants were still there.. Her children barely remembered who she was, and she had to fight hard to earn their trust and confidence.

Little Scheherazade had been most quickly won back.

"Mommy, Mommy," Scheherazade had shouted when Tahirih entered the house. "Here are flowers from the garden outside. I take care of them myself. Aren't they beautiful? They are for you."

Tahirih had swept her eight year old child into her arms, sobbing silently while praising Allah for allowing her this moment of sheer ecstasy.

"My sweetest Scheherazade," she had murmured, "how wonderful, beyond belief, it is to hold you again," and she had kissed her daughter over and over. Being kissed was an experience the child had not enjoyed for five years.

The twins were more reticent. Having been infants when their mother disappeared, they were not sure just who this new woman was. Quickly, however, Tahirih established herself as someone much nicer than the other woman in the house. Tahirih never sent them away as soon as their father left for work, and she allowed them to call her Mother. Little by little, the twins too were exhibiting comfort in her presence, as they noticed that their father treated this woman very nicely. More nicely than he treated the other woman these days.

Husayn, however, considered himself beyond needing a mother. He was now eleven years old, and everyday he accompanied his father to the bazaar. In his young eyes, he was a man, and he certainly had no need for a woman telling him what to do. Just short of disrespectful, he remained aloof from Tahirih. Although he believed that whatever his father told him was correct, Husayn did question why he was constantly being reminded to be more amiable toward his mother.

Upon Tahirih's arrival, Mahvash was remotely polite, as if dealing with an unwanted relative who had come to stay briefly. Tahirih was no longer taken in by feigned courtesy, and she likewise maintained a distant attitude. Each woman presided over her own area of the house, and Tahirih was delighted to find that her sleeping quarters had never been taken over by the second wife. Indeed, she was distinctly grateful that Ismail had built the large addition to the house.

"Tahirih," Mahvash commented one day, "the servants have become accustomed to my supervision. The ones that you had are no longer here, except for Parvin who returned with you. Do my servants do your bidding properly?"

Tahirih missed her servants, who had been not only loyal but capable. Mahvash's definitely were not. It was to Mahvash's great surprise that Tahirih one day said simply, "I have discussed the servant situation with my husband, Mahvash, and our previous cook and his daughter Zahreh will be returning next week." The fleeting look of shock on Mahvash's face was enough to delight Tahirih for hours.

At breakfast that morning, Ismail announced that his friend Haji was in town, and would soon be stopping by to visit. With him would be Talat, who now had three children of her own, while she continued to care lovingly for Haji's disabled son.

"I know, my dear Tahirih," he said, directing his comments to her, "that this will be a very special evening for you. You were so worried about Talat, and even though I told you that she had married this Haji, I suppose you never quite believed it. So now you can see for yourself."

"Ismail, when will they be coming?" Tahirih was beside herself with excitement. "Three children? Will they be with her?" She peppered Ismail with a thousand questions until he finally laughingly assured her that they would come the following evening, and then she could interrogate Talat instead of him.

When they arrived, a newly hired servant escorted them to the large salon where the freshest fruits were arrayed, and the smell of cardamon tea suffused the air. Tahirih leapt up as she saw Talat enter. The young seventeen year old girl had become a ravishing twenty-three year old woman, and Tahirih looked at her in awe. Talat's serenity was manifest, and Tahirih escorted her to a corner of the room where they could talk alone, while the men discussed their own issues. Tahirih was disappointed that they had not brought the children, but this did allow the women to talk more easily.

"Talat, you are so beautiful. It comes from within you, so it is obvious that you are content. Tell me what has happened with you."

Talat was embarrassed, but by this time had come to accept what had occurred to her at Tahirih's home many years before. She had heard that Firidun had been murdered, so had no qualms about returning to where her torment had begun. Ironically, that event had been the beginning of a whole new life, and Talat was happy to share her contentment with a woman she knew had suffered many travails of her own.

"Tahirih Khanem," she answered, still addressing her former mistress in a ceremonial manner, "please pardon me for disappearing so abruptly with no explanation all those years ago. I apologize for whatever strain my departure created. You have since been told what caused me to leave, and I know you have forgiven me."

"Dearest Talat, I was so miserable about what happened to you in my house, and I apologize for not understanding when you asked for a lock for your door. It was so ignorant of me, and overwhelming guilt still abides within me."

"Please, no, Tahirih Khanem," Talat exclaimed, in anguish that her former Mistress should blame herself for what had happened, "my life has become wonderful, and I could ask for no finer man than Haji to protect me. We have two fine children of our own, and he has accepted the one I brought to him as a present from Allah, just as I have come to love Mak, his son from the wife who burned her house down. My life is now perfect."

Tahirih's eyes filled with tears as she allowed herself to believe Talat's avowal of happiness. It was obviously true.

"Being separated from my children was unendurable, but that, too, is now past and little by little they are getting to know me again -- "

Just then Mahvash entered the room and came unbidden to sit with the women.

"Talat, welcome back to your former place of residence," she said, not caring that she had interrupted a private conversation. "Now you have servants caring for you -- that is a change, is it not?" The impertinence of this greeting left both Talat and Tahirih speechless for a moment, then Talat answered.

"Mahvash Khanem," she answered simply. "For a while, this was indeed my home, and I am deeply appreciative for the many things I learned here. Then Allah guided by footsteps elsewhere and my life is now much different. My husband," and she nodded to the prosperous man at the other end of the room, "provides well for me and our children, and it has been many years since I became his wife, not his servant."

"Yes, such fortune is rare. And fleeting sometimes. I hope that for you it lasts forever." Then she departed, leaving the two women wondering just what she meant.

After a moment, they resumed their own discussion while their husbands talked animatedly at the other end of the room. Ismail was curious about Haji's farming methods, which were resulting in colossal yields from his fruit orchards.

"What is it that you are doing so differently from your neighbors?" he asked with great interest.

"Perhaps you remember my nephew Habib," Haji answered. "The lad's father was killed in an explosion in the palace kitchen a number of years ago, and Prince Masoud, in one of his kinder moments, took him as a private valet. Well, somehow the boy talked His Highness into allowing him to learn to read, which was both good and bad for the lad. It made him a misfit among his fellow servants, which was hard on a gregarious child like Habib. But, when His Majesty the Shah went abroad to Europe a couple of years ago, he ordered Habib to accompany him. They were gone for quite sometime, and when they finally got back, the Prince had found someone else to carry on as valet. Poor Habib was out of a job, and when I heard about it, I invited him to come live with me."

"Fortunately for me," Haji continued, "some of the material he was reviewing for the Shah was about modern farming methods, and with his excellent memory, he was able to share the knowledge with me. He told me about the way Europeans irrigate their lands, and how they use worms and insects to aerate the ground. My crops have been abundant for several years now. With Allah's grace, may it continue forever." Haji added with a smile.

Ismail was impressed. "Many of my neighbors here in Shiraz still believe that anything European is befouled. It would be good if they could learn of your experience, but they probably would not listen anyway. It is such a shame that we are so insular." Ismail looked remorseful as he considered how much people could learn if they would only allow themselves to trust others.

"I have heard," Haji declared, "that you travel to Russia and England a great deal on business, and that your esteemed second wife Mahvash frequently accompanies you. Is that really true?"

"Well, for the last few years it has been," Ismail replied. "However, I believe that in the future I will be going alone. Although Mahvash is able to give good business advice, her presence is sometimes overpowering, and I believe that in the future I will just get away by myself for a while."

Noting Ismail's reticence to discuss the issue, Haji changed the subject. "I see that the Shah has begun building railroads. If they really do expand to the point that they crisscross the entire country, it will be a great boon to me. I could ship my fruits to other cities with great ease. I have enough production now that I could manage to meet the demand from all across Persia. I could become even wealthier, and the Shah could collect yet more taxes from me." Again he laughed.

"Haji, my friend, may we both live to see the day when our beloved Persia again becomes the world leader she was in centuries past," Ismail declared with much exuberance.

After the guests had left, Tahirih was supervising the cleanup, and she made an offhand remark to one of the servants.

"I thought I remembered that the carpet in this room was the one Ismail particularly loved. I wonder what happened to it; I don't recall seeing it anywhere."

This was carried back to Mahvash, and its meaning became distorted.

"I understand that you are accusing me of removing carpets from my husband's home," she remarked angrily the next day. "Is that an appropriate way for you to express appreciation for my tolerance of you in this house?"

"Mahvash, perhaps it is time for us to discuss this issue," Tahirih replied after a moment's consideration. "Let us go out to the garden where we can speak privately."

"Go ahead, if you wish. I will not be coming. You may have been first wife at one time, but your heresy lost you that position. I am now the woman in charge of what happens in this house, and you had best learn that."

Tahirih laughed. "Assertion is not the same as reality," she answered, and she went on about her daily duties, ignoring Mahvash for the rest of the day.

CHAPTER FIVE

"Mahvash Khanem," the servant timidly whispered. "Please forgive me for interrupting. What did you want us to prepare for tomorrow's main meal?"

Mahvash had to pull herself back from her daydream, to the miserable realities of living in Shiraz. It had been so nice there, in her thoughts, where she had become very influential. Her sons were important diplomats, her father praised her for enabling the family to regain its status, and everyone spoke to her with great deference. Tahirih and her brats had been relegated to the status of servants. Mahvash smiled briefly, then remembered that these things had not occurred. They were still in the future, and right now one of the servants was asking her something.

"What did you say?" she snapped.

"Tomorrow's meal, Madam. What did you want us to prepare?"

"Don't bother me with such foolishness. Ask the other woman. I don't care what anyone eats," and she returned to her fantasizing.

The servants had learned in the year and a half since the first wife had returned to rely on Tahirih Khanem for judgment, and gradually their loyalty had been weaned from Mahvash to the one who was so much nicer to work for. Some of the servants who had been there before had come back, and all now worked well together. A few months ago, the elderly servant who had come back with Tahirih Khanem had passed on to the next world. Tahirih Khanem had arranged for an extraordinary burial service to honor her servant. None of the servants expected that Mahvash Khanem would ever do such a thing for them.

So Tahirih Khanem was consulted about preparations for the meal, and she quickly gave instructions. "You know what Ismail Agha prefers. Prepare two of his favorite lamb dishes, and some sweet rice. Cucumbers and tomatoes are abundant right now, so make a salad with those. For dessert," she added with kindness in her words, "make the saffron flavored pudding that little Mo loves."

The servant left to inform the kitchen staff of the orders, and it was soon known that Tahirih Khanem was doing something nice for the older son of the second wife. The child had become ill a few days before, although his own mother had barely noticed his fever. On the other hand, Tahirih Khanem had charmingly cajoled him into drinking an herb tea, which helped him feel better immediately. The servants noticed and commented among themselves on the difference in the ways the two women treated each other's children.

When Ismail came home at noon, he immediately asked about his ill son, but Mahvash did not seem to know how the child was feeling. He went to find the child and was surprised to find Tahirih in the room, telling the little boy stories and encouraging him to smile a little.

"Tahirih, you are a good woman," her husband pronounced. "I give thanks to Allah every day that I came to my senses."

Tahirih smiled at him. "Allah teaches us in many ways. My life with you is perfect, dearest Ismail, and I could ask for nothing more." Together they took the little boy's hands and took him to the garden for a few minutes.

As they approached, Mahvash saw them and became infuriated that Tahirih was with her child. "I will thank you to leave my children alone. You can spoil your own if you must, but not mine." Her venom filled the room.

"Mahvash, please, do not be foolish. The child was not feeling well, and I was just playing with him a little. Showing attention to a sick child is not spoiling him."

"Look at your own Husayn. If ever there was a spoiled child, that is the model. He doesn't obey you, and he speaks of you with contempt in front of the servants. No child of mine will ever behave like that," Mahvash spat.

This stung Tahirih, and she hung her head momentarily. However, Ismail intervened.

"If Husayn is spoiled, it is because of the way I have dealt with him, Mahvash. I, too, have noticed his truculence. It is wrong for him to treat his mother as he does, and I fully intend to do something about it."

This retort startled both women. Later, during dinner, both

remained silent, but one was with joy and the other fury.

After a while, Ismail began to talk about an upcoming trip to Haji's home. On this trip, Tahirih would be accompanying him, he announced, and Mahvash would remain in Shiraz.

"I have heard," he said to no one in particular, "that Haji's new home is even grander than mine. I'm not sure I can tolerate that." That had been said with a smile. "Perhaps I will enlarge this one, and then no one will ever find anyone again." He laughed at his joke but got little reaction from the women. "Mahvash, what would you like me to bring you from this trip?"

Mahvash thought to herself that she would most like him to leave Tahirih there with the former servant and come home alone, but she did not say that. "Ismail, you provide so skillfully for us. There is nothing I want that I do not already have. Perhaps just a little trinket of some sort. However, I would be happy to go with you. I have never been to that area of Persia, and it would be delightful to see it."

Ismail answered as diplomatically as he could. "Perhaps while I am gone would be a good time for you to go to Tehran to visit your parents. I promised your father that you could return at least twice a year, and it has been a long time since you were last there. Your family loves to see you and your children. You could remain for a couple of weeks."

"Ismail, my husband," Mahvash retorted instantly, "you know that I always prefer to be with you. A wife belongs with her husband, not her parents." Indeed, Mahvash had felt a sudden panic that possibly Ismail was sending her back to her father permanently, just as he had once done to Tahirih.

"A wife belongs where her husband desires her to be," Ismail had answered. "I will be going to Haji's home with Tahirih, and I would be happy to know that you are safe with your father while I am gone."

That was the end of the conversation. Mahvash darted bitter looks down the table toward Tahirih, who ignored them. While Ismail continued talking about business at the bazaar, the wives ate in silence. Tahirih noted a few things he said and decided to discuss them with him at another time, but she did not want to antagonize Mahvash any more just then.

Ismail had again begun seeking advice from her on a regular basis, and this had increased his business success even more. She now helped him keep his books, which permitted him to ferret out one supplier who was cheating not only him, but several other merchants at the bazaar as well. Exposure of this supplier to his fellow bazaaris had increased Ismail's stature even more.

"Tahirih," he later commented, "regarding Haji, they say, if you suffer too many losses, don't try again. But for Haji, he lost two wives and had the courage to marry once more. Look how well it has worked for him. He and Talat are perfectly suited to each other. I guess it means we can never give up."

With this, he arose from his seat in the garden, stealthily kissed Tahirih with great passion, and left for the afternoon at the bazaar.

Tahirih went to her room and began checking her books to be sure she had added the figures properly. After half an hour she sat back in satisfaction, looking at her handwriting, the neat columns of figures, and the final totals, which increased week by week.

She left the books where Ismail could review them when he came home. Even though he could not read quite so well as she, he took great pride in her ability. Could this really be true, she thought to herself. Who would have ever dreamed it?

She took a Baha'i prayer book from its hiding place. Soraya had given it to her, and she read from it daily, although by now she had memorized every prayer it contained. Ismail knew of its existence and said nothing, but she had to be sure that no one else in the household was aware that she followed the beliefs of the Baha'is. It would be disaster for all of them if anyone ever found out.

CHAPTER SIX

"Tahirih Khanem, welcome to our home," Talat said welcomingly. "It is so wonderful to have you here. Please, come sit by the fire."

The day was cold and rainy and Talat felt badly that Tahirih and Ismail had been traveling in such nasty weather. She did not want her former Mistress to become ill just because she and her husband made the journey to visit.

"I am fine, Talat. You know I am a hardy soul, and a little rain will not hurt me. You see, already your fire has warmed me," she assured Talat, as she removed her outer wear. "I want to meet your fine children. Where are they?"

"Mak is outside playing with the children next door. It is amazing. A doctor came last year and was very interested in Mak's condition. He said that there was extra fluid on Mak's brain, and that some of it could be drained off. Somehow he did it, and after that, Mak was able to move around by himself. He even started talking. Now the neighbors no longer shun him, and he is allowed to mix with other children."

"How fantastic. Was the doctor trained at the House of Science?" Tahirih asked.

"I think so, at least partly. Then he went to Salzburg to study some more. I understand that our little Husayn will be going to the House of Science next year. Is that really true? It would be so wonderful."

Indeed, he was their little Husayn. Talat had been such a help in raising him in the early years, and she slipped easily into that wording. Tahirih smiled as she confirmed Talat's assertion. "Yes, he will be. Ismail wants him to learn not only the school subjects, but also how to live with other boys. He thinks that will help prepare him for the future, too."

"I had not thought of that, but I am sure Ismail Agha is correct. He is such a wise man." Talat acknowledged her former employer with honor.

"What about your other children?" Tahirih asked. "Are they as mischievous as the ones you raised in my house?"

"Absolutely," Talat laughed, and she began to recount tales of roguish behavior which soon had both women doubled over in mirth.

Ismail and Haji, accompanied by Habib, were outside inspecting Haji's fields. Habib was discussing crop rotation, and again he affirmed how fortunate he had been to learn to read. "Without being able to do that," he asserted, "I would still be in the palace, holding the Prince's coats and suffering beatings whenever it pleased His Highness to administer them. Instead, now I am here helping my own family to live a more comfortable life. Truly I have been blessed."

Later, Ismail made his own contrite acknowledgment. "You know," he said to Haji, with both admiration and penitence in his voice, "I can hardly believe there was a time when I thought reading was useless. I was really hard headed, and my dearest Tahirih suffered because of it. So did I, but she far more than I. Now when I think back, I so bitterly regret my intransigence."

"Ismail, my friend. We learn. Do not be hard on yourself because it took you longer than you think it should have. Trust in Allah's time, not yours."

"Yes, of course. You are right. Dear Haji, your wisdom has always been a boon to me. Now tell me, what about your --"

Just then a servant came to announce dinner and they broke off their conversation to enjoy a magnificently prepared meal.

Looking at the abundance, Ismail protested. "We won't be able to eat all this in ten years. Do you think we are gluttons to be stuffed?"

Haji relished the acknowledgment of his bounty, and answered. "Ismail, my friend, as I recall, you can eat all this and twice more. Now come sit down and enjoy some country cooking. Habib, sit next to our guest, and you and he can discuss business matters if you wish. And the lovely women -- he nodded appreciatively in their direction -- can keep the conversation from straying too far toward mundane matters."

They savored the delicious food and covered many subjects as the meal lasted for more than three hours. The servants continued to bring in one dish after another, and Haji kept laughing as Ismail protested that he was already full.

Between dishes, Ismail talked lengthily with Habib and was impressed by the lad's wisdom and intelligence. He asked if the boy got to Shiraz very often.

"Not very frequently, actually," Habib answered. " However, I was hoping to visit there in a couple of weeks to meet with some people who share my interests in farming methods."

'When you come, you will stay with us," Ismail commanded, genuinely pleased at the prospect.

After ten days, Ismail and Tahirih had to return home. When they arrived, Mahvash was nowhere to be seen.

"Please take the bags to our room," Tahirih gently ordered. "I have not seen Mahvash Khanem. Where is she?"

"She remains in Tehran at her father's home," was the almost joyful reply.

This response astonished Tahirih, who had been so sure that Mahvash would be there to make life as difficult as possible the instant she and Ismail returned. She looked to her husband for an explanation.

"I notified her father that I wish for her to remain at his home for a while longer," Ismail interjected, before Tahirih could ask any questions . "I will discuss this with you later. For now, go and rest. You have just returned from a long journey."

Gladly, Tahirih obeyed his instructions, thinking how different this return was from the last time she and her husband had gone away together. This time he was solicitous of her well being, and a second wife was not the foremost thing on his mind. Indeed, the second wife appeared not to be on his mind at all.

As Tahirih entered her room, she thought back to both good and horrible things that had happened to her in that room. Babies conceived and born, one baby lost, the horrendous scene with Ismail when he had banished her, then the glorious night when she had returned. Does life really change so easily, she wondered? Is this all really one lifetime, or have I been reborn over and over again? She fell asleep with these questions dancing in the back of her mind.

Three weeks later Mahvash still had not returned, but her children had been sent back to their father, at Ismail's command. Indeed, it was Mahvash's father who had brought the children back, and he could be heard in lengthy, often loud, discussions with Ismail. Nonetheless, Ismail remained adamant that he wanted Mahvash to remain in Tehran for a while longer. Life had become tranquil in his home, which Ismail learned to treasure. He was not interested in having his second wife continually brewing yet another problem. He needed a respite from Mahvash, perhaps even more than Tahirih did. How had Tahirih always coped, he wondered, as his admiration for her grew.

As promised, Habib arrived after a couple more weeks, and immediately fit into the household comfortably. He introduced Ismail to other farmers in the area who were following new techniques, and Ismail found that the ideas they discussed were creative and likely to lead to better production. As he listened carefully to the different thoughts Habib had gleaned from books written by both Europeans and Persians, Ismail reflected how much more refreshing Habib was to have around than Mullah Mohsin had been.

Ismail had even consented to allow the Baha'is, Soraya and her husband, to come to his home, and he chuckled to himself as he recalled how horrified he would have been two years before to even contemplate such a visit. He was still a little nervous that consorting with known Baha'is might result in trouble for him, but he had found that they were truly extraordinary people, and he had enjoyed talking with them. He truly appreciated how much Soraya had helped his wife over the years, and told her so.

One evening Soraya and her husband had come for dinner, and Habib was still there, so the talk was lively and thoughtful. They were discussing a book written by a British author named Dickens in which he portrayed the poverty of his city so movingly. They had all been amazed that there was a part of London like that, so unlike the London they had heard of with the pageants and royal processions.

"If not for Tahirih," Ismail said lovingly, "I would never had been able to learn about things like this."

"Well, if not for Soraya, neither would I," Tahirih responded.

"All right," Soraya laughed, "let's give the credit where it is due, which is to my dear husband," and she patted his hand in affection and appreciation.

"Well," came the response, "I do what Baha'u'llah teaches, and so long as I do that, I have no problem which cannot be resolved."

They all laughed, but they knew that the words came from genuine conviction.

"Soraya Khanem," Ismail said, "you have helped move the

shadows away from this house, even though at one time I thought you were the cause of them. From the bottom of my heart, I thank you for being a comfort to my wife, not only right now but so many times in the past."

"Ismail Agha," Soraya responded with gravity, "each of us is here on this earth to do just that, make life better for someone else. It is so true that the journey often makes it seem as if the shadow blocks us from the sun like a wall, but we often need that blocking until we are ready to be able to absorb the warmth of the rays that will eventually break through."

They all sat is silence for a moment, considering these words, until Habib said something humorous that allowed them to return to the gaiety of the dinner. Afterwards, Ismail remarked to Tahirih, "Soraya has an inner beauty about her, and so does her husband. Do you suppose the serenity in their lives is related to their religious convictions?"

"I don't know, Ismail, but I can tell you that the peace that comes to me because of my beliefs has not been destroyed by anything that has ever happened to me, no matter how horrible it may have been. Whatever strength you may think you see in me comes from the surety I feel in the eventual rightness of what will happen, whether I see it at the moment or not."

"I love you, Tahirih," her husband replied, with absolute conviction in his heart and voice.

CHAPTER SEVEN

Three days later, Habib returned to Haji's home. Later in the morning a fellow merchant came to Ismail's stall at the bazaar with a whispered warning. "Ismail Agha, I overheard some mullahs talking last night. There are rumors that you invited heretics to your home recently. The mullahs sounded very angry and one of them even said they should burn your house in retaliation for such behavior. You had best be careful."

Ismail left the bazaar immediately and almost ran to his home, where he quickly called to Tahirih.

"Tahirih, gather the children, pack bags for all of us, and pay the servants two months wages. We must leave quickly. We have been denounced as shelterers of heretic, and there may be danger very soon. We will go to Tehran, and decide from there what to do.

Instantly, Tahirih called the servants and set them to work packing suitcases with clothes and special mementos. Not wanting to alarm the children, she told them that they were going to Tehran for a long visit, and had each of them select something special to take.

Was Ismail really doing this, she wondered? Was he going to give up everything he had worked for and accompany her to who knew what future? He could just as well denounce her as the heretic and remain safe in his home. What had changed his heart? Allah allowed humans to decide for themselves how they would respond to His requests. Was it possible that Ismail had understood this test, and was responding from love, not fear?

These thoughts raced through her mind as she urged the children to hurry. Tehran was the logical place to go. Did Ismail plan to stay there, or would they have to leave Persia entirely? Tahirih knew that Ismail would not abandon Mahvash. Wherever they went, surely Mahvash would go with them. Perhaps they did not have to leave Persia. Could they not move to another town, somewhere where she would remain silent about her beliefs.

Ismail returned, looking distraught but determined. While continuing to pack, Tahirih voiced her concerns. "Will we have to leave Persia, Ismail?" she asked with trepidation in her voice.

She was shocked at his answer. "Soraya and her husband have managed to live in Shiraz for many years as Baha'is. However, I don't think that we can do that. You and I will go to London where we can live in relative peace. Some Baha'is must stay in Persia, and others must go elsewhere in order to keep the Faith alive. The mullahs will win if they are allowed to intimidate everyone into silence. People around the world must hear about what they are doing. We are both Baha'is and we must . . ."

Tahirih did not believe her ears. "Ismail, did you say that we will live as Baha'is? You will accept the Faith as your own?"

With a smile, Ismail answered his wife. "I did a long while ago, Tahirih. I just never said it out loud, neither to myself nor to you. At last I have. Now hurry, we must leave quickly."

They gathered all the children together, paid the servants four months wages instead of two, and told them to leave the house immediately for their own safety. As they slipped around the corner, they saw black robed mullahs and street hooligans heading their way. They managed to turn into another side street and avoid detection. Not long afterward, they saw smoke rising from where their home had been.

"We will stay with Mojtabeh for a day or so until I can make arrangements for transportation to the coast, and then a ship will take us to London. I have decided that Mahvash may accompany us to London if she chooses, but I will not force her."

When they got to Tehran, Ismail first assured the safety of Tahirih and all the children, then went to his father-in-law's house. Again he noted the dismal outer appearance, and thought that perhaps his first impression of this home had been correct after all. The beauty was transparent, and if you looked closely, it was banal. There was no real warmth here.

Dispensing with courteous behavior, Ismail asked immediately to talk with Mahvash in private. When she appeared, she looked disheveled.

"Mahvash Khanem," he said formally, "my family and I are about to leave Persia. We are going to London. If you wish, you may come with us. We will be leaving tomorrow morning."

"Why have you decided to do this, husband," she asked

jeeringly. "Does the first wife want to travel where I have already been?"

"No, Mahvash," he answered sternly. "Like Tahirih, I have declared my belief in the Baha'i faith, and I now find it safer to live with my family overseas rather than here in Persia. Although it breaks my heart to leave the country I love, it is the only way we can survive at this time. Perhaps one day we will be able to come back, but I have no idea when that may be. If you choose to come with us, it is possible that you may never return to Persia."

Mahvash, for once startled into silence, instantly decided not to forsake the luxury of living in Persia. "If that is what is important to you, then so be it. My children and I will live with my father."

"Your children, Mahvash, will remain with me. Unfortunately, I am forced to say that they will be much better cared for than Tahirih's were. Very well, good bye to you, Mahvash. I wish you a good life."

Two days later, as she clung to the railing of the bounding ship, Tahirih wondered where all this would lead them. Resting her head trustingly on Ismail's shoulder, she sighed, knowing that she did not have to know all the answers right now.